I0445630

This is a work of fiction. Names, characters, places, and incidences are either a product of the author's imagination or used fi ctitiously. Any similarity to actual organizations and persons, living or deceased, is entirely coincidental.

Published by

CWG Press / Seventh Street Press

1204 NE 11th Ave #2 Fort Lauderdale, FL 33304 www.cwgpress.com

Text Copyright © 2011 Mike Palecek

Cover Art Copyright © 2011 Anthony LeTourneau

ISBN 13: 978-0-9801354-9-7 ISBN 10: 0-9801354-9-4

Printed in the U.S.A.

To Sacred Heart School, the building, the bricks, the steps, the playground, the marble water fountains, milk cartons on the chalk tray, the gym, the library, T.A.B. books, the smell of paper towels and hand soap, *Captains Courageous* for Christmas, flip-up desktops and so much more.

To Sister Monique, Sister Luwellan, Sister Phyllis, Sister Pedro, Sister Briana, Mrs. Widhalm.

To Ray the boiler guy and factotum and friend.

To morning Mass and play practice and Valentines Day boxes and football practice with real football pants and pads.

To memories that stay though the building is gone.

To Mary Pat and Kevin and Jane and Neil and Mike and Tom, Larry, Deb, Patricia, Sally, Lori, Carla, Jill, Steve, Michael, Kenny, Barb, Don, Tim, Margaret, Sue, Theresa, Charlie, Terry, Vicki, Bernadette, Chuck, Pam, Gary, John, Paul, and all.

Johnny Moon

*... and the continuing adventures
of Jimmy, Bobby, Tommy,
Timmy, Danny, Michael, Jane, and Susan*

by Mike Palecek

We choose to go to the moon.
We choose to go to the moon in this decade
and do the other things, not because they are easy,
but because they are hard ...

— PRESIDENT JOHN FITZGERALD KENNEDY
Rice University, Sept. 12, 1962

"But in a very real sense,
it will not be one man going to the moon, if we make this judg-
ment affirmatively, it will be an entire nation.
For all of us must work to put him there."

— President John F. Kennedy,
speech to Congress
May 25, 1961

" ... We face in the Soviet Union a powerful and implacable
adversary determined to show the world that only the Communist
system possesses the vigor and determination necessary to satisfy
awakening aspirations for progress and the elimination of poverty
and want. To meet the challenge of this enemy will require determination and will and effort on the part of all Americans. Only if
our citizens are physically fit will they be fully capable of such an
effort."

— PRESIDENT JOHN F. KENNEDY
Sports Illustrated, Dec. 26, 1960, "The Soft American"

———————————

The President's Council, on Physical Fitness recommends hiking
as an excellent activity for improving physical fitness and is pleased
to note the current
interest in that form of exercise.
Begin by walking a distance — and at a pace — that does not
result in undue fatigue. Day by day increase the distance and the
vigor. Before undertaking long hikes, be sure you are wearing the
proper shoes and socks.
A fifty-mile hike is a fine challenge for the Marines and other
persons who are in good physical condition. The Council is pleased
to note the number of people who are sufficiently fit to cover that
distance.
WASHINGTON, D.C.
IMMEDIATE RELEASE
February 12, 1963

Someone woke up very early in the morning and went right to the guns to see they were still there and all right and safe and clean and happy.

Someone called someone and talked over a final note that had kept them from sleeping past three that morning.

Someone else awakened with a smile to think of the cumulative power of all the months of preparations, finally coming to fruition.

Two persons worried that all the details were in place and what could possibly go wrong.

One person woke up at the alarm clock, wondering for a moment where he was, and rolled to the bed table to check departure times once again.

Someone else asked someone at the end of breakfast: What about the children.

I'm not sure I know what you are talking about was the only response before they crumpled white napkins and tossed them along with a couple dollar bills onto plates and went off to meet the plane.

———————

Catholic school construction heated up around the United States during the whole first half of the 20th century.

People were glad they had survived the Second World War and everyone was excited to expand, to move into a new place, buy a toaster and get on with the exciting new prospect of living.

And in the 1960s every berg and ton and ville in the Midwest boasted a Catholic block of school, rectory and convent.

The sisters and priests and bishops and parents energized each other to offer a firm alternative to the suggested boogeyman, anti-religion communism. They constructed a cozy campfire of Catholicism in the middle of town and invited all to join, to come sit around the fire and warm their hands and their feet around the pulsating heart of Jesus.

Then a Catholic President was elected and Pope John XXIII called the Second Vatican Council.

The United States had recently introduced the universe to nuclear weapons and Tide and the new Catholic President talked about going to the moon.

Civil rights and Vietnam turned the cozy campfire into a forest fire.

In the heat of it all the stout soul in the basement, the school boiler, pumping proudly, like Boxer, on a frozen Midwest morning.

If the mostly unseen boiler did not work, Sister would send a classroom representative flying downstairs, leaping whole sets of steps, to tell Mr. Somebody that there was NO HEAT in Sister's room.

With *NO HEAT* everything rumbled and dragged to a halt. The learning did not go on without the pulsing of the heart of the boiler in the school basement, next to the school stage and the kitchen where the Catholic Daughters made the triangle funeral sandwiches.

The school janitor charged downstairs at five a.m. by the light of the full moon to stoke the fire, proud of the task he had been given by the priests and sisters after he moved to town from the farm.

The moon, the man, and the boiler, the basics, the fundamentals of Catholic education, worked together to send the heat to what would soon be the sacred symphony upstairs, directed by the celestial, exotic nuns who all came from somewhere else to be with these town kids in their snowsuits and fourteen buckle overshoes.

A tune and melody repeated in hundreds of cities and towns each morning, thousands of lighted flames, culminating, generating upward in one big homecoming bonfire of 1960s glory in The United States of America.

And that was how life began, out of that primordial ooze of snow slush flavored with radiation, colored by Rambler exhaust and cocker spaniel piss. Remembering the past, yet rushing with arms wide toward the future, caught between The Flintstones and The Jetsons.

Captain Marvel, My Favorite Martian, The Twilight Zone, Bewitched, aliens, Roswell — a world wanting to know how far it could go — on the edge of science fiction, of fantastic ideas about time and space and society, race, poverty, war and religion.

These innocents in the upstairs classrooms assumed the best from America.

They looked at JFK on TV, smart, handsome, smiling, funny, and just knew they were in the best place and time there had ever been

— or maybe they just assumed it was always this way and always would be, maybe that was it. Maybe they did not think so much as feel.

And when they grew up not too long from now they were going to the moon and outer space and to dances and football games and they were in love – it was just the best place ever and it was just going to get better. They couldn't wait to grow up – they so much wanted to be alive, to live.

All this and the Beatles, too.

And every morning there were the old people at Mass, the persons these young people were resigned to someday becoming — half-kneeling in the back in the shadows, watching the children, someone they used to be, watching, banging their elbows and rosary beads on the wooden pew backs, still confident of their own specialness, of being Catholic, of going out in a blaze of glory.

[Chapter One]

Say, it's only a paper moon
Sailing over a cardboard sea
But it wouldn't be make-believe
If you believed in me
— "Only A Paper Moon," Harold Arlen, E.Y. Harburg, Billy Rose

*N*ow just let me say that Johnny was a fat boy.

A fat young boy in the third grade.

Who thought he could fly. Because he saw things that others did not.

Not because he was so special, just that he cared enough to look.

It's true the world is not as we see it. We see it, but it's different. Way different. Like that.

If you want to know the truth.

And the truth is that Johnny could in fact fly, but he looked like he could not, and so you might assume that he did not.

But he did.

He looked less like Superman and more like a, well, a fat robin, big-boned, wearing buckle overshoes and a snowsuit.

But his snowsuit was blue, not red like a robin, so maybe he was a puppet, a flying blue Sesame Street puppet, with special powers.

And a corduroy cap with a button on top and a buckle strap under the chin.

A fat young third grade boy headed down the steps of his home wearing a snowsuit and buckle overshoes in late November, trying to run as best as he could, carrying his sack lunch in one hand and trying with the other to buckle his hat strap under his chin as his mother had just shouted from the doorway.

Who took off down the sidewalk, shuffling under all that weight — which actually wasn't all that much — but he thought it was, and that's all that ever really mattered.

He was inspired and he wanted to do something about it, and to do other great things, too.

Well, he took off from his front porch with his arms up and out, one hand holding that lunch sack, like Superman headed to work.

Not that Johnny actually thought he could fly, but he thought some people maybe could and you never really knew until you put your arms out.

He had tried it before. Put his arms out, so he kinda already knew that much about himself.

But he was inspired and he wanted to try again.

So he took off, again, his eyes wide and his arms out and up, though already they were getting a little tired, with the blood draining down his arms to make his face red.

He would try to fly, settle for a little running until he got really tired, and then he would walk.

He would walk as far as he could, but would that be far enough?

He did not know because he had never done this before.

But he was finally going to try.

He was going to try.

And he smiled.

Goddammit.

He smiled as he chugged down the broken sidewalk, across the street and out of sight of his white-painted home as his mother checked the sky, folded her arms across her chest and ducked her head against the sudden chill to head back inside.

He pitched his chin and gritted his teeth and looked straight ahead, down that sidewalk that stretched straight to forever almost. He could just see the railroad tracks at a rise in the flat landscape and he saw the school and the cross atop the church that Johnny told himself, not anyone else, looked like a radio tower for space aliens.

And he smiled again, this time only internally, just to himself.

Not to brag, in case anyone would see him smile too much or too often and send him to the retard workshop not real school, but he knew he would make it.

He might not exactly fly, but he would do the other things.

He would lose weight, get in shape, and maybe go to the moon. He did not have to be able to fly to lose weight or go to the moon.

And he would start by walking to school this morning. No problem.

He was an American, and he was special. He just was. What could he say?

But still, between Johnny Moon and the school and the church were a few blocks of Russians and Communists and UFO space aliens and chances that he'd go to hell, and fat, blocks and blocks of being out in the wide open and being fat, and there were kids and people with money and people who were not nice, he had been told they were there, who told all manners of lies and engaged in deceit and well, lies ... and well, deception.

And they would just as soon kill you as look at you. That was from either ... Jack LaLane or "The Tonight Show" or "I Love Lucy," he was not for totally certain.

But Johnny Moon did not let that bother him, because he was special.

He was an American.

And a Catholic, too.

But positive thinking only gets you as far as that one store that has screwdrivers.

[CHAPTER TWO]

Yesterday, all my troubles seemed so far away. Now it looks as though they're here to stay. Oh, I believe, in yesterday.
— The Beatles

*W*hile Johnny walked to school, the rest of the country was rubbing its eyes and waking up as well.

What a beautiful day in the big city.

November and temperatures like this?

Margaret Kelley almost fractured her arm in three places patting herself on the back congratulating herself on the good sense she had shown in planning her big move.

Margaret tossed a pillow at her roommate from the doorway and missed. She had been awake since five, but surely could not have pinched Susan in the buttocks until now.

Susan and Margaret were new to the city, both coming not that long ago from separate midwestern towns.

They worked as secretary temps in one of the new high-rise buildings in the downtown on Commerce Street. They had found a small home to rent in a nice enough section, called Oak Cliff not that far of a bus ride in the morning and afternoon.

Today they would not have to work.

They had planned for weeks to go to the parade through downtown. When they had learned about it, they had gotten out their "Cats of the Southwest" calendar from the refrigerator and laid it flat on the small kitchen table with the red and white covering and centered their whole month around it, like a concert or a play or a trip to the Black Hills.

Margaret got up, took a quick shower, got dressed and got the coffee and the toast going, then flipped on the radio when she heard Susan in the shower.

The announcer talked about the day's big doings.

Margaret got the paper from the porch. They couldn't afford it, but there was a special and they were planning to cancel after that.

She sat down with her toast and coffee and waved without looking as she heard Susan walk in, reading the front-page stories about the day's activities.

"Oh, my!" Margaret gasped, spilling her coffee and looking everywhere for something to wipe with.

"What? What-what?" Susan ran over.

Together they stared down at the full-page ad in the middle of the paper, with a black border running all around.

"It looks like a funeral announcement," Susan said, getting onto one knee to help Margaret wipe up the spill.

[Chapter three]

"There are two kinds of people in this world: Those that enter a
room and turn the television set on, and those that enter a room and
turn the television set off."
— "The Manchurian Candidate"

*T*hat's it.
It's over.
He tried and it just didn't work.
Johnny Moon didn't have what it takes.
The Russians would win.
Yes, he did.
The Communists would be defeated!
No. He did not. Just like always.
Shit. Oh-no. He looked sideways and up and down to see if any-
one heard that.
Johnny skidded sideways like they did in the Olympics.
He stopped.
The salt in front of the hammer store helped to grind his boots into
the ice.
He sucked hard, pulling frosty air into his lungs, which can't be
good for you. He let it out in a locomotive stream. He checked him-
self in the store window. Maybe he was skinnier already.
Something was not quite right.
Something besides his not having what he should have, and if he
didn't have it he might as well not go to school at all.
He dug his fat fists into his sides like a Lewis & Clark explorer,
pushing all the way in. He could touch his bones and it made him
feel skinny.
Johnny couldn't believe he'd done it again.
In fact, he hadn't. It was here. It had to be.
He shoved his right hand into his left pocket, his left hand into his
right pocket, then both hands into both of his pockets.
"This is how the Russians win," Johnny said out loud to himself.
"It's my fault. Oohh, brother, I am in big, big trouble.

"Jesus. Oh, sorry, sorry."

He crossed himself quickly and looked around to see if anyone was around.

Johnny waved at Dave and Isom in Dave's robin's egg blue pickup. They were going to pick up the old people at the Catholic nursing home out on Thirteenth Street.

Johnny could see Dave pushing on his steering wheel trying to beep-beep, but sometimes it didn't work if it was cold.

Everyone knew that they brought the dead old people back to school and shoved 'em in the boiler in the basement to heat the school. They used to use coal, before it got darn expensive.

He began walking back, toward home, looking down on the sidewalk, over to the gutter, up against the building.

He looked up and saw his Dad's car coming down the street.

Johnny turned around and continued walking toward school as he had been, shooting looks left and right at the sidewalk.

"Hey!"

"Hey-Johnny!"

Hands waved out tops of windows and quickly pulled inside again.

"Beeeep ... beep."

Johnny raised his chin and his lunch sack at his dad and brothers and sisters on their way to school.

"Go-Johnny-Go! Fifty miles! You can make it! Whooo! Johnny!"

They think I'm brave for walking to school. I'll never make it, Johnny thought. I'll never be perfect like them. I'm just a big fucking loser. He slapped both hands over his mouth and looked around, then shook his head and shuddered at what he had just risked, a venial sin for sure if anyone heard him. He could even get a mortal. God hears every-*fucking*-thing.

As soon as Johnny thought his dad and the rest couldn't see him he stopped again.

He shoved his hands again into all his pockets, pants, snowsuit, inside his hat.

Why he had to wear a snowsuit in November when it had only snowed a little once, he did not understand, and boots, big black ninety buckle shitting farmer engineer boots.

He took off his mittens and shook them out. He scuffled over to the side and sat down with his back against the blond bricks.

With his cold, wet hands he worked to unbuckle his boots. Raising each boot way up over his head he pulled them off, sat there with his red, bare feet and stuck his hands inside his boots to pull out his socks, then shook each boot with both hands.

Johnny chewed on a deep breath to consider his life options.

He dug into a pocket and retrieved a couple days old piece of candy still in the wrapper. Unable to get all the paper off he began chewing and decided paper does not taste.

He looked up at the white moon, smiling down, or smirking. Johnny waved with one hand, then put both hands up higher and waved. He stopped to dig for more candy.

Something was not quite right. It was like in the Wizard of Oz when Johnny sat on the floor staring up at the screen with his eyes almost closed just before he knew the flying monkeys were going to be right there.

The sky looked kind of greenish-yellowish, the way his mother had said always meant a tornado and they had to go to the basement and light a candle and begin the rosary.

"In the name of the father and of the son and of the holy spirit," his mother and father would start and then the children knew when to come in.

There are no tornadoes in November. Not usually. Uh-oh. When you do get one, it's a doozy. Someone said that. Prob'ly Jimmy Purple.

He couldn't just not go, sit there and then go home at three-thirty, could he? Or, maybe there would be nucular war, whatever that was, and he would die and nobody would ever know.

He didn't have his fifteen cents.

Johnny wiped sweat from his forehead with a plump, whitish-reddish, fatish fist.

He held several ideas and plans and worries inside his head, concentrating on all of them at once, like a good pinball turn.

There were Communists everywhere, but you couldn't see them. They could be anyone. You might even live with one or two, like Johnny did.

You would never know until they cut your throat in the middle of the night with that string that goes around the baloney. They can do that. Communists can use every part of the bologna. That's what Jimmy Purple said once.

Or you could eat snow and die of radiator poisoning from the nucular bomb testing.

Johnny wished he lived in the olden days when they could eat snow. He did eat snow before. In fact, he ate it almost every day last winter, and he didn't die.

But last winter he had wanted to die because, well, he couldn't remember now, but he recalled a general malaise, nothing to do in this house, nobody to play with, old boring toys and world-weariness.

But this year he wanted to live because he had heard the president on the radio or maybe it was the television or maybe it was his dad and mom talking about it, but he had heard about it, and he was going to lose weight and walk fifty miles whenever he went anywhere and he was going to go to the moon. Maybe not really, but ... no, yes, he was *going to the moon*.

Johnny breathed, deep.

He made a fat fist and lightly tapped the side of his jaw like a fighter, taking a punch, like his brother did sometimes.

He battened down his buckles: one-two-three ... four-five ... six. Then took a deep breath to reach the other foot, then rolled over to push up to stand.

Johnny spied his grey mittens in the slush and sand where he had been sitting and went to one knee to get them.

As he pulled them on he buried his nose into the wool like wet mothballs or cats.

Johnny's eyes and mouth went wide as the bells chimed a Latin conga.

He thought of the world that awaited him. The one solid block of the Catholic school, church, rectory and convent, Father and his intimate relationship with Jesus and God, and the other-worldly Sisters, none of whom were from around here, all from somewhere else, dressed in their crazy garb, gliding around as if they were on roller skates or skis, asking the children to consider that there were more to this life than what they could see on the tips of their noses.

He could do this.

He had to do this.

Missing Mass, would that be a venial sin or a big one, on a school day. What if you were late, what did that count for? He'd ask his brothers and sisters, they'd know.

Maybe he'd ask somebody else.

That's just what the Communists would want. They want you to be late for Mass and missing Mass and they might have taken his dime and nickel or maybe it was three nickels for bowling.

Johnny took off again, trying to roll up his lunch sack to cover up the "Johnny Skis" — complete with quote marks — that his mother had marked in different colored Magic Marker – red, green, blue, yellow — because she had once heard the kids calling him that once when she walked up to school to meet him after kindergarten when he probably pooped his pants.

That was a long time ago!

He rolled and rolled with one hand and pumped with the other, leaning into the slight hill before the tracks.

He still couldn't believe it.

He didn't have his fifteen cents.

Again.

He didn't have his — he whispered to himself while mouthing wide, "god-damn" — fifteen cents.

"A strong boy makes a strong man makes a strong country," he quickly followed up the god-damn.

Johnny whooshed a stream of locomotive air ahead of him and he jumped up, almost leaving the ground, more coming to his tiptoes inside his boots, to touch the fluffs with his corduroy hat button.

At the tracks Johnny rubbed at the red rocks, needing to see something shiny.

The train horn blew like a cow monster, and Johnny looked and saw the light way down the line. He smelled the creosote on the ties that reminded him of going with Dad to fill up the Rambler, and set his sack down to show off for the few cars idling past.

He stretched both arms to balance and stood with his boots on the tracks feeling the edges of the steel with the bottoms of his feet, like a high-wire trapeze so high up that if you fell you would die. You would.

Johnny pulled his right foot out from behind his left, looked back to see who was watching, then back to where the train was, then set the foot down and picked up the left.

He was famous for this with all the car drivers who slowed down to watch him and then called their whole family to tell them as soon as they got home.

The train engineer gave a little toot as he approached the intersection two blocks away. Johnny pulled out his left foot and leaned way out into dangerous leftness. Johnny waved his right arm in circles to bring himself back, then fell onto the rocks in his boots, which burned hideously from the hot lava rocks and volcano fire.

The church bells rolled out another warning like thunder running. Someone was burning leaves at this time in the morning, probably old people. Johnny looked around for the smoke.

Johnny pumped his arms and ducked his head as the chimes rang louder: "COME-ON! COME-ON! COME-ON!"

Johnny swung both arms and skidded to a stop.

He opened his mouth and eyes wide to look over his bulky snowsuit space suit to see his lunch sack perched perfectly on the shiny, cold brittle, deadly railroad track.

Like James Bond, Johnny quick-looked up to the sky for incoming missiles then back to the train.

"Aaaahhh!"

"Aaa!" The engineer in the green and yellow engine pulled his cord and looked hard at Johnny, who had now lost his lunch and forgot his fifteen cents. They both looked at the sack, then back to each other.

"Rrrrnnhh!"

"Rr! Rr! Rrrrr!

Johnny felt his stomach rumble.

"Aaaaa! Aaaaa! Aa."

The engineer locked eyes with Johnny as Johnny took one defeated step toward his doomed peanut butter sandwich, apple, Chee-tos, all in separate Baggies, and maybe three Oreos. Two.

Johnny faced the train with clenched fists at his sides and watched the big, round steel disks as big as a Volkswagen Bug squish his lunch and stuff squirted out.

Johnny wondered if the engineer was a Communist with that hair and that big mustache. He could be a space alien. Some have jobs and live here. Others probably go back and forth from where they live and then stay home all weekend. He watched the hairy alien Communist turn his attention to the next intersection and toot his horn.

Johnny took one step toward his dead lunch. The chimes banged out over the cold and the snow dusting and the ice. Johnny turned and walked fast, almost running, his head down, arms pumping and legs swishing in his blue-plaid snow suit — trying to ignore the buckles on his boots that had come loose, yet watching them with each lurch of his overstuffed legs.

Johnny stopped at the busy intersection across from school.

He puffed and huffed and waited for the cars and station wagons pulling up to the curb to let children off.

A dog trotted up and stopped, sitting down on the snow next to Johnny.

They both watched the traffic, looking for an opening, then at each other, then back to the street.

Johnny touched the dog on its head with his wet mittens. It wiped the ice with its tail.

The dog wiggled its nose and ears and whimpered, its eyes on something across the street.

Johnny looked and saw two boys from the fourth grade waving at the nervous dog, now pacing back and forth, worrying.

The two boys, bundled in winter wear, laughed together. One put a knee on the ground and held a candy bar and waved it at the dog, urging him to cross through traffic.

"C'mon, boy, c'mon, c'mon."

"You can do it. You want this? C'mon, come get it."

"Here it is."

"Hey! Don't do that!" Johnny yelled though they could not hear him above the car tires and slamming doors and revving engines and "Seeya, have a good day!"

Johnny looked at the excited dog and then to the rush of cars coming and going, dropping off, spinning on scarce ice patches.

One of the fourth grade boys — Johnny recognized them from serving at Mass — gave Johnny the middle finger beside his jaw.

The other yelled something at Johnny, holding up a fist to tell Johnny to get away from the dog, or else.

Johnny knelt down and tried to coax the dog to him with an open wet mitten of nothing.

"C'mere, boy, c'mere-c'mere."

The dog sniffed Johnny's mitten, licked it once, then looked back at the boys across the dangerous intersection, waving, laughing, urging him to cross the deadly stream.

The dog wagged its tail and gathered itself.

Johnny lunged from his knees. He wrapped his arms around the dog's shoulders and pushed his nose into the dog's soft, brown fur that smelled like rotten something.

The dog yelped and struggled and yelped and Johnny let go.

The dog skidded on the ice like a cartoon character and ducked its head and shoulders to rip into the street just as a brown station wagon pulled from the curb after disgorging a stream of kids from the back seat.

The mother behind the wheel judged her chance and plowed ahead, looking right and left as the dog zipped into her path.

"Hey! Hey-dog!" Johnny yelled, sprawled on his stomach. "Brownie!"

The dog stopped. It turned and looked at Johnny.

The boys across the street punched each other and pointed at the dog sitting in the middle of the street with cars whizzing by.

Johnny pushed up to his knees and rushed into the street.

He chugged into traffic in his giant boots and moon space snow suit, his hands outstretched, into the way of the onrushing brown station wagon, the mother intent on her next appointment, strangling the steering wheel at nine and three.

Johnny stopped at the blare of a horn, and a car slipped by. He charged on. He reached the dog, leaned down to wrap his arm around it. He grunted and picked it up as the station wagon driver saw them and slammed on her brakes and made her eyes big.

The boat car floundered on the ice.

Johnny watched the woman's mouth yelling at him, just as the grill plowed into his stomach. He kept hold of the dog in his arms, absorbing the weight of the world in his snow space suit padding.

As he fell and flew Johnny turned in mid-air like a Green Bay Packer. The dog whined and ran in the air.

Johnny landed with an oomph! on his back on the ice and cement. He lost his breath and his arms flew open.

The dog scrambled and scampered between stopped cars, splitting the two fourth grade boys standing with their mouths open. It grabbed the Mickey Mantle card from the bigger boy's fingers, and disappeared around the school corner.

The woman in the station wagon threw open her door and ran to Johnny. She helped him up and offered to walk him to the other side, dabbing at his face with a Kleenex that smelled like lilacs.

"No thank you," Johnny said.

"I'm okay," he smiled.

He took the woman's hand and shook it and waved over his head at the other drivers as he waddled toward the other curb.

The bigger boy stepped to Johnny.

"Your dog got my Mantle card."

"Not *my* dog," said Johnny.

"Here," the other boy handed Johnny a Hershey bar. "Don't tell Sister."

"I don't need that," he said. "I'm losing weight," he patted his stomach. "I need fifteen cents."

"Hey," he pushed the bigger boy's shoulder. "I'll get your card for you for fifteen cents you gotta pay me now and I'll get it."

The boy, his eyes still glazed and staring, put his hand into his pocket, pulled out some coins and held his fist over Johnny's open grey mitten hand.

The boy began to leave his trance, saw Johnny and his own hand hovering over Johnny's hand, blinked his eyes, then went ahead and dropped the coins into Johnny's hand.

Johnny looked at them and shut his fist tight.

He walked between the boys, heading off down the sidewalk as the bells dribbled out the Agnus Dei like steelies on marble stairs.

"Strong boys make strong men makes a strong country," Johnny said out loud to himself as he pounded on, in between the old people and other kids and dogs headed toward Saint Luke's for eight o'clock Mass.

He snuffed up snot, knowing it would be his last chance for a while.

Johnny chugged on, his head down, the pennies and dime smothered forever, fossils inside his sweaty wool mitten.

He slid on the ice with his hands out, "Squaw Valley!" he whispered to himself and passed the side entrance to the church. It would have led right to where his class sat for Mass, but they had to go in the front door, "like gentlemen and young ladies, not someone sneaking into the beer joint from the alley."

Johnny mentally checked his soul and decided it was still white from confession last Wednesday. He put his head down farther and pumped his left arm harder to turn right around the sternly cut hedge.

"Hey, Skis! Skis!"

Johnny looked up and around.

"Hey! Wait up!"

One of the old people pulled the front door and Johnny saw the sharp brightness inside framed inside the darkness outside like matting on a picture, and the cherubs playing in the painting on the convex ceiling above the altar way in front.

The bells rang, insisted, nagged, implored.

Ding-dong. Dong-dong.

Ding-ding. Dong.

Johnny found an opening in the foot traffic and headed for it like Jim Taylor.

A hand on his sleeve tugged at him.

"Hey, we're early."

Johnny looked, annoyed, and saw Jimmy Purple.

"Moon-skis," Jimmy said. "Where you goin?"

"Church," Johnny looked at Jimmy and shook off his grip.

"There's lots of time," Jimmy said. "Let's skip."

"Hemanooo the maaab-nificent!" Jimmy said, putting his face close to Johnny's.

Johnny pulled back.

Jimmy referred to the animated movie the school had seen in the school basement called "Hemo The Magnificent," about the blood in the body and how it is powerful and gives life and the movie took them on an incredible trip through the body along the bloodstream. Johnny and Jimmy had made a good joke for themselves after the movie that they had repeated the whole rest of the day about pretending to be riding in blood as they walked through the halls.

Jimmy asked Johnny if he had seen "Voyage to the Bottom of the Sea" that week and how Admiral Nelson had flown the flying submarine.

Johnny shook his head.

"Mr. Wizard?" asked Jimmy. "The ghosts-and-dreams whatcha-ma-jig thing they had?

Johnny said, no, that he had been out playing.

"My Favorite Martian?" Jimmy grew impatient.

"Yeah, not this week," said Johnny.

"Okay," said Jimmy, "did you see where Uncle Martin and Tim go in that one time machine …"?

Johnny looked toward the church and back to Jimmy and back to the church door.

"Nnh-uh," Johnny said.

He knew that Jimmy didn't want to go into church.

He said every time he goes in there he feels some kids from the ghost class pushing him and poking him in the sides, trying to get him mad and in trouble.

And Jimmy was scared of the cherubs on the ceiling above the altar because they made him think of the ghost class. And when he would get scared he would point at the cherubs and call them "Johnny," even though they all looked like girls, probably to make himself feel better.

The ghost class, with ghost nuns, was the very first class coming through the school, back in the … long time ago.

They were all downstairs in the kitchen, next to the gym and the stage and the locker room and the boiler room.

They were making paper mache turkey heads for Thanksgiving they say.

The old boiler that the priest had got from another school that had bought a new one, 'sploded.

It shot hot air and fire right through the cement wall from the boiler room right into the kitchen and burned all the kids and the nuns, right in place, like Bombay.

And now they just ran everywhere, wherever they wanted, all day long, and the two nuns who were with them chase them all over the school, all day long, except when they take breaks to sit on the roof of the priest garage to watch Sister Mark pitch kickball. That's what Mark says.

Johnny turned from Jimmy and headed toward the open door, mixing with the horde of kids, parents and old people.

Johnny dipped three fingers into the holy water sponge inside the door and touched himself on the right places. One finger was for people who thought they were too good for God. Two fingers were for the Pope, Bishops and Cardinals, only.

It's a rule.

Johnny ripped at his hat and gloves in a well-worn flurry, revealing red face and hands, like the embers of a campfire. He gripped the wooden railing on the side and pounded up the hard vinyl steps.

All steps were stomps.

Each boy and girl jabbered like a monkey in a zoo, and they pounded up the stairs like so many cattle headed to Mass, and clomped their feet like horses.

The girls searched and traded and made last-second alterations and inventions to put something on their heads, a napkin or hand-kerchief, with bobby pins, before daring to show themselves to God inside.

Johnny pushed through the wooden double doors then headed left, smelling the old people section in the back like cigarettes and coffee and Rolaids and gas and rounded the corner, passing under the ivory icons for the stations of the cross, then began smelling the incense and the burning white and red candles that cost a dollar and five dollars depending on what you needed. Lots of times the old people would be up there lighting candles and banging coins down the metal tube that were as loud as 'roshima, Johnny's Sister had said.

He headed down the side aisle. He crushed his cap at his side and felt again for the coins in the other fist.

Johnny put the brakes on to keep from breaking into a jog down the incline that resembled the angle of the Rialto aisles.

Jimmy bumped into him from behind.

"Sorry," Jimmy said.

"Watchit, geez, fucker."

"I-said-sorry."

Johnny then began to pick up his feet, not wishing to sound like someone going out to feed the cows.

Johnny and Jimmy both half-genuflected, bowed their heads and blessed themselves and slid into the last two spots of the third row of third graders. They knelt on the red-cushioned kneeler, crossed themselves, bowed their heads, crossed themselves, then slid back onto the wooden pew, all the while keeping their heads down like they knew they shouldn't even be alive but they were and sorry, but what could they do about it.

Johnny looked at the altar, took a deep breath, kept his eyes on the altar and began placing himself in the presence of God while searching his pockets for a place to stick his fifteen cents so he didn't lose it.

He took a deep breath the way Sister said and closed his eyes and began to drift away from the dock like she said, drifting, breathing, lying back in the boat, in the moonlight, listening to the crickets and the owl.

Johnny opened his eyes and saw that everything around him was the same.

Jimmy had his arm on the outer armrest like he was in a bank, not church, but Johnny didn't feel like saying anything.

"Got yer money this time?" Jimmy asked with a knowing smirk.

Johnny showed him the open mitten with the pennies and dime.

Jimmy shot an elbow into the aisle and turned around to growl at the empty pew behind them, then started playing with the metal hat snaps that they weren't supposed to use for their hats because, well, Jimmy snapped the holder and it echoed around church. They both put their heads down and tried not to show they were breathing by their backs moving up and down.

They waited and waited, then raised their heads.

"That's not fifteen, lemme see," Jimmy hissed.

Johnny showed him the open mitten and the dime fell onto the floor. At the sound all the third grade girls in the two rows in front of them turned around.

The coin took off.

Johnny turned red.

The ten cents rolled under the next pew, downhill, then hit a pew leg and began to spin. The spinning noise echoed, louder than the coughing, grunting old people and the frantic bells and the cars honking outside.

Johnny watched the dime spin.

It stopped and he slid ahead, just hanging by the edge of his butt to the pew, then lunged with his knees for the red kneeler.

Johnny dived under, grazing the seat with his head. In the darkness he reached and grabbed a girl's leg. The leg shook and he let go.

"Ooohh!" he heard squealing above him.

A head came down from the pew. Just the head.

"Eeeewww!"

"Siiissstteerrr!"

He saw the silver sparkling in the dim light from the stain-glass windows and shinnied toward it on his stomach. He reached, reached. Almost. "Oooh, ooh," he urged his body forward, feeling boot slush go down his neck.

He reached one finger to the coin, pinned it to the floor and pulled it in.

"Pull me back!" Johnny whispered to Jimmy. "Pull me back, pull me out! Help!"

Johnny lunged backward on his stomach. "Ooo! Ooo!" he grunted and got his legs up over the kneeler and found his seat, breathing heavy, sweat on his forehead.

He looked at Jimmy and smiled, holding up the coins in his hand.

"Got it," Johnny said.

"See?"

Jimmy wasn't looking at Johnny or his money, but over Johnny's shoulder, like he was watching "The Birds," alone at night at home with all the lights off and he saw beaks sticking through the front door.

Johnny looked over his right shoulder. And he saw a finger. The giant pointer finger of Sister Mark. As if it were pointing at him from up on the Rialto screen, in 3-D, down at him seated in the front row and peeing on the floor with both hands.

"Jonathan Moon!"

Sister Mark's face shined red, throbbing within the wimple facemask headpiece like a cat with its face stuck in the back door headed out.

Johnny's face swelled, engorged with horror. Silently screaming as if a Negro were climbing in the bathroom window in the middle of the night.

Sister hissed.

"You report to my room after Mass, young man," and then whipped around and sidled back down the row, holding up her robes with one hand, fingering her beads with the other.

Johnny turned around.

He stared straight ahead like he had been shot but not sure yet where the bullet had gone in.

He squeezed his fifteen cents and a tear slid down one cheek.

One of the fourth grade boys from the street curb pulled the red velvet cord at the opening to the sacristy and the bells rang. Everyone stood. The two fourth grade boys led Father out from the back room.

They came around to the front to bow to the altar and kneel, then Father marched straight up to the altar to begin his private meeting with his friend God.

The green vestments and the red candles burning in front of the statues of Mary and Joseph on either side set the stage, along with the flowers collected by The Catholic Daughters from the funerals from the previous week and the American flag next to the altar, the cherubs and the chimes.

Johnny tried to follow along and watched the two altar boys to see how they worked. Next year they would be learning to serve when they were in Sister Mark's class. At least they were supposed to. You had to learn a lot of prayers and serve at either daily 5:30 p.m. Mass with the old people or 8 a.m. Mass with the whole world – unless there was nucular war with the Russians and the world ended and he didn't have to. That's what Sister Mark told the fourth-graders, and that's what Johnny's brother had confirmed.

Jimmy looked to see if Sister was watching and put one of his feet up on the kneeler, which didn't allow Johnny or the others in the row to push the kneeler up and it cut them at the shins.

Johnny watched the action on the altar and began to wonder if he had fasted long enough to be able to take communion. He had ice cream, strawberry swirl cake flavor, while watching "My Three Sons," and then nothing, but was that long enough?

Oh, shit, he put his hand immediately over his mouth at the bad words thought.

He ate a spoonful of meatloaf after the ice cream. If it was after midnight it would be on Friday and he couldn't eat meat on Friday or he would go to hell if he died before getting to confession again.

One, two, three, he began flicking his fingers out of his fist to count the hours. If he didn't go up with the group everyone would know he had done something wrong.

Johnny smelled Smith Bros. cherry cough drops and looked to see that Jimmy was sucking one in his cheek. You weren't supposed to.

At the Hosanna everyone knelt. Jimmy looked behind Johnny down at their nun, Sister Mary-Michael, with her head bowed, and half-sat back on the pew.

Johnny pressed his fists together with his money still trapped inside the sweaty mitten.

At the homily the children all watched, intent, holding their breaths. Father did not always give a talk during the week, saving his best stuff for Sunday, but sometimes he did and it meant a longer Mass.

On this morning they bowed their heads in sorrow as they saw Father headed toward the pulpit, grinning, thinking of what he would say.

"The blessed Sisters of St. Francis," he began as the children wiggled their butts like hens to get comfortable in the hard wood, while the old people in back grinned at the chance to listen to Father's story once again.

"… they don't like me saying this, but" – they are truth seekers, pioneers, coming from far away to come here – to this "distant planet" to be with us."

Father smiled at his own words and looked down at his notes.

"And let me tell you … that having supper with these women, these 'supernatural' women with their amazing skills, and how they fly all around, zip here and there and do all these super things, simply amazing, is like … how shall I say it … is like … hmmm, if we could all … say … go to the basement of the school and climb inside that old courageous boiler and fire it up and ride it, burrow down into the earth! And go underground … deep down … down, down, down … into the very bowels of our earth and our being … "

Father looked out over the sea of faces, then down seriously, then back up.

Johnny looked back at Sister Principal-Something, seated almost back with the old people, thinking she would be happy that Father was talking about them. She looked mad.

Father pointed right at the third grade section.

"Don't any of you do that though!" His face was serious. "I think it'd be a little hot," he managed half a smile.

"You know you can tell time by the layers of the earth – like a tree's rings – each layer is for a certain period of time – well if you could go down, down into the earth you might be able to journey back into time and find out what really happened, in our history and the history of the church."

Again Father chuckled in anticipation of what he was about to reveal.

"That's what supper at the convent is like – not that I don't recommend it, they are wonderful cooks – but their knowledge and awareness is simply beyond what 'normal' people are capable of … I'm convinced of that.

"They inspire me."

Children and old people strained pupils and retinas and blood vessels to see out the sides of their eyes to see how the Sisters, seated behind their classes, were reacting.

"Well, anyway-then, let us pray."

At communion time Johnny stood with his row, his fifteen cents still clenched in one hand. The rest of the children bowed their heads and just touched their foreheads to the tips of their first fingers with their palms pressed together.

Johnny held one hand up, the one on the side of Sister Mark, seated behind her fourth graders, and Sister Mary-Michael seated just behind Johnny and Jimmy's last row of third graders.

He pressed his left fist against his open palm and touched his sweaty forehead to the fingertips of his one hand, his eyes half-closed in adoration and scouting the skies for any admonishment warheads headed his way.

The two lines in the middle aisle inched down the incline toward the altar, toward Father handing out the hosts with the two fourth graders on the sides, one hand over their heart and the other holding a golden plate on a handle under the chin of each supplicant to keep Jesus from falling onto the wet, grimy blue carpet.

The servers are like soldiers protecting you from the Russians — trying to save you from a mortal sin and the eternal burning fires of hell licking at your feet and your head for ever and ever time without end like hot scorching tongues — like your guardian angels.

He too could become a guardian angel if he made it through server training boot camp in the fourth grade.

Johnny inched closer and closer, his fist against his palm, not able to keep his eyes from any other eyes that might possibly be seeing that his hands were not properly folded.

He exchanged awareness with the fourth grade server on his side, the one who had handed him the money.

Johnny looked away then back, away … back.

"The body of Christ," Father said.

"Amen."

Johnny tilted his head back, not way back, he was not a bird in a nest. He stuck out his tongue. Not way out like the most hungry little starling.

Like a skilled surgeon, Father placed the host on Johnny's tongue.

Johnny pulled his tongue in, not like a lizard, but like a human being.

He crossed himself with his right hand, not the left fist of the devil. He sucked lightly on the host, letting it dissolve subtly. The host is not a sucker, it is The Body of Christ. Would you like to be chewed, your arms, your head, your legs? Would you? Wouldn't you rather be sucked and then dissolve?

He did not chew like a cow with its cud, and rounded the corner and leaned into the incline up the side aisle, keeping his eyes down in holy adoration, searching subtly frantically for his home pew, not wanting to go way past and almost being lost, having to go home with the old people or living in the locker room with the Negroes.

His heart leaped when he saw his familiar spot with his crushed hat. He dived in, went to his knees, crossed himself and with his eyes closed felt Jimmy plop down and begin to whisper.

They stood to receive Father's final blessing.

"You've got to go to Mark's room," Jimmy said too loud.

As if Johnny could not remember.

The children began to gather their things for the walk over to school. Johnny sat to re-buckle his boots and cast a glance down the row toward the middle aisle. Sister Mary-Michael M&Ms pursed her lips sympathetically and nodded gently to indicate that he may go, that she knew what was happening.

She mouthed the secret word to Johnny.

He couldn't hear her, but he knew what she was saying.

It was the secret word she gave to her class each year. Each year got a different word. It was the secret between the children and her.

They were to say it to each other to keep each other's spirits up, to encourage each other. She felt it brought them closer together, like a family, and might enable them to get along better, not battle each other, and perhaps accomplish more.

She thought it was at least worth a try.

Johnny nodded to let her know he had received her message.

Johnny stood on the kneeler to get around Jimmy, still seated in the pew, taking his time getting on his gloves.

"You're gonna die, Moon-Skis," he looked up at Johnny, so high up on the kneeler that he felt the whole world was watching him headed off to the fourth grade classroom for crawling around in church before Mass, as no one in history had ever done, up to now.

"How was your fifty-mile hike?" Jimmy added as Johnny stepped down into the side aisle.

"It's only a few blocks," Johnny said.

"I'm losing weight," he said softly so no one could hear as he touched his stomach and stepped from the kneeler into the aisle, and then turned sideways to go against the oncoming third, second and first grade traffic bound for the front door of the church to exit after Mass like young boys and girls, while he headed to the side door, a pagan baby, in need of everyone else's nickels and dimes.

[CHAPTER FOUR]

Well, boys. I reckon this is it. Nuclear combat — toe to toe with the Ruskies!
— "Dr. Strangelove"

*M*argaret and Susan got safely out of the house, leaving the dishes until they returned, as well as some sort of crochet project that Susan wished to start, lying on the kitchen table so she would not forget.

After they had eaten, they each ran in different directions around the little place, picking up, dusting, putting away.

They grabbed light coats and out the door they went, giggling, running, walking, then fast-walking to the bus depot.

The bus had a terrible time making it over the freeway and into the downtown. In fact, the driver turned to everyone as soon as he got to a place he could stop and said, this was as far as he could go. He let everyone off.

Margaret and Susan had wanted to be farther into town to watch the parade.

They looked at each other and at the map of the route from this morning's paper.

"We could just stay here, at the end," said Susan. "Whatdya say? We'll still see the whole thing, otherwise we have to walk, and through all these people."

Margaret agreed and they found their spot, right there, in a big park-like open area.

They each picked their new cameras from their white purses and showed each other, like Secret Agents 007 and 008.

Then they walked out into the big grassy open area.

If they could find a spot where there weren't many people, Margaret said, maybe they could really get some good footage to show their families.

"Sir Lancelot will notice us and smile for our movies, you think?" she put a hand on her knee and posed.

"You are so naughty," Susan smiled.

They both ran together, as best they could in their good shoes, holding their cameras, their coats flapping.

Johnny hurried out the side door. He waited for a few steps behind some old people holding on to each other over the one ice spot in sight, then bolted to the lawn and around the cannon to be rid of them.

31

He slid with arms out over a patch in front of the rectory and saw the fourth grade server boys vault over the back porch railing, letting the sacristy screen door bang.

In the still-dark morning the sacristy lights blared. Johnny saw the top of Father's head coming toward the back door and took off fast, shuffling, sliding, Colorado-skiing just as the sacristy turned black.

Johnny remembered to jump over the section of the sidewalk that had the hollow underground tunnel from the priest's house to the convent. He landed one boot safely, then the other with an "ooh."

The ice turned rough, unsafe for Colorado-skiing. Johnny saw Dave the janitor headed back toward the school swinging an empty white five-gallon bucket with "San" scrawled on it in light-blue pen.

Johnny tried to catch Dave in his long, skinny strides with his rapid, thigh-rubbing, ten-thousand buckle, wet-mitten-holding-fif- teen-cents shuffle.

"Dave!

"Dave."

Dave stopped and turned and looked straight back. His eyes shooting three feet over Johnny's top button on his snap-under brown corduroy cap.

"Hey!"

Johnny called out, breathing hard, face red, taking another try at sliding over the sandy ice.

Dave looked down.

"Oh, there you are. I thought I heard something. You supposed to be in Sister Mark's room?"

"I'm going," said Johnny.

Johnny stopped and looked straight up – saw Dave from under him – right under his nose – breath puffs, sweat on the tip of his nose. It dripped. Johnny pulled his head out of the way, just in time.

"It was on the news, that's how I know," Dave said. "WRUR, the Daily News, the Herald, TV, too.

"Johnny Moon."

Dave extended his arm and made his yellow-gloved hand into a "C" and drew it across left to right to build a banner headline.

"Johnny Moon walked fifty miles to school, almost late to Mass, just makes it, but in big, big trouble with Sister Mark for crawling around on the church floor before the start of Holy Mass."

"WILL DIE."

Johnny stepped back.

"It did not?" he said, his eyes half-open, hoping he was not on the news. He would be in big trouble.

"Yeah, really," Dave said. "There will probably be TV cameras up there when you get there. President Kennedy's not going to like this, makes him look bad, Catholics on their stomach in the mud on the church floor."

"Yeah, but."

Johnny put his head down and pumped his arms, trying to take bigger steps in his giant heavy boots and sweating snowsuit, wool mitten and corduroy cap.

Dave hurried up next to him.

"Not really, Johnny."

He squatted down and put his arm on Johnny's shoulder.

"It's okay. You'll be all right."

Johnny took a deep breath and opened his eyes wide to say, "Really?"

He took off again down the walk like the most determined, blue-plaid snowball.

Johnny passed the familiar grey painted and re-painted wooden door of the entrance to the old maroon brick part of the school and plowed ahead into the vanilla brick zone.

He put one boot up on the slick cement and reached to grab one of the double glass door handles. He grabbed with both hands and leaned his behind out over the two cement steps.

He stood on the steps and pushed his nose into the glass. He knocked lightly on the glass with his left-hand mitten fist. The glass punched him in the face. He stepped back and grabbed his nose as a big kid, a fifth or even sixth grader, pulled on the handle and walked in.

Johnny scooted inside just in front of the closing door. He followed the big kid the first flight of grey cement steps with dips where a million kids had stepped, some in big trouble.

Johnny recognized this part of the school. Over there was the library where they came every Friday. Johnny had "Pinocchio" and "Paul Bunyan" checked out as usual. He wondered for an instant where they were.

Johnny stopped.

In front of him spread a wide stairway with grey steps and a brown handrail leading up. On his left was the corner around from the library, and there was the door to Sister Principal-Something's office. Off to his right was the long, narrow hallway to the boys lavatory and the girls lavatory, the audio visual office and nurses room, and the balcony over the gym where the teachers stored their colored paper and other craft supplies, and where Johnny might some day run the lights for a school play, but Johnny did not know any of this.

Straight ahead like a waterfall fell grey stairs to a side entrance. Unlocked. Unattended. Outside there were no troubles, no worry, only people working at interesting jobs and not getting yelled at.

He gritted his teeth and crunched his fists at his sides and pushed his feet into the hard, grey paint.

He heard music. He looked down and saw he was melting, getting the floor all wet.

He moved toward the music. Maybe it was fourth grade after-Mass music and this would be over quickly.

He stopped at the top and leaned over to hear. He saw the gym door where he would go to get the milk when he was on morning duty, in that fourth-grade fantasy world that seemed so untenable now.

The music came from the locker room where the seventh and eighth graders dressed for P.E., but Johnny didn't know that. He just knew it as the home of Isom and Anthony and Earl the Negroes, who played basketball for the junior college and helped coach them sometimes and do physical fitness.

Johnny heard laughing, talking mixed with the music.

The Negroes in the Catholic school basement locker room always had white girls down there, Johnny knew. And they smelled bad and they were kind of like gorillas and monkeys and chimpanzees. And they were from far-away towns and why didn't they just stay there. He didn't know why they wanted to hang around with girls.

"Hey! My man!"

Johnny startled and looked up and saw Isom towering above.

"Hi, Coach," Johnny waved and said in a small voice.

The man squatted to put his face level with Johnny.

"What's up, Johnny. Mr. Moon, Johnny Moon."

Johnny didn't say anything, amazed and aghast that even the Negro coach basketball players knew that everyone called him Johnny Moon because he once said he was going to go to the moon like President Kennedy said. He had said he wanted to be the one to go, the first American on the moon.

"You lost, little man?"

Johnny nodded.

He had never been this close before to the black man who lived with a couple of friends in the school locker room because nobody in town would rent to them.

The man had tight, curly hair with shiny stuff on it. It looked "squeaky" to Johnny he decided without telling anyone. The man had big eyes and smelled like honey and black olives.

"I'm in trouble," Johnny admitted in a whimper, then asked where was Sister Mark's room, that way?

The man took Johnny's cold, clenched fist that housed the coins into his large, strong hand and led him up the grey steps of the new school section that the parish had been able to build a couple of years ago as more and more Catholic families had moved to town. The tip-top floor even had high school, but a new school was also under construction on the edge of town since there really wasn't anymore room right there in the downtown.

Johnny didn't know how he felt being led up the stairs and down the halls holding the hand of the Negro coach, whether he was proud to be with the coach or embarrassed to be led by the hand past the big kids like some dumb little creep.

Isom got Johnny as far as the fourth grade hallway and knelt on one knee next to Johnny. He didn't really look like the Negro on his sister's Johnny Mathis albums, but more like on Wild Kingdom.

Isom pointed like Sacagawea toward Sister Mark's classroom and nodded solemnly like it was bad medicine or the witch's castle in the forest and he could go no farther.

Johnny stuck his chin up and then down and moved off, slowly, like a chunky ship from port, hugging the wall like one side of little dog magnet set.

The fourth grade hall felt sophisticated and learned, and quiet, like you don't need to yell if you know a lot. On the walls were historical hand-made student depictions of the Pilgrims feeding the Indians on Thanksgiving, Moses and The Burning Bush and Washington cutting down the cherry tree.

Lockers made up one whole wall.

Johnny scuffled along and kept one finger running down the wall for balance.

He came to the giant vanilla wooden door with a window. It looked kind of like the door to the medical clinic that Johnny feared because it meant mystery, the smell of alcohol, needles, fear and pain. On the window, etched into the glass it said, "Sister Mark, Fourth Grade."

Johnny took a giant deep breath, looked back down the quiet hall, saw that he was all alone, and thought that maybe Sister Mark and the fourth graders and the TV cameras weren't back from Mass yet.

Oh, well, he had been here, that's what he would tell Sister M&Ms, Sister Mary-Michael. He went there. They weren't there, but he went there.

Oh, well. I guess it's over now. He was there. They weren't even there yet. Oh, well, he really would have liked to have visited with them to gain the advantage of their experience as to how he could improve his deportment.

His toes felt sweaty and squishy inside his boots and his underwear was just turned all around.

He breathed again and stepped up to the door.

He tapped lightly with his grey mitten fist so that even he couldn't hardly even tell he was knocking.

He scanned up and down the hall and relief burned in his heart. He wasn't that good but he wasn't that bad and now that he would live he would make every reasonable effort to maybe do a little better.

The door pushed open like the giant inside had exhaled, causing Johnny to dodge out of its way with an exaggerated step like jumping a mud puddle.

Sister Mark filled the doorway like a forest nun Johnny had awakened. Her arms were crossed. She scowled, looking down at the notorious church crawling little creep criminal kid from the third grade classroom in the old section.

He thought of his own warm, bright room and Sister Mary-Michael's smiling face and then in an instant was yanked back by Sister Mark's stamping of her severe, worn black shoes on the tile floor.

Sister Mark pointed down at a line, a white piece of tape on the Linoleum. Johnny stepped up and put his grungy booted toes on the line, just short of the line, not daring to touch the line.

He looked up and there was the whole fourth grade, rows and rows of them, with their hands folded, teeth glowing, eyes reflecting the light from the giant glow in the dark plastic Jesus on the wall, in the shadows of the fourth grade cave.

They grinned ironically as if they were waiting to rule on whether they should allow Johnny's loan application to go through on his sharecropper farm. They stared at him like Johnny had killed God, sitting there in their connected rows, like sleighs, toboggans they had taken to Mass and had landed back here, dry, in perfect rows.

Johnny's heart pounded and he hoped he would not pee his snowsuit as he had wet the floor of the kindergarten class all those years ago.

"What do you have to say for yourself, young man?"

Sister glared down at Johnny like the hardest nun on Mount Rushmore.

He looked for a moment into the stone faces of the one million fourth graders, the girls in blue plaid dresses and white blouses and the boys in dress clothes, then to the back and to the front, to Sister's desk, with a small statue of a saint and a box of Kleenex and a prisoner Matchbox red and white Chevy.

He looked up at Sister, then down.

He tried to move his toes enough to see them through the rubber boots, wondering if he might lose circulation and have to maybe have his toes cut off. Maybe his feet needed to breathe. They had been in there a long time. His stomach began to hurt, or maybe it hurt before but he was just now noticing it. He felt light-headed and warm. He started to worry about appendicitis.

His lips begged permission to quiver and his teeth wished to rattle like a skeleton.

Johnny refused.

His knees asked to be able to crumble to the floor and he shouted, No!

The room sat quiet for hours and hours, like the whole weekend in a storage locker at the meat packing plant.

Johnny saw the framed photos of the President, and General Washington, the detailed graph on the blackboard behind Sister's desk of how the world was made in seven days and what was created on each day.

On a card table in the corner the class T.A.B. book orders were arranged in neat piles ready to be handed out.

And he saw the Pope and a crucifix above the cloakroom along the back wall. He spied drying boots sitting upside down on the radiators under the windows. For a moment he admired the fourth-grade drawings of the parting of the Red Sea, Jesus Walking on Water, and Noah's Ark in big, sculpted waves.

It didn't seem as though anyone was ever going to talk and soon they would have to listen to the morning announcements and morning prayer through the new intercom box, so Johnny just waited.

He swiveled his head and looked all around the room like a small-town kid in Time Square. He saw Holy Card depictions on the wall of Jesus Feeds the Five Hundred, Jonah and the Whale, and Jesus Raises Lazarus From the Dead, and the little children at Fatima who knew Jesus' Mom.

He smelled gum. Cherry. Wild. Stolen. He followed the aroma to a boy in one of the front row seats. The boy stopped chewing upon making eye contact and looked at Sister.

"What should be done with him?" Sister asked the class like Poncho Pilate.

"Is there anything wrong with crawling upon the floor on your stomach like a grasshopper in church before Mass?"

A few unseen girls tittered. The boy who had been chewing raised his hand and stood by his desk in one motion.

"It helps the Communists," he said. "This boy might be a Communist. He probably is. And the devil. The devil benefits by his actions."

He sat down. Johnny could see him shove his gum deeper into the side of his mouth like a miscreant gopher.

A front-desk girl with glasses and a watch stood by her desk without raising her hand.

Johnny could only hope her testimony would be disallowed.

"The President would not like it," she said. "Because the Kennedy family is all Catholics and he never laughed in church or did anything like that. He was captain of his own boat!"

She sat.

Johnny looked down and saw a puddle around his boots, disrespecting the white tape line. He scooted back and took inventory to determine it was only slush water.

"Was it a sin?" Sister flicked her headpiece with a toss of her head as if she and Johnny and the fourth-grade class were filming a Breck hair commercial.

She pulled magically a handkerchief from nowhere to wipe her flaming red nose.

"If a truck hit Johnathan," she began.

"Or a train," one of the children offered.

"Or a train," said Sister. "Hit Mr. Moon today ..."

"Or if a building fell on him," somebody chose to add.

"We'll just stick with truck and train, for now," she said.

Johnny shook his head subtly to sneak Sister the information, that wasn't his real name.

"Would he be in a state of sin and suffer the eternal fires of hell?"

She finished wiping her nose and somehow disposed of the handkerchief without pockets.

Through the open closet door Johnny saw a big brown box of brown paper towels, a mop, extra long erasers and a Nixon poster.

"He's fat."

The sound, like jabbing a scissors into a balloon, came from one of the invisible girl gigglers.

"We're suppose to get in shape," said the gum-chewing boy, to fight Communism and go to the moon."

"The moon," someone said and someone else laughed.

The boy looked back to see who was laughing.

Sister turned to Johnny and stepped toward him.

"Just why *do* you walk?"

She twisted and ground her heels into the floor and raised her toes up together like Dorothy.

"Why do you walk to school in November of the year while your siblings and all the other children ride to school with their parents at the same time in the morning, and always arrive to Mass on time?"

Her jaws showed through her skin.

"Why? It's cold out there."

She stared and rubbed her sore nose with the back of her hand.

"Amazing," she whispered and shook her head.

Johnny looked at her, then at the class, then down at the lake he was making.

It was my first day, he thought, and denied a request from his eyes to become wet.

"A strong boy," he began.

"Please raise your head and speak to the class and not to the floor, young man."

"A strong boy … makes a strong man … makes a strong nation, umm-country."

Many of the girls snickered.

The gum-chewer chipmunk and two boys near him who looked like they could be twins laughed out loud.

"And yet," Sister stepped in front of Johnny and turned her back to him to address her class like a prosecutor before a jury.

"And yet, you deem to crawl on your stomach in — are we to know if your snow attire was filthy when you put it on this morning — on the floor under the pews of church, just prior to the onset of the Holy saying of the Mass of our Lord.

"Just to get money," gum-chewer growled. "Would Jesus be on the floor grubbing for money in the dirt and mud?"

"Boo-owling money," an invisible girl chimed in, confident the information was lethal.

Sister swirled to Johnny in the dock.

"Is that so?"

Johnny touched eyes with Sister Mark and nodded slowly.

"Bowling," she said as if saying poop-cicle.

She returned to her class and began to pace.

"For the President's Council on Physical Fitness, I assume?"

Johnny shrugged then nodded quickly when she turned on him again.

"Bowling's not a sport anyway," a boy in the second row stood to recite then sat.

Johnny watched Sister until she looked at him and then nodded, yes-it-is.

"Coach Isom takes us," he said.

Sister turned sideways, half facing Johnny and half her very own class. It was probable she had decided she was prepared to pass sentence.

She produced a giant navy blue jar of Noxzema, took out a dab and painfully touched her nose. Johnny looked away for one moment to follow a sound of a pen being clicked like a gun cocked and the jar disappeared. His eyes began to burn.

Sister rubbed her chin, found a pimple and began fondling it.

"The third grade will not be going bowling this week," she declared.

"But Sister Mary ...", Johnny blurted.

"I will speak to Sister Mary-Michael," she said. "The money will instead be given to the missions."

She walked toward Johnny as a gunslinger in the street certain his foe has no gun.

"Where is your money?"

Johnny held up his sweaty grey mitten fist as high as his nose and opening his hand, revealed the dime and pennies like the black jack and ace.

Sister leaned herself into a "C" as a blue jay over a robin's nest.

"You only have fourteen cents," she said. "You weren't going bowling anyway. You may return to your room," she said as a titter fever spread through her room.

Johnny took one blind step backward as the door slammed, leaving him alone in the hall with The Burning Bush, The Cherry Tree, and an unseen dripping faucet.

He turned and trudged down the fourth grade hall like a Russian soldier headed home across a million miles of taiga, wondering how he would ever find his own room.

It wasn't on this floor. Maybe if he just kept going.

He kept going, walking slower and slower as he grew more confused.

Like Jesus wandering in the desert, smelling water, like a cowboy sniffing the log fires of home, he followed the aroma of brown paper towels and dispenser soap.

[CHAPTER FIVE]

I've known a secret for a week or two,
Nobody knows just we two.
Listen, do you want to know a secret,
Do you promise not to tell, Whoa . . . . .
Closer let me whisper in your ear ...
— "Do You Want To Know A Secret," The Beatles

*M*argaret and Susan sat down on the grass.
They drew apples from their purses.
They munched and crunched and enjoyed the sun and could not get over a day like this in *November*.
"Nobody would believe me," Susan said.
Susan talked about her family back home and what she would be doing right now if she were still there.
"Scooping snow," she laughed.
Margaret talked about her family. The brother who was sure he wanted to join the Army when he graduated from high school in May.
"My twin sister's a nun," she said, snapping her head toward Susan and smiling.
"You never said!" said Susan. "A twin! You're a twin? There's two of you. Oh, heaven help us!"
"Yeah," Margaret looked at the ground and took a chunk out of her apple and chewed contemplatively like a cow with too much education.
"She's pretty," said Margaret.
"You are pretty!" Susan pushed Margaret's shoulder and almost fell backward herself.
"You're a twin, you stoop!"
"She's really pretty, though," said Margaret. "You should see her."
"Why'd she be a nun?" said Susan, biting her apple and looking all around at the cars whizzing past and the helicopter overhead and the time and temperature on the huge sign on top of the big red brick building over there, up the short, inclined road.

"She's special," said Margaret, looking at Susan and waiting until Susan stopped gawking all over and looked at her.

"Yeah, right. I'll bet she can fly and tell the future," Susan said, tossing her apple core into the street.

"You can't do *that*," said Margaret.

"I don't know, but she's just … different, and so smart and so … *interested* in everything … and everybody."

She looked at Susan again and waited.

Susan looked over and bobbed her head a little, to say, go ahead, I'm listening.

"Well, it's creepy sometimes, you know? She's a teacher."

"Teachers are creepy," Susan grabbed a hunk of grass and threw it up to judge the wind direction, then swiping the bits off her clean skirt and blouse.

"No, not that. It's just … so intense. I actually wanted to get away from her for a while, you know? Get a break. But today, you know? I miss her."

"Awww!" Susan pushed Margaret again.

Margaret pushed Susan back and tossed her core into the street. It landed right next to Susan's.

"Ooooh!" they both screamed when a city bus smooshed their trash.

Together, synchronized sitters, they wiped the juice from their faces with the backs of their hands, then swiped their hands in the grass.

[CHAPTER SIX]

"… in some dioceses it meant exclusion from the sacraments for parents to send their children to the public schools.

"… near each church, a parochial school if it does not yet exist, is to be erected within two years from the promulgation of the Council, and is to be maintained in perpetuum …

"… a priest who, by his grave negligence, prevents the erection of a school within the time or its maintenance, or who, after repeated admonitions of the bishop, does not attend to the matter, deserves removal from that church.

"… all Catholic parents are bound to send their children to the parochial schools …

— Congregation of Propaganda, Second Plenary Council of Baltimore, "Instruction to the Bishops of the United States concerning the Public Schools, 1875

*J*ohnny spotted Dave in the fourth grade Boys lavatory, on his knees, then on his back, holding a wrench to the bottom of a sink. A battered red toolbox lay wide open as if sacked by Visigoths, with all sorts of tools, including a non sequitur handsaw and bike chain covering the white and black tile.

Johnny stood in the doorway, sweating, soaked, covered in dried slush mud, his hat unbuttoned from under his chin and all cockeyed. He wore one wool mitten on a clenched fist, mentally touching and counting again the beleaguered coins.

He stood there for a while, watching, then looked down at the water around his feet.

Dave grunted then began talking and Johnny asked himself if Dave had eyes in the back of his head.

"Hey, I'm seeing you everywhere today. You okay?"

Johnny nodded.

"You in trouble? Still?"

Johnny nodded.

"You lost?"

He nodded again.

44

Dave held Johnny's fist in his hand as he guided him down the third grade hall.

"Well, here you go, Mr. Moon, then," Dave said.

Johnny looked up at him with a gallows demeanor.

"Just kidding. You have a good rest of the day, okay-now?"

Johnny nodded.

He stood outside the big brown shiny wood door, Sister Mary-Michael's class.

He hung his hat on a hook attached to a long board on the wall. The other hooks sported drying hats and gloves. The boots sat in two's with toes pressed to the wall.

Johnny heard Sister inside the room, her cheerful, light voice doing times exercises, the class answering her together.

Johnny sat on the floor against the wall to pull off his boots. He stood in his socks and pulled down his snowsuit, hung it up then slipped his feet into his shoes waiting for him on the floor.

He tilted his head this way then that, staring down at his feet.

They were kind of big, maybe.

He worked hard to open his cramped hand and touched each coin, counting in his head up to fourteen.

He shoved the coins into his front pocket and dropped the mittens on the edge of his boots to dry.

Johnny stood alone in the hall, dark and long and quiet except for the dripping of coats and hats and gloves from the three other rooms besides Sister Mary-Michael's.

Through the open door to Sister Celeste's second grade class Johnny heard her talking about stuff he already knew.

Johnny heard steps coming up the stairs and grabbed the loose black metal knob to go inside his room.

He pulled the knob a little and opened the door a crack.

All eyes went instantly to him like you see in a scary show when something happens in a window.

Silence poured out the little crack in the door like air out a hole in a passenger plane.

He looked back around and listened hard. It sounded like little voices and laughing and little black clacky shoes on marble.

Jimmy said he saw one last week, one of the kids in the ghost class.

Johnny heard the clicking sound of whoever was coming getting closer and pulled the door open, then stepped inside, blindly closing the door behind him.

He was home, finally. The big bright, open, not overly supplied room, felt warm. Not the institutional too-warm feeling of a radiator stuck on wide-open, but the sort of wood-smoke, logs on the fire warmth that came from familiarity and caring and okay.

He watched himself step ahead on the shiny wooden floor. He sort of smiled at his classmates. Photos of the Pope, the Beatles and President Kennedy Mona-Lisa-grinned at him from three sides of the room like grampas who lived with you.

The string and paper car races each row ran against each other on the front blackboard stood where they had been yesterday with Johnny's row one length behind the first-place row, so he had not missed too much yet.

Sister twirled and hurried to him, not quite running, her long brown habit and cords and rosaries and her veil flapping and banging like a missionary weather rooster on top of the barn.

Sister Mary-Michael smiled and squatted, then knelt on one knee and hugged him. She took his hand and walked him to her desk and gave him a boost to sit in her wooden rolling chair.

She pulled out warm, dry socks from somewhere in her desk and helped him in taking off his shoes and wet socks and putting on the new, warm ones, while shielding him from the curious stares of the others so they did not see Sister touch his bare feet.

Sister touched Johnny's knee and grinned and nodded to say, watch this.

She looked up over the desk at the class.

"Third graders!"

The voice came from the intercom above the blackboard.

All the children snapped to attention and looked up with frightened countenances. This might be it, the end of the world.

"James Bambi-Boxers! Sit up straight!"

Sister snickered and Johnny looked at her and caught a glimpse of her adam's apple bobbing too much.

Jimmy sat up and looked all around, his eyes wide.

"That's not my real ..."

He looked all around and up at the brown intercom box.

46

"That's just what they ca …"

Johnny took his eyes off the frantic class and the intercom to watch Sister M&Ms.

"Michael Irish! Zip up your fly! Your cows will get out … and we don't think God the father, son and holy spirit would care much for that, would they, young man? Or the holy mother of us all? To have to chase cows, your cows, on a Friday morning, young man?"

Her mouth did not move, maybe a little. Her adam's apple jumped up and down like a bobber with a bite.

Michael Irish ducked his head way down below his desk, then turned sideways to zip up his pants, then turned back to the class as if he were going to die, right there.

Then she put both her hands over her face, ducked her head below her desk and turned red and burst out laughing behind her hands.

The whole class stared up at the intercom as if they had had a vision. A vision of hearing. Maybe it was a miracle. They waited for what happens next.

Maybe a ghost would come through the blackboard, or little baby Jesus in the manger with cows would float down through the ceiling, or apple pies with white plastic forks would appear on every desk.

Some watched the ceiling. Some watched their desks.

After about ten seconds they forgot about it and remembered Johnny, over there at Sister's desk getting very extra special treatment.

The class looked over at Johnny together, sitting facing straight ahead, turning only their heads, as if a producer had pointed in that direction.

He smiled at his classmates and waved as they all stared over at him. He kept waving, like he was on a ticker-tape parade down Broadway and he was on the Yankees and they won.

He was a major leaguer. He was famous. And his big feet were warmer than they had ever been. And the back wall of windows was filled with light and blue sky.

Then he saw the mission jar on Sister's desk.

And if there were not a hundred people dying right this moment somewhere from something everywhere in the world that you didn't know where it was or who they were or why they were dying, it would have been a grace-filled moment — except that now you

47

remembered that people were dying everywhere and you recalled that you had not been thinking about them until just now, but now you remembered, and you also remembered that you were going straight to hell, just as soon as God found a not-too-obvious way to dispose of you, because you were living for yourself and ... your ... self ... only.

And nobody was going bowling today.

Johnny wiggled his feet inside his new white warm socks and looked at the glass peanut butter or something jar on Sister's desk with the homemade cover of people with forlorn looks and he felt his clenched left fist and his not-enough bowling money.

Johnny slid down from Sister's chair as she moved back to the front of the class to get things rolling again.

He walked to the back of the room then turned up his aisle to his desk. He slid in and pushed up his desktop, revealing his private domain, the Kennedy sticker, peeled at one corner, his Fruit-Stripe Gum collection, his ring collection, Magic Marker collection.

Johnny felt like a star for the first time in his life. Holding the desktop up with his left hand he looked right, at Jane Lincoln Frogs to see if his new status would make her like him, which ... it ... had not.

He saw Jimmy Purple a couple of rows away, digging into his desk with a straightened-out paper clip. Michael Irish smiled at Johnny.

Timmy Eagle Pest Crest-Nest waved at Johnny. Tommy Turdner, Susan Mishal-hmm-hmm-kakowski, and Danny Glasshopper all stared at Sister, hands on their open workbooks, pencils in hand like convicts working for parole.

Johnny pulled out his arithmetic workbook and let his desk down.

He stole a look at the door, wondering if they had already heard from Sister Mark or whether they would yet, or maybe they never would.

Johnny looked at Sister when she was looking at the class and when she turned to write on the board he began placing his dime and four pennies in his pencil groove.

Also on Johnny's old desktop was a large, dug-out "Mark," so that he could not even write over that spot with one sheet of paper because it would make holes in his paper, and the round hole in the

upper right corner that everyone had that you could put almost anything in there that you wanted if you were in Sister Mary-Michael's
class but in some other classes you couldn't hardly put anything in
there.

Johnny began placing his collection of rings around the hole. He
had about five or six and he wore them all at once sometimes, even
the thumb, especially the thumb. He was trying to get the kids to
call him "Ringo," and he'd be famous for that.

"Just a minute, please," Sister smiled, raised a finger in the air and
said as she almost always did, "hold that thought," and nobody had
been thinking anything.

She then galloped to answer the knock on the door that nobody
else had heard, carrying her workbook, the breeze filling her gar-
ments.

Johnny could see that Sister was talking to a fourth-grade messen-
ger, Johnny's angel of death.

Sister Mary-Michael closed the door and turned back to them, her
workbook pressed against her chest and her head bowed in discern-
ment. She reached the middle of the front of the room in a flourish,
shot her head up and smiled, pleased with the idea of whatever she
was about to tell them.

"There will be no bowling today," she said.

"Aaaaa, Ohhhhh," came back the general reply.

Sister kept smiling and stepped two steps closer to them, smiling
yet wider and brighter.

Johnny curled his toes and felt his hands getting cold. He clenched
them into bread dough clumps of fist. He brought his feet out from
under his desk and stretched his legs back, digging his toes into the
tile. He tried to place his head directly behind the head in front of
him, matching all the moves.

"Likely we will be going next month," she continued, "but it has
been suggested by Sister Mark, and I wholeheartedly agree, that
we should support our President in his call for a greater interaction
between our country and the rest of the world."

She then entered one of the aisles, right up close to the desks and
with alarming alacrity continued her monologue.

"Our reaching out to the rest of the world, and also to the rest of
the universe."

She stopped at Johnny's desk, but did not stare down at him. She even turned her back to him.

"Which is what going to the moon is all about, a reaching out to explore and to extend our helping hands. Isn't that so?"

"Yeee-eesssSiiissterrr."

"And so, we will go by rows up to my desk to drop our bowling money into the mission jar. We give with joyful hearts just as Jesus did, isn't that so?"

"Yeee-eesssSiiisstteerrr."

The first row stood up on the right side of their desks and processed over to Sister's desk.

The clanging of the coins into the jar was not the gallows construction nail pounding that Johnny had anticipated, but rather a ringing affirmation.

Somehow Sister M&Ms had made it all right.

He loved her.

She stayed at the front of the room, her workbook clutched to her chest with both arms, smiling, watching the third-graders bang their fifteen centses into the mission jar.

As the jar became fuller, the noise lessened, but Jimmy Purple and some others on that side of the room found a way, even though they were the last ones, to clang the jar with each one of their coins.

Sister retained her cherubic pose.

Johnny watched her and imagined her with hair and arms and legs and a body. She turned and smiled right at him. He hid behind the head in front of him, then peeked out and she was still there. Johnny raised up his hand, keeping it in touch with the desk by his palm and waved at her. She brought her hand down to her hip and waved back.

He mouthed the secret word and she nodded clandestinely.

Johnny turned red, put his hand to his brow, bowed his head and told God that if he wanted him to go to the moon he would do it for Sister … and for America. And he would lose weight if they needed him to fit in a little place.

Sister then walked to the door and on her way looked back over her shoulder towards them.

"You may put everything away," she said as she stepped into the hall and pulled the door closed, stopping the door at the very end and easing it into place like the last burglar out of the bank.

The room filled with the busy noise of desks opening and shutting, pencils hitting the floor, and workbooks fluttering, falling, giggles and shhhshes.

Sister danced back to the middle of the room and announced they were going to have Science Class.

Her veil and robes fluttered as she put up double quote marks and galloped around.

The children looked at each other with puzzled looks.

The front row girls quick-looked into their desks for their science workbooks. They were not there. They had lost their science workbooks. They would get down marks for deportment.

Two of the front row girls turned deep red all over the place, one got blotches.

Sister took her yellow chalk out and ran to her desk to retrieve long, unused beautiful sticks of pink, blue and green chalk. The children shielded their eyes against the sensory over-stimulation.

She wrote ASTRONOMY in huge letters across the top of the blackboard.

Sister drew the earth and the sun on the blackboard, and the moon and the planets. She described the orbits and movement of the planets and together they figured out how far it was to the moon and how long it would take for earth astronauts to travel there if they would go the daytime highway speed limit.

She asked them to raise their hand if they had heard of the "Fan Alien Belt."

They stared at each other for a count of one-thousand-five.

"I'll have to look it up," she said.

And the children looked at each other, in shock that a teacher did not know everything.

"Michael, big eraser," she clapped her hands at the boy nearest the cloakroom and put up her hands like a ballplayer. Michael threw the eraser overhand end-over-end.

Mary-Michael caught the eraser right in front of her face, giggled and shut her eyes when it threw dust on her nose and cheeks, then swirled and used big swooping motions to erase the board.

Then she used the pink chalk and the green and blue and red and yellow to draw a group of Egyptian-like people with like old-time under-water helmets on, the big round ones, and a cave and a boxy something inside the cave, no, on the wall of the cave, like the people had drawn it on the cave wall.

To those who had gone down to Dave's workroom to get the big box of Christmas decorations or a pair of new light bulbs, it resembled the boiler, the biggest thing in the workroom, big and steel and with tubes and wires and ducts going in and out and around, like a grandfather in the intensive care unit.

Sister smiled and laughed and whirled and had them get up and do skits and go stand by the window in a long line to stare up at the sky. When the hour was up it seemed like a little less than an hour.

After she had finished the lesson they all worked to erase the board, and while she put away her chalk she asked two of the bad boys to wash the board with wet rags.

After arithmetic and milk break and spelling Sister asked the class to by rows go to the cloakroom to find their wraps and line up along the chalkboard for noon recess.

As Johnny struggled to put on his snowsuit and get his hat and gloves and everything in order, Jane Lincoln Frogs turned up behind him, her outdoors clothes already on and ready, and handed him a glove that had fallen to the floor that was not his.

"Maybe you should go to the moon, Johnny," she smiled. "You really should. Are you going to?"

"Yes.

"Yes, I'm going to."

Johnny took the damp glove and forced it on and felt his face glow and throb.

"I'd like to."

"Then you should just do it. *I* would."

[CHAPTER SEVEN]

Patty: "Try to catch snowflakes on your tongue. It's fun."
Linus Van Pelt: "Mmm. Needs sugar."
Lucy Van Pelt: "It's too early. I never eat December snowflakes. I always wait until January."
Linus Van Pelt: "They sure look ripe to me."
— "A Charlie Brown Christmas"

*M*argaret and Susan got quiet.
They sat back on their hands and looked around.
Up there on the overpass were some people just standing around. Over there were people in windows, looking down on the street.
"Hey," said Susan.
"There's the Russians! And Cubans!"
"Where!" said Margaret.
"Up there," she pointed.
"And there's the Chinese."
Again she pointed to the top of one of the buildings.
Then she pointed at somebody in a window.
"And there's the Iowans and the Oklahomans."
"And there's the jail."
She pointed way up to their right at a big white building with hundreds of small windows on all the floors.
"No. Really?"
"Yah-huh, the city jail, ye-eepper. When's this thing start, you hungry?"
Margaret pointed out a man carrying a walkie-talkie just across the street and then a man with an umbrella.
She looked at the sky and asked Susan if she had heard the forecast.
Susan shook her head and continued looking all around.
"No, I didn't hear," she said
"Your sister would like this."
"Yeah, she would, she really would," said Margaret.
"Could have brought her kids, you know her stuu-dents," said

Susan. "How does she do it, you know, if she's such a knock-out. You know."

"I dunno. She's very talented. She was the best dancer at any of the school dances we had. Everyone wanted to dance with Mary Kelley. I even slipped in there when she got tired. Nobody knew."

Margaret sat up straight and shook the needles out of her hands and arms.

"I hate that feeling," she said.

"Yeah-fuck," said Susan.

"You, know, I don't know how she does it, or why, or how," said Margaret.

"You *said* how," said Susan.

"I know, how."

"You said how twice, that's all, no big deal, don't have a con-niption-fit. She must be a saint. Maybe she's a saint. Saints can do anything, no big deal."

"Oh, I don't think she's a saint, not by a long ..."

"When does this start?"

"Oh, I'm sure it has by now – see look, they're cutting off the traffic," said Margaret. "That's a news helicopter. Or weather," she said, looking over again at the umbrella guy.

Other people moved in next to them, in front of them. They stood and found a good spot right by the road.

A railroad engine blew its whistle, a piercing warning, sort of out of place in a big-city downtown, Margaret thought. Maybe it was the start of the parade.

"No. It's already begun long ago," said Susan.

"That must just be a switch engine working," said Margaret.

"What's a witch Injun?

"Sss-witch-engine. My dad used to work for the Chicago North-wester, anyway, I just know, don't' worry about it."

"I'm not worrying, believe me."

They could feel the space filling in around them, a red pickup parked on the far curb behind them, all the spaces taken, people stopped walking, in cars on the overpass over there.

Somebody was smoking.

"It smells good," Margaret smiled at Susan.

"Where's it coming from?"

Susan pointed across the street, behind the fence.

"The wind must be blowing this way, just perfect, I can really smell it," said Susan.

"Yeah, uh-huh, hey, here comes something."

[CHAPTER EIGHT]

"The coal-fired boiler in the 1948-49 building, which became the junior/senior high school when the elementary school was built, was converted in 1959 to an oil-fired boiler, and later converted to gas. The remaining heating equipment dates to the original 1948-49 construction. A new west wing was added in 1980, which was comprised of four classrooms, a band room, and wood shop. A steam-to-water heat exchanger was added to the building steam system to supply hot water to heat the new wing."

— Johnston Boiler Co., Ferrysburg, MI

*F*ather surrounded his coffee cup like bad news over breakfast. Leaning low, he circled it with his arms, and feathered it with just his top lip like a horse on a salt lick.

He sat at the regular table.

Right up next to the big front window at the Corner Café.

In his regular chair.

Jim walked in, ringing the front door bell. He clicked to the table, sat down, leaned back in his chair and raised a hand to ask the waitress for coffee. Jim reached to the ledge under the window for the paper and flapped it smooth onto the table.

Father touched his cup then put both hands around it, pressed it and pulled it to his chest.

Tim parked his Mustang right in front of the window, mostly cutting off Father's view of the street. He sat next to Father and said, yes, coffee, please, and a glazed donut.

They were joined one by one by Dan, Bob, Tom, and John.

Around the table in comfortable silence sat the banker, publisher, realtor, insurance man, car dealer, and radio station manager.

And Father.

All together again like the apostles and Jesus at coffee break, looking around again at the cactus and the figs and the donkeys, hoping maybe today one would talk or one would turn to gold.

They drank and watched out the window and acknowledged infidels at other tables. Two of them squinted against the low sun, shining right in their eyes for a short moment.

"So, how's Father today?" said Tim.

Father nodded, gripped his cup, turned his head and said he was doing just fine.

"Gonna snow?" Tim asked around the table.

One man scrunched up his mouth and his eyebrows to say how should I know.

Two men shook their heads that they had not heard. One turned the page of the paper in a rustle.

"Could," Father said.

"Yeah," said Tim. "Hey, how's old Sister PMS-Something doin'?"

Father looked hard at Tim.

"Don't remind me," Father said.

"Prezdent's in Dallas," the man with the paper said, keeping his eyes down, grumbling at the wrinkles in the paper, folding it in half and running a hand across it, creating a small tear.

"Lombardi," he pointed at something in the paper, almost touching it with his finger.

"Knights play tonight?" the car dealer sipped his coffee and peaked around the cup at Father.

"Friday," Father said.

"Oh."

[CHAPTER NINE]

"...there is hope for the future. When the world is ready for a new and better life, all this will someday come to pass, in God's good time."

— Captain Nemo

"Hey! Hey!"

"You're up! You're up!"

Someone hollered at Johnny, sitting on the ground against the priests' garage while the rest of his team took their turns kicking.

Sister Mark served as permanent pitcher for both teams today. Sister M&Ms stayed with the kids in the merry-go-round, monkey bars, swings area. They supposedly rotated, but Mark most often grabbed the kickball game.

Mark's cheeks gleamed rosy red, framing a wide smile. She had tied her black shawl around her waist and her black gloves were cut off at the knuckles. She pounded the white ball in her hands.

Johnny continued to play in the dirt, messing with the ants, naming them, watching what they did, where they went, who they associated with, while he doodled in the dirt with a stick, making pictures of space alien ships, My Fav'rite Martian little antennas and laser beams and Moses and the Burning Bushes.

Johnny imagined being one of those ants down there, working hard, finding this one twig like it was the golden twig, the twig of all time, pulling that twig around all day long, thinking there must be something special to be done with this amazing twig and just looking and looking and nobody telling him nothing.

"Who is *up*?" Sister hollered out, breath puffs hanging in the air above her head like cartoon dialogue boxes.

"Who's up? Let's go!"

She pointed at Johnny with his behind turned toward her, on his knees with both hands on the bricks pushing and grabbing to stand, trying to whistle the intro music to "The Andy Griffith Show."

Johnny found his way up and shuffled up to take his turn at bat.

He stepped up to the rubber-mat home plate on the blacktop and backed up three long steps.

"Cuuu-moo-on!" someone yelled.

"Why does he always have to do that? He just stands against the door? Geez!"

Johnny pressed his heels against the white garage door.

Sister leaned over and wrapped the ball in her left hand and arm. She shuffled and slid like a bowler. At the end of her release she flicked her wrist. The ball spun as it headed toward Johnny, clunking toward the ball in his snow boots, buckles clattering.

He saw the ball and opened his eyes wide and tucked his tongue into the corner of his mouth. He clenched his hands and extended his arms like a field goal kicker. He drew his leg back and kicked at it just as the ball turned right.

Johnny looked up at the pigeon club swooping over the school. He held out his arms like a blue whale pigeon. He cracked the small of his back on the blacktop as Sister whipped around and slapped hands with her sycophant first-base girl.

Ribbons of color shot across Johnny's eyes. He caught his breath and realized where he was. Johnny sat back on his hands looking out at Sister.

"Missed it by a mile!" someone said.

Johnny wanted to play for the Yankees. Here he was sitting on his butt on the playground with Sister Mark chewing confiscated Fruit-Stripe Gum, maybe his gum, glaring at him, just a dumb little kid.

While he sat there Johnny locked eyes with the third basemen, the fourth-grade boy who had given him the fourteen cents to find his Mickey Mantle card.

"Get up!" the boy yelled at Johnny.

With her head down Sister toed the pitcher's rubber green chalk mark on the blacktop. With one hand she caught the ball fired back to her from the catcher on Johnny's team.

Johnny heard giggling and "C'mon, let's go, let's go. We want to bat, too!"

Johnny rolled over to push off to stand.

He returned to place his heels against the white garage door.

"Johnny Moon! "C'mon, Johnny, hit it out here!" someone said.

Sister coiled into her stance and began her approach. Johnny shuffled fast toward the ball. The ball took a screwball turn. Johnny sat on his hands in a haze.

The third time Sister deigned to make giant slow-motion gestures showing that she wasn't doing anything strange with the ball and Johnny took a giant lunge-kick and popped out weakly to the second sacker, wearing a blue plaid skirt, black shoes, white blouse and bright red button-down sweater.

"Moon Shot! Not!"

Johnny sat down on the blacktop against the garage.

He stretched out his legs, with his giant snowshoes pointing straight up. He put up his left hand in front of him like a partial parenthesis and placed the middle finger of his other hand just inside the parenthesis to show the second base person.

"Siiiissteerrrr. Johnny Moo-ooonnn."

Sister Mary-Michael's fingers-in-the-mouth whistle signaled the end of noon recess. She waved her hand twice one hundred and eighty degrees to tell Sister Mark to stop pitching and help her gather the children to go inside.

Sister Mark pounded the ball with both hands on the pavement and pointed to the next girl in line.

"You're next!"

To say that girl was the first batter in tomorrow's recess. But it was Friday and by Monday maybe, the girl could only hope, Sister Mark would forget whose turn it was.

Sister Mark pointed at each of the rubber bases and home plate then marched off tall and straight dribbling the kickball as she went, toward the fourth grade entrance, followed by her sweaty, jabbering class.

In the classroom, after the coats and hats and boots were put away and the last of the outside-type stories told, the third grade boys and girls found their desks and began to steel themselves for what was to come — a whole afternoon of English, arithmetic and vocabulary.

Sister Mary-Michael hit her mark in the center of the room, in front of the class, between them and the blackboard. At least she got to see out the windows at the grain elevator and the bank and the radio tower.

Sister-Something-The-Principal appeared miraculously in the doorway.

Her brown robes gracefully just-skimmed the floor.

She folded her arms at her waist, each arm presumably tucked into the opposite sleeve, where Kleenex and absconded Magic Markers and Matchbox cars were also stored.

Sister Mary-Michael hustled over, like a ballplayer to a coach.

The two whispered.

The children fidgeted with feet stretched back, turning around to talk, poking someone in back of them with a pencil and smiling, looking behind with a mirror. It looked like all were silent and serene from a distance – like the earth from the moon – but up close all were engaged in some sort of activity, surreptitious and not.

Johnny messed with his rings. He wished he had enough for all ten and wondered if Jimmy Purple would take him to the dime store and show him how to "cob" things. Jimmy said he went down with a winter coat, just messed with something like he was looking it over to buy, then just pushed it down into his sleeve. He walked out of there with his sleeves full of cool stuff, pens and gum and markers and ink pads.

Johnny wanted a couple more rings.

Sister Mary-Michael turned toward the class, her head down, her hands folded together.

She slid back to the door when Sister Principal-Something stuck her head back in and held her arm out with a fistful of Kleenex.

"For the girls," she whispered and nodded toward the class.

Sister Mary-Michael found her spot directly under the clock above the chalkboard. It said 12:40.

She looked up to the class.

She had red, shiny eyes and her nose was running. She wiped tears away with her wad of Kleenex.

The children tried to figure out what was wrong. Maybe some kid and his family had been killed in a car accident. Maybe this morning's Mass did not count because of Johnny Moon and they all were getting venial sins for missing Mass on a weekday. Maybe bowling would not be held next month either.

But, for sure, Sister was crying, in public, in class, and they grew nervous, like horses in a barn with a tornado headed their way.

"Class. Girls and boys," she said.

She took a deep breath, which they could tell because her robes moved.

"The President has been shot."

"Ohhhh!" the class sat with eyes and mouths wide open, staring hard at Sister.

Then to each other.

"What?"

"What did she say?"
"The Pres'dent?"
"*The* Pres-i-dent?"

Sister fell to her knees on the hard wood floor, found her rosary, crossed herself and began. "In the name of the father and of the son and of the holy spirit."

Each child slid out of their desk to kneel on the right side. Each folded their hands and bowed their head to just touch the tip of their noses with the tip of their index fingers, like expectant young angels at the feet of God's almighty throne.

Jimmy Purple slid off the left side of his desk, putting him right next to a girl he liked and refused to yield.

Sister led the class in the Sorrowful Mysteries of the rosary. She then pulled and pushed herself up by one of the front row desks and stumbled over to her desk. She disappeared behind the statue of Saint Michael the archangel that the other nuns had given her on her last feast day.

They heard Dave in the hallway through a crack in the door left by the principal, talking about whether to bring in radios or TVs to the classrooms and where they would get them and whether the cords would reach.

"We are all going to die," someone whispered.

"There will be a nu-cu-lar war. Nice knowing you."

"The Communists did it."

"It's because of the Beatles and Castro."

"Oh. Brother."

"We'll never go to the moon now, so forget that," a girl in a front desk turned and stuck her whole body into the aisle to look at Johnny.

"We never were," said someone else.

At the same time the boys and girls realized they would be soon rounded up by Russian soldiers and made to line up in the playground and say there is no God. A boy and a girl shot from their desks and ran to the window to stand on their tiptoes and pull themselves up by the ledge to try to see down onto the street and up to the sky.

Sister wiped her nose and began to ask them to please return to their seats, then asked if they could see anything.

Johnny curled his toes inside his shoes and clenched his hands into Kung-Fu dinner roll fists.

"We choose to go to the moon," Johnny whispered, "and the other things …"

He couldn't believe he was doing this.

"Not because it is easy … but, because it is hard."

Johnny pushed himself out of his desk to his knees.

The children turned their heads into the aisle to see.

Johnny flexed his fat hands and placed them flat on the wood floor. With the back of his hand he swept away some of the dirt and playground mud.

He leaned over his hands and stretched back his legs to stand on his tiptoes. He kicked out his legs and shook them out like a sprinter getting ready for a race the way Coach Isom had showed them. He checked the back of his pants and gave a yank to make sure he didn't "Moon" everyone like he had done once during exercise with Coach that one day when Coach Isom could be there.

He took a deep breath and let himself down.

"Johnny Moon can't *do* a pushup," one of the boys said.

Johnny's face glowed radish red and his hands turned whiter. His arms shook as he brought his nose down to just touch the wooden floor.

He exhaled and pushed up. His legs shook.

"Not because they are easy, but because they are hard," he said in a rush, as he reached the top and held it.

Again Johnny let himself down and pushed himself up, and again and again, as the other children watched him with their mouths open.

Jimmy Purple and Michael Irish plopped to the floor, their joints cracking, and began doing pushups, their behinds high in the air like cows rising.

Sister Mary wiped her eyes with the tail of her headdress, pushed off from her desk and walked to the front of the room.

She stared down at the three boys on the floor. She stretched out her arms and dropped to the floor like a cliff diver, smacking her hands on the tile, and began doing pushups, pausing on one arm to throw her veil out of her eyes.

The children flooded the aisles, began kicking each other to have enough room and stepping on each other's hands to have enough room and farting, on accident and then on purpose, in order to have enough room to do pushups.

A few minutes later they all sat in the aisles breathing hard. Sister Mary-Michael sat with her back against the front wall, her legs bent upward, both hands clutching her rosary, staring out the windows at nothing.

They heard amplified noise, coming from the brown box intercom above the cloakroom. First they heard messing with papers and a loud thud and a chair scooting and whispering. Then they heard Father's voice and Sister Principal-Something, as if they were arguing.

"In the name of our Lord Jesus Christ."

That was Father.

"Please! Silence!"

That was Sister.

And then a couple of frantic whispers back and forth.

"President John F. Kennedy has died.

"Let us pray."

And the principal began leading them in the rosary. Sister Mary-Michael and the children willed themselves again into kneeling position on the floor and followed along on the Hail Mary's.

[CHAPTER TEN]

"I can no longer sit back and allow Communist infiltration, Communist indoctrination, Communist subversion and the international Communist conspiracy to sap and impurify all of our precious bodily fluids."

— Colonel Jack D. Ripper, "Doctor Strangelove"

*M*argaret and Susan heard the crowd roar before they saw anything. People up on the hill began smiling and waving and screaming.

Everyone around them stood and moved closer to the street.

They watched the first car almost stop to make the sharp left-hand turn.

They saw the big, long, shiny black cars and the flags fluttering.

Margaret got right up on the curb and then she spotted John F. Kennedy and Mrs. Kennedy in pink, closer, on their side of the street.

In a reflex her hand shot up in a wave even though they were still far off.

She really wanted the President to see her.

She stepped into the street and pulled away from Susan's hand touching her elbow.

She stepped ahead and aimed her camera and then looked up over her camera and smiled and waved and then she saw him.

He smiled and waved from one side to the next.

She focused and aimed and looked up over the camera and then their eyes met. He smiled right at her and waved and her heart caught somewhere in her throat.

They had a moment. Time stopped and he — from riches, from the White House, from fame, from TV, from PT109, from her dreams — locked eyes with her.

And then he turned away to wave, and then firecrackers popped.

Margaret scowled, angry that someone would make such a joke.

Then the motorcade stopped and she wondered if they had planned a fireworks display and the cars were stopping so the president could see. Maybe it was children, a class from an elementary school, going to do a quick program.

And then louder, sharper cracks echoed in the small area, like an arena made of buildings.

Margaret felt Susan next to her and they told each other without speaking to keep shooting.

Then through their camera eyes they saw the President's head explode, like a hammer through a watermelon.

Splats of blood sprinkled their camera lenses. They looked up and

around and at each other as all the long, shiny, black cars roared past
and then they were gone.

Susan wiped at Margaret's arms and hair and face and clothes to
get off the blood.

Margaret shielded Susan's hands away and looked all around.

As Margaret's twin sister, Sister Mary-Michael Kelley knelt with
her students on the shined wooden floor of the third grade classroom, crying, praying, hoping someone had the power to come
through the door and tell them to get up, it did not really happen,
that it had all just been a national emergency test, Margaret and
Susan sprinted with a crowd across the street and onto the grass, up
the little hill, toward the smoke.

Margaret first, then Susan, they led the charge up the concrete
steps, to the wood fence.

A policeman stopped them, saying there was nothing to see here.

Margaret pushed around him.

The policeman back-tracked one step and grabbed her arm and
said forcefully that she should go back, now.

Margaret and Susan backed away, each dangling their cameras at
their sides.

Seven or eight men in suits and police uniforms surrounded them
and demanded to have the cameras.

Afterward they soothed their guilt at having given up the new
cameras and the film of the President smiling at them and what
followed by telling each other that maybe what was in the cameras
would help the men with their investigation.

Then they stood together, silent, in shock, at the road, just watching the place where it happened and seeing the traffic rolling past,
down the slight hill, as if everything were back to normal.

They waited and waited, not wanting to leave, thinking that maybe they should not go yet, that there was something they should do.

But what.

A television team showed up, out of breath, from the local station,
and started asking people questions.

Margaret and Susan walked over closer to listen.

"We saw it all," Margaret said out loud when she was satisfied
that the people being interviewed had only just arrived.

The lights and camera people and reporter with the microphone switched quickly to surround Margaret and Susan.

Later the two adventurous young women moved by rote to the bus stop.

When a bus finally wheezed to a stop in front of them, without consulting each other they let the bus go and embarked on their journey home, an ambling, in-no-hurry saunter through the dazed crowds and the traffic and the screaming lights and sirens, like being inside an anthill that has been kicked over.

People running back and forth, across the street then back again, each with a piece of leaf or stick in his mouth.

[CHAPTER ELEVEN]

"If my requests are heeded, Russia will be converted, and there will be peace."
– Mary, Mother of God, at Fatima

*A*s Johnny walked home after class he kicked a rock until he lost it down a sewer drain and watched the sun hide behind the elevator like Sister Mary-Michael at her desk.

He decided to sit and looked for a place.

He kicked another rock as far as he could and followed it to an empty wooden spool next to the power company shed.

Johnny watched the traffic and winced against the sun when it came out from behind the elevator.

He saw his dad and brothers and sisters go by in the new white Rambler. They didn't look or wave and Johnny didn't yell at them.

The world was ending. Maybe in some time zones it already had.

It's what Father had just said when he talked to the whole school from the office over the brand new intercom system that the Knights of Columbus had sacrificed and worked so hard for, just before dismissal, five minutes early in honor of the dead president of the United States of America.

At least that's what Johnny thought he had said.
President John F. Kennedy was dead.
Somebody killed God.

God was young and handsome and Catholic and nice and smart and he smiled and joked.

Johnny remembered back to kindergarten in the public school. Miss Joe Hansen had written in big, thick, flaky, new yellow chalk on the blackboard that was so big Johnny could not see to the other end.

PRESIDENT JOHN FITZGERALD KENNEDY

It wasn't the first day Johnny was there, but it was the first day he could remember.

And he remembered how big that room was and the windows and that the door was the first one on the left when you went into Lincoln school.

Johnny's group table was the green one.

His mother had drawn green across the toes of each of his tennis shoes to help him remember. He had hoped the kids wouldn't notice, but they immediately saw the green marker on the tennis shoe toes, knew what it was for, and started right in on Johnny like inmates on the tier.

In December his mom gave him a string of colored beads to decorate the Christmas tree that went all the way to the ceiling. The room was decorated with hundreds of Santa Clauses that the children had drawn on construction paper, taped to the windows, the blackboard, the door to the closest to their tables.

At Easter there had been ten thousand construction paper Easter Bunnies and they had looked for plastic eggs on the playground that had numbers inside that matched prizes in the principal's desk.

His rug for naptime was red and yellow and green and ... he could recognize it when it was time to pull them out of the rug closet.

He peed himself once standing at the green table for the Pledge-A-Legions when Miss Joe Hansen showed the class the crack of her butt when she leaned over to wipe up Jimmy Purple's puke that he said he did on purpose, and he had to walk past a big red dog on the corner on his way home at about noon.

Jimmy and Johnny and the whole class went down some steep windy wooden stairs to make clay hands. Johnny's broke when it fell off the wall once during a hailstorm.

That was all so long ago.

"A strong boy makes a strong man, makes a strong country," Johnny said out loud as he put his hands on his knees to prepare to push on them to make himself stand to go home.

But he didn't want to go home. He stuck his hands somewhere else. He tried his pockets, but his snowsuit didn't have them. Then he folded them in front of him, but thought that was a bit melodramatic.

The President being dead was the worse thing anybody had ever seen.

Johnny sucked in his stomach and wondered if he had lost a bunch of weight already or not.

He put his hands under his bottom and sat on them. That's warm, he thought.

It had scared Johnny to see the nuns and Father crying and all the adults too who were picking up their kids.

He saw Dave's old blue pickup headed this way. He spied a dark figure in the passenger side that had to be Isom. Dave sometimes gave him rides to school or practice or the grocery store, or to pick up the dead old people and shove 'em in the boiler with pitch forks and rusty spades.

Johnny jerked his hands out from under his butt and waved when they got close even though he didn't think they would see him.

Dave smiled and waved his hand way up out of his open window. "Hey, Johnny!"

He quick jerked the wheel to turn across traffic and hopped the curb to pull up close to Johnny.

"Hey, Johnny," Dave pulled the driver's side up next to Johnny seated on the wooden spool. Isom waved across from the other side. Johnny waved back.

"You don't look so good, champ," Dave said.

Johnny shook his head at Dave and saw that Isom didn't look so good either. Isom looked the other way out his window.

Johnny looked at the ground and then pawed in the dust where he was looking.

"Yeah, I guess you're right," Dave said. "I know how you feel. 'Course ... in a way ... oh, never mind."

"I wonder who would do that?" Johnny looked up at Dave. "Jimmy Purple sai ..."

"They got the guy, didn't you hear?" said Dave.

"Lee ... Haahvey ... Ozzwalt, the radio says now," Isom said, then shook his head and looked out his own window at the slow, meager traffic, thinned out since the school rush was over and the bank and Chevy lot and elevator had not yet dismissed their employees for the weekend.

Or maybe they were already home.

Dave shut off his engine and opened his door. He looked back at Isom.

"We got a little time, right?"

Isom didn't respond, but looked back out his window.

Dave got out, closed his door softly and walked over to Johnny.

"Mind if I sit?" he asked.

Johnny scooched over on the round spool.

"How'd it go with Sister Mark? She gonna let you into heaven? How you sittin' for purgatory?"

Johnny shrugged his shoulders and stared at the ground.

"It's sad, so sad, everyone is so sad," Johnny said.

"It is that," said Dave. "But at least now he knows."

"Who?" Johnny looked up.

"The President," Dave said. "John F. Kennedy. At least now he knows what's what."

"Oh, c'mon, man!" Isom moaned from the truck. "You should not ought to ..."

Dave put up a hand.

"Now just a minute, brother, this here is not some ord'nary kid. This is Johnny Moon. He understands things. Isn't that right, Mr. Moon?"

Johnny stared at Dave, looked at Isom, then back to Dave, trying to figure out if he was being made fun of. He remained silent, staring at Dave, still trying to figure him.

Dave removed a pocket knife from his pants and began to cut nicks into the wooden spool.

"Whether there is a God, heaven, all that, Johnny. Now he knows, you know?"

Johnny smiled.

"There's a God! Geez, c'mon. I know that already. We learned that in first grade."

"Yeah, maybe you did," Dave tended to his whittling.

He crossed his legs and looked to Isom in the truck. "You okay yet? You can roll those windows up, turn it on and crank the heater. It's not so bad, really."

Isom shook his head and put up a hand to say he was fine.

"Well, and there's other stuff, Mr. Johnny Moon," Dave said. "Just so many things, about life, death, the sky and stars, the ground, the rivers, what's under the rivers? Stuff like that."

He stopped and cut into the wood.

Johnny waited, furrowed his brow and thought for a while.

"The ground? The President already knew about the ground, Dave."

Dave looked up and smiled.

"I suppose he did at that. Yeah, you're probably right there."

"What's under the rivers?" Johnny said.

He stood and found a rock. He reached his arm way back to throw it at a power line. He missed and put his head down to find another stone.

"Yeah," said Dave. "Like what's down below."

"The devil," Johnny said matter-of-factly. He already knew and didn't wish to be reminded.

"Rocks. Mud," Johnny said and put his hands on his hips to look at Dave and then back to Isom to see if they were trying to think of more stuff under the rivers, like Sister had them brainstorm about what things for everyone to bring to the Thanksgiving party.

"There's just some people who know," Dave said. "Say, some people who have attained a certain station in life." Dave looked at Isom and saw that he was listening. "You might say that, right Isom?"

Isom nodded.

"How the world works. What … is … truth, what is real. They got built-in boo-shit detectors, you might say. Sorry for swearing, Johnny."

"S'okay. Jimmy Purple says way worse than that, lots of times. Like what's true? This is real, right?"

He put his arms out. And put his eyes in the top of his sockets to think.

He brought his arms down.

"Football practice. Ice cream," he smiled. "TV. Cars. People in the radio, church, Sister … and dogs." He took a deep breath like his was tired. "This is *all* real. Right?"

Dave smiled and switched crossed legs. He folded his arms over his chest and looked out over the flat town.

Johnny saw Dave's chest go up as he took a deep breath and let it out.

"But then John F. Kennedy was never going to learn that way, not like me and Isom … and you … some other folks. Right?" he looked at Johnny.

Johnny shrugged his shoulders up around his ears.

"But he was beginning to learn," Dave continued. "The long way around. And that's a dangerous way to go. As you can see today."

Johnny tossed a few more rocks at the power line. Dave looked back to his wood work.

Isom appeared over Johnny.

"Everyone asks thenselves, what if?" Isom's voice was deep and full, came from way down in his throat, and commanded attention.

Johnny and Dave stopped what they were doing to listen.

Isom bent down, picked up a stone and fired it at the wire with his left hand, striking it dead-on. The rock ricocheted and landed on the metal building, thundered down the roof, onto the ground.

"What if what, Coach?" Johnny said, looking up at him like a little kid asking his parent to continue the bedtime story he was telling.

"Oh, things," Isom said. He looked at Dave. Dave nodded go-ahead.

Isom sat down in one motion, not in parts like some other adults. He sat on the cold ground in his new blue jeans rolled into cuffs, and wearing his new junior college team grey sweatshirt. He bent his knees up and rested his arms on his knees like they were on a campout or something. His sitting revealed his hightop black canvas tennis shoes with white laces that had torn and been re-tied.

"Things … like," he began.

"What time is it anyway, janitor man?"

Johnny had never heard Dave called that. He looked at him to see how he would take it.

Dave didn't mind. He looked at his watch. What time you got to be there?"

Dave didn't wait to hear Isom's response, but indicated that he already knew. "We got some time, but, yeah, maybe we should be going anyway."

"What things!" Johnny said. "What things are you talking about? What things!"

"Just stuff," Dave said. "You might not understand."

"Yeah, but I might," said Johnny. "C'mon!"

To switch the mood and subject, Isom started to sing low and soft, a folk song that Sister Mary-Michael liked. She brought a record player in one day and played it for them, then left the record player in the room, over by the fish tank and the window.

"I know that song," Johnny said. "See. I know some stuff."

"Things like flying saucers," Isom smiled. "And the guv-ment. That's some of the things."

Isom thought again and waved his hand at them and shook his head.

"No, go ahead," Dave said.

"He is a child!" Isom said in a bass tone from way down low.

"Who's going to tell him if we don't?" said Dave.

"Who?"

Dave uncrossed his legs and closed his pocket knife. He disposed of it somewhere before you knew where, just like Sister with her Kleenex.

He leaned forward and put up one finger.

"This child, this young person, has had one hell of a day, Isom. His mom makes him wear a snowsuit on a nice day."

"And buckle shoes," said Isom.

"And buckle overshoes," said Dave.

"And he gets his lunch smashed by a train, gets hit by a car while

trying to save a dog, gets in trouble at Mass, falls on his butt —
twice — at recess."

"That hurt," said Johnny. He rubbed his behind like a genie's lamp
to bring back the memory of the kickball game.

"And who knows how many other injustices, like needles, poking,
poking through the day," Dave continued. "I think you know what I
mean?"

Johnny looked to Isom just in time to see him nod in affirmation.

"And then his President gets murdered," Dave sat up as punctua-
tion.

"His President, that he has had since kindergarten, gets shot
square in the head in broad daylight, in his own country, murdered
by the very people who were supposed to protect him."

"Lee Haahvey Ozzwalt I thought," said Johnny.

Dave continued.

"His very country is taken from him and he is in the third grade.
Nothing will be the same ever again for him. When he charged
down those familiar home steps with such bravely self-manufac-
tured high hopes he did not know he was heading into a hornet's
nest, a trap, a shooting gallery.

"I'm talking about you, Johnny Moon," Dave looked down.

"This is all about you."

"A strong boy makes a strong man, makes a strong country," said
Isom in a voice that made it sound like it was really true, not just
some thing like wearing ten rings and having nine flavors of gum in
his desk or pens with nine different colors just so they might forget
about his fatness, his slowness, his not having a new Sting-Ray or
living out in Sunset. Or about that stupid thing he said that one day
about going to the moon.

That's why he wanted to die last year, now he remembered.

The moon.

Johnny Moon.

Johnny Moon-skis with the big feet and the big butt and the big
head. He couldn't fit in a moon rocket ship in a million years and it
wasn't fifty miles to school like he was supposed to walk, it was five
blocks or something and he even got tired doing that.

[Chapter twelve]

"There was a fantastic universal sense that whatever we were doing was right, that we were winning . . . And that, I think, was the handle — that sense of inevitable victory over the forces of Old and Evil. Not in any mean or military sense; we didn't need that. Our energy would simply prevail. There was no point in fighting — on our side or theirs. We had all the momentum; we were riding the crest of a high and beautiful wave . . . So now, less than five years later, you can go up on a steep hill in Las Vegas and look West, and with the right kind of eyes you can almost see the high-water mark—that place where the wave finally broke and rolled back."
— Hunter S. Thompson, "Fear & Loathing in Las Vegas, A Savage Journey Into the Heart of The American Dream"

"Are you going home?"
Dave asked Johnny.
Johnny shrugged his shoulders and kicked at a wrapper.
"What time you got practice?"
Isom shook his head like he was okay.
"How 'bout you?" Johnny asked Dave. "What are you s'posed to be doing now? I thought you were gonna go with Father to get the church Christmas trees that's what we heard Sister-Principal-Something telling you in the hall."
"Cancelled," Dave said. "Prob'ly tomorrow."
"Want us to give you a ride?"
Johnny shook his head. The look in his eyes was all about how sad his house would be right now with his whole family in the living room watching the small black and white television and The News. None of the kids would be allowed outside to play and he had used up all his money for the month yesterday at the gas station on peanuts and pop.
He opened his mouth and eyes wide, then shrunk his shoulders and tilted his head back and closed his eyes.
"What?" asked Dave.
"Nu-uthin'."

74

"Well, then," Dave said, slapping his leg. "There is no time like the present, right?"

Isom sat silently on the pavement with his arms wrapped around his legs, looking down, studying the tiny rocks.

"For what?" said Johnny.

"To lose weight and go to the moon," said Isom, looking up.

"That's right, said Dave. "To have a better day!" He smiled and for a moment Johnny caught sight of a likeness to President Kennedy when he made jokes with reporters on television.

He climbed into his pickup.

"Well, c'mon, guys. You're shotgun," he pointed at Johnny and nodded at the passenger side. Isom pulled himself up and put one large hand on the side of the pickup and hopped in.

Johnny got in and pulled himself up by both hands to look back into the pickup bed for the old people bodies, all crinkly and white.

He turned back around and grabbed the door handle.

"Here we go!" said Dave.

Dave pulled up to the grey metal screen door that led down the steep concrete steps to his maintenance shop.

Dave went down first, then Johnny. Isom stayed behind for a moment to look around.

"Coach, coming?" Johnny looked back.

Isom stepped inside, then looked one more time out the door, around, up, back and forth.

The sloped ledge down to the shop was packed with cans of paint, rags, various lawn and fix-it tools, one long extension ladder, too big for anywhere else.

They entered another grey metal screen door at the bottom. Dave hurried across the room to get the light.

Johnny stared. He'd never been down here. There was the huge brick boiler that somehow sent heat up to all the rooms. It was round with pipes and wires and tubes running in and out.

"It looks like a big goldfish."

Dave stopped messing with the tools on his table and twisted around.

"Yeah, I guess it does."

Isom sat in one of the school desks scattered about.

"Where's the tail," said Isom.
"Uh, I do not know," said Johnny.

Johnny continued to look around, walking a little bit here and there until he got to the dark, the edge of the light of the one bulb over Dave's grey painted workbench.

He saw screen windows and more ladders and more paint cans with the color dripping down the side. He smelled dust and cold and wood.

Johnny put his hands over his eyes and looked in between for the spare old people lying on the floor or the pallets of bodies they needed for tomorrow. He thought it was nice of the old people to contribute to the school this way. He had seen the signs on the tables in church about considering the church and school when you die.

He smelled dead old people now, just their slime, after they melt, like Vicks vapo-rub.

He looked at Isom, sucking on something in his cheek, old people gristle.

He returned to stand next to Dave while Isom worked to get himself free of the desk he had jammed himself into.

Johnny opened the door and found himself in the hallway that led to the milk room and the other way to the stage. He stepped into the hall and there was the gym. It was dark. He heard the mimeograph machine working somewhere, probably in Principal-Something-Sister's office.

"We got to get him back home," Isom said, boosting himself up onto the top of the desk to sit, his long legs dangling to the floor.

"Whatever you say," Johnny said, "they're nice, they won't get mad. The other kids are there anyway. I always don't get home very fast. I like to look around.

"It'll be okay," he smiled and gave Isom's knee a soft punch with a fist.

Isom quick covered himself with both hands, thinking Johnny was going to hit him between his legs.

Dave continued working to tidy up for his guests, his workbench, hanging clamps and saws on the wall and shoving screwdrivers and hammers into drawers. He ran his hand along the table to scoop nails and shavings and screws, nuts, bolts into a box on the floor.

"Owww," he licked his hand.

"Y'okay?" Johnny said.

"Yep," said Dave, rubbing his hand on his grey railroad-type coveralls.

He lifted Johnny up and sat him on the high bench.

Johnny looked straight into Dave's eyes. Over Dave's shoulder he saw the goldfish boiler and the stairs and the thick block glass windows at the playground level.

Up close Dave looked even more kindly than he did in person, before, from down at Johnny's level. His old Conoco cap sitting askew just like Dave placed it every day, his thin face, and lines everywhere, bent nose, black stubble whiskers, thick eyebrows, serious dimpled chin.

Dave stepped back to give Johnny some room.

Johnny swung his legs and smiled at Dave, then Isom.

He was already having a better day.

Dave began to pace like Perry Mason, like Sister Mark.

"Johnny, you know when you dream?"

Johnny nodded and jutted his jaw and knit his eyebrows to think.

"You ever notice that you do way more in your dreams than you do in the day?"

Dave looked at Isom.

"We use about two percent of our brainpower," Isom said. "Umm, during the day."

"Less than that, yeah," Dave said, stopping in a skid in the dust and paint chips. "And when you dream, your brain gets to go crazy! You go all over, do all these things."

"I fly," Johnny said, not sure if he should.

"Yes," Dave pointed at Johnny.

"You fly. Do you?" Dave asked Isom.

Isom shook his head.

"Me, neither," said Dave. "I sat in class in my underwear once, twice … probably a thousand-million times."

Johnny and Isom pointed both hands at Dave.

"And," Dave continued to pace, wrapped his arm behind his back and bowed his head, then brought his hands in front and straightened out. He put a finger to his chin and tilted his hat even more. He scrunched his eyes and tried to scratch his nose with his bristles just above his lip.

"Let's say when you dream, it's like a movie, and you're everyone, the producer, director, all the actors, the lighting, costumes — do you realize that your mind has to do all the parts of the other people?"

Isom nodded and Johnny dropped his mouth wide open.

"Yeah," Dave said. "It's only you. It has to be you that does all the parts. How do you think you do that?"

"How," said Johnny.

He looked at Dave and they both looked at Isom.

Isom shrugged his shoulders.

"I thought you knew," Dave said.

"Not that, I didn't say," Isom said. "It just happens."

"But we can do so much more than we think we can, that's the point, Johnny," Dave said.

"Right?" he looked at Isom.

He clapped his hands together and Johnny sat up straight and back a little. He gripped the table with his legs and hands.

"You ever see the ghost kids?" Johnny whispered to Isom.

Isom stared at Johnny.

Dave hollered over from on top of the boiler.

"He sees 'em, he hears 'em, he talks to 'em!" Dave yelled over the basement boiler room sounds.

"He just won't admit it."

Johnny looked at Isom and Isom looked at Johnny.

Isom slowly nodded up, then down.

Johnny smiled.

His stomach rumbled and he wondered for a minute about the cookies and milk his mother would have waiting for him on the kitchen table. Maybe not today she wouldn't, but maybe. Mmm, Oreos, creamy middle. Crunchy chocolate on the outside.

"It's the future, or it's what we did that day," Johnny said. "Dream. That's what Sister said. She said she doesn't really know, but she thinks that's what sign-tists say. She said she would try to find out and tell us. We just talked about dreams last week I think it was."

"Really?" said Dave. "Pretty," he said, looking at Isom, who took a deep breath and looked at his feet.

"Anyway," Dave said, jumping down from the boiler top.

"Ground and under the rivers," Johnny reminded him.

"Yeah," Dave pointed at Johnny with a yellow-gloved hand. He shoved both hands into his underarms and pulled them out, then caught the gloves before they dropped and tossed them up on the desk next to Johnny.

"Oh, and, time, your parents, Johnny." He put his hands into quote marks. "When we came down the steps time kind of stopped. It's hard to explain, but your parents, not that they won't miss you, but you'll be back there, kind of like how you left off."

"You say I'm smart and you try to tell me stuff and then you say stuff like that, Dave, and act like you have to lie to me like a little kid, c'mon, Dave," said Johnny.

Isom smiled.

"That's why he was trying to explain dream," Isom said in a booming soft voice, putting his hands up in quote marks.

"We tried to explain all this to Sister Mary-Michael, see, Johnny. Maybe you can tell her some-too," said Dave.

"Kind of teach her, in a way," said Isom.

Johnny held both hands up in quote marks. He had seen Sister do that.

"And it did not happen when we came downstairs, that's an exaggeration," Isom said.

"Yeah, that's what I was trying to get at," Dave said.

He moved up to the work bench, next to Johnny.

Johnny turned, putting his feet up on the bench, working hard with both hands to pull them crossed. He watched Dave lean over the bench to something on the wall, with a straight screwdriver in his mouth and a big, red, tattered crescent wrench in his hand.

He grunted and swore to himself, then straightened up, changed tools, stared at the glassed meter he was working with, then stretched and leaned and cussed, then stood up.

"That should do it," he said. "Now we're okay."

Johnny looked at the wall where Dave had been working.

"That's not a time machine," said Johnny. "It's just a meter thing."

"That takes some doing," Dave looked at Isom.

79

Isom crossed his leg to re-tie the laces on his left shoe.

"Okay," said Dave. "I suppose we should get started, huh?"

He looked at Johnny.

Johnny turned back around and swung his legs.

"They take milk, mix-up milk orders," said Isom.

"Who's that?" Dave said.

"The ghost class and their nuns," said Johnny.

"They were the first class here," Isom continued. "They came from Germ'ny, Are-land, Czecho-slow-baak-yeah ..., Norway-maybe."

"Africa?" said Johnny.

Isom shrugged his shoulders.

Johnny nodded and listened.

"All gone, all burned," said Isom.

They still couldn't afford to totally replace the boiler, just fixed it some, until they got this one," said Dave.

"And now it's haunted," he shook his head. "Ain't that the beat."

Johnny nodded once and said, "Uh-huh," thinking of black and white cookies, and now of chocolate or maybe *straaaw*-berry milk.

"They play basketball all ... night ... long," said Isom. "'magine how fun that would be? And not get tired?"

"Which first?" Dave looked at Isom and then at Johnny.

"Which first what?" said Isom.

"You want to see the truth about the past or about the future?" said Dave.

"How about past?" said Johnny.

"Well, then we need to crawl into the goldfish," Dave said.

"To go underground?" said Johnny. "In the school's boiler, right there? To see what's under the earth, like Neemo?"

"Yeah-yeah, like that," said Dave. "You'll like it, someone like you. It's like looking through one of those kaleidoscope things they have at the dime store. You know?"

"Yeah, Jimmy Purple has nine of them in his desk," said Johnny.

"Or, you think, what if?" said Dave, talking with his mouth and his hands and his eyes and his feet. "Or something big happens, like someone dies ... when you are taken out of your routine, what you do every day ...

"Or you remember. Or you think about what it will be like when …

"Or when you walk to school.

"Or, if you are poor, or black, or have a job that your children are not proud of. Or if you are a woman who loves God and has to wear certain clothes and do whatever Father tells her, even though she is way smarter than the man.

"You turn sideways, you see things differently, for a moment, like getting the sun in your eyes but it scares you or something and you want it back to the way it was even though you didn't really like it the way it was, but you felt comfortable, safe, back there.

"Well … we … Isom and me … we don't have any choice. We see things that way all the time, whether we want to or not.

"People like you, well you have a choice, Johnny Moon. Just like John F. Kennedy, and you can choose to see things the way they really are.

"Or you can choose to see things the way others see them, the ones who really can't see.

"That's the Ground we was talkin' 'bout. That's the now."

"What's the others?" said Johnny.

"Well … there's Underground, that's one," said Dave.

"And there's *Skyyyy*."

"What's *Skyyyy*?" said Johnny.

"You know, like, when you dream, maybe, like Sister said. "I'm not totally for sure," said Dave.

"Oh," said Johnny.

"To see the future, the truth of the future," said Dave, "not the lies of the future, the lies they are going to tell, to really see the truth …"

"David!" Isom shouted.

Dave took a deep breath, let it out in a whoosh and ran through his next sentence like he was sprinting through a graveyard at midnight.

"You … we … would need to go to the roof … of the convent."

Johnny's mouth gaped wider yet. His eyes bugged out wider than anyone's eyes had ever bugged out in his town.

He pictured walking through the kitchen of the convent and seeing Sister Mark in sweatpants and T-shirt and walking past Sister Mary-Michael's room with the door open and seeing her in there smoking cigarettes and drinking whiskey, and walking past the upstairs Nun's restroom and looking to the left and seeing Sister-Mary-Principal-Something …

"Past. Past-then. Past-past-past! Let's climb inside the boiler goldfish," Johnny said, knowing that when someone wants to play a game, takes the time and imagination to come up with a game, it's good to go along and show respect for their work.

"Not so fast," Dave stuck a finger into the air.

"Have to shut everything down. It'd be a bit toasty in there just this moment."

"It was warm in the room today," Johnny smiled. "I'll bet the old people like to go back to the past, don't they?"

Huh?" said Dave, "umm, yeah. I s'pose."

He hurried over to the big maroon brick boiler and began working his way around it, rubbing it like a magic lantern, twisting, grunting, cursing, turning this and that.

Steam whooshed out the top like the boiler was farting, like the radiators in the room, Johnny thought and looked at Isom to see if he thought the same thing.

Isom sat and watched, folded hands in his lap.

Johnny put his hands in his lap.

Isom held up two sticks of gum to Johnny.

"Cherry," Johnny said.

Johnny held out both hands. Isom tossed it underhand. Johnny caught it and smiled wide. They both unwrapped their gum and folded the paper into their fists.

Isom wrapped his arms across his chest. Johnny pulled his shoulders up around his ears. He tried to see his breath.

"The Twilight Zone," Isom called out to Dave, on top of the boiler, squatting, using a red pipe wrench on a giant nut.

"Huh? What'd you say!"

Johnny hopped down to the cement, sending shivers up his ankles. He walked around the tables and old desks and brooms and dustpans partially filled with detritus. He stood below Dave up on the boiler.

"Twilight Zone!" he said.

"Twilight Zone! You know!" Isom shouted.

"Oh, yeah," Dave nodded. "It's scary," he mumbled to himself.

"What'd he say?" he looked down at Johnny.

"He said, Twilight Zone!" Johnny cupped his hands around his mouth.

"It's like! The! Twilight Zone!" Isom shouted. "How to explain it! This!"

Isom waved both hands at Dave, showing the whitish undersides of his hands like angel wings in the dark.

"This here boiler!" Dave shouted to them while straddling the top of the boiler, his thumbs in his pants pockets.

The boiler rumbled and shook under Dave's feet. He seemed not to notice, but continued speaking loud.

"This here boiler system came to us! Can you hear me?"

Isom nodded at Dave and looked at Johnny and shook his head. Johnny shrugged.

"It came to us … from Chicago! Hear me!"

Johnny nodded at him.

"There's a God," Johnny said to Isom.

"Say what?"

"You guys were talking about if there's a God."

Isom nodded toward Dave to say him, not me.

"It was Sister Mark's old school. She went there and then later she taught there when she was first a nun, then she came here!" Dave said.

"They closed that school down-see, St. Stephens or something I think, anyway, it was haunted or something. They especially wanted to get this boiler out of the school basement, gave it to us real cheap. We took it.

"They said it was evil, that it glowed. Imagine that? An evil boiler?"

He stepped lively as the soles of his boots began to get warm.

"Fuckin' nuts I say," he said to himself.

"Well, Fatima," Johnny said.

Isom nodded.

"We learned about Fatima. If there's no God and stuff, then those kids were lying. I don't think they were lying. Somebody said they were lying. I think Sister M&Ms said they weren't lying?"

"They brought it by train, from Chicago, long ways, by train. Right? I said, right!"

Isom nodded at Dave then looked back to Johnny.

83

"Some of the kids play Fatima on the playground. I got to be the little boy once, but I didn't see nothing."

"Then it took a month for the parish council and the priests and everyone else to get it down here and get it going!"

"I saw Jane Lincoln Frogs standing on a snow pile wearing Sister's black shawl and pink snow boots. That was about it."

"M&Ms?" said Isom.

"Mary-Michael."

Isom grinned and hummed.

"Maybe Mary of God wears pink snow boots," said Johnny. "But I doubt it and I heard somewhere there's no snow in heaven. There's a song like that. Maybe the sun was in my eyes, the other kids were all crying, like they saw something. I didn't see nothing. Not really.

"So I think we should name the boiler Fadama, too," said Johnny.

"Why is that?" Isom said. "Too?"

"Well, too because it's already Neemo from "Twenty Million Miles Under The Sea," that one book. I ordered it from T.A.B. It's got a giant octopus on the cover. You seen it?"

Isom shook his head.

"Used to use coal, now it's those bricks, special bricks, lots of 'em, heat 'em up, works pretty good, kind of like a sauna I guess! Anyway it works that's all that counts I guess.

"Can you hear me!"

Dave jumped down.

He walked back to them, wiping his face with a handkerchief.

"Becauuussse," Johnny said. "What's wrong, Dave?"

"Nuthin'," Dave said, "go ahead, you was sayin'?"

"Becaauusse ... we can go find the truth in Neemo, down below and it should be Fadama, too, because those kids ... well ... they did some hard things. People didn't always believe them, that they saw God ... or I mean God's mom Mary. And I think when we come back people won't believe us if we tell them what we saw."

Isom looked straight at Dave.

"Johnny Moon is wise beyond his years."

Dave nodded and rubbed his chin and dug at nothing on the cement floor with a boot.

"It's too dangerous," he said. "It's too hot. We'll just take you home, Johnny, maybe some other time, huh?"

"No, let's just wait!" Johnny said.

"It's not working that great," said Dave.

"It never is," said Isom.

Dave looked at him, wiping his face again.

"Al-mos' never."

"I'll tell you what, Mr. Johnny Moon," said Dave.

"You let us take you home, maybe we'll come back here and work on ol' Nemo, see what we can do and just as soon as we get her in operating condition again, we'll pull you out of class to come on a ride.

"Okay," said Johnny, smiling.

"What class you want to be pulled out of?" said Dave.

"English-no-arithmetic … no-music," said Johnny.

"Music."

"Music it is," Dave said.

They each grabbed Johnny under an arm to let him down from the bench.

Johnny had a nail in his hand and walked right over to the boiler and began to scratch on it.

"Don't, Johnny," Dave said. "I don't want to start that, gettin' writin' all over it now."

Johnny kept going.

Dave and Isom walked over behind him and watched him work.

Johnny stepped back in accord with the other two.

"NEEMO FADAMA," Dave read. "Sounds good to me."

He put a hand on Johnny's shoulder and turned him toward the steps.

They got in line to walk up, one hand on the rail, head down, scuffling, hearing the boiler mumble and then cough, like an old man getting up in the morning.

At the top Johnny reached to flick off the light.

Dave stopped him with a hand.

"We're coming back."

They climbed back into the light blue pickup. It started up and rattled over the playground blacktop like rocks down a slippery slide.

They pulled up to Johnny's curb.

85

Johnny reached to the outside handle to open his door. Isom hopped out. Johnny saw a neighbor lady on her porch stop her journey to her mailbox to pick up her newspaper to pause and stare at Isom.

"Maybe we'll try it some other time," Dave leaned across the seat to wave at Johnny.

Isom ruffled Johnny's hair and waved to the neighbor lady and smiled, then got into the pickup. Isom waved again as they went past the lady.

Johnny waved at them and smiled too, then turned to consider the front of his house and touched an ice cube in his chest that he had forgotten was there.

He heard the TV on in the house and saw figures inside the front curtains gathered around the screen in a semi-circle.

Johnny squatted to consider an ant hole, then looked back up at his house. Someone peaked out the parted curtains. He got up and walked up, taking long slow steps, holding the railing.

Johnny pushed the door open over the carpet and stepped inside the dark front room. Hassocks surrounded the black and white set like curious Apaches around a wagon train. Johnny heard someone sniffling.

His father looked at him then back to the TV with a wild, scared look in his mouth and his eyes and his hands like he was directing a missile strike headed right at his own house.

His mother hunched right up front leaning forward over her knees, clutching a Kleenex, watching the newsman with a microphone standing in front of the hospital in Dallas.

Johnny tiptoed into the kitchen and carefully made himself a peanut butter sandwich, filtered his way back into the TV room and sat in the back.

When the TV went to commercial Johnny's mother said, "Well, I had better make something for supper, hadn't I." She got up and everyone began moving around, changing places, going to the bathroom.

Johnny opened the front door just enough and slipped out.

[CHAPTER THIRTEEN]

The answers are there for those who are willing to dig ... after spending several thousand hours knocking on doors, asking questions, meanwhile reading the Report, we believe audacious actions were taken by the Commission lawyers and the chairman obfuscating the evidence left after President Kennedy, Tippit, and Oswald were killed.

— Penn Jones, Jr.

*T*he next Monday in school Johnny sat at his desk during milk break working hard concentrating on opening his square chocolate carton without fingernails.

"Hey! Hey-hey!"

Johnny and the other children looked to the door and saw the heads of Dave and Isom and hands clutching the doorframe like the edge of a bridge.

They continued to hiss and whisper.

"Hey, over here."

Their eyes looked for Sister Mary-Michael.

"Siiisssteerr!" one of the girls in the front desks called for Sister. "Sooommeboooddyyy'ss hee-eerree."

"Shhh!" Isom put a finger over his mouth, then pointed at Johnny.

"C'mere-c'mere!"

Johnny looked around to see who Dave was talking to.

He looked back and saw both Dave and Isom pointing at him. Isom curled his finger.

"C'mere-c'mere."

Johnny pointed at his own chest and Isom nodded, up and down, up and down.

Sister Mary-Michael turned from straightening the children's clothes in the cloakroom and smiled. She fluffed her headpiece back with both hands and hurried over to the doorway like a junior high girl on a Saturday afternoon delighted to finally be relieved by a diversion from extra chores.

"The room is perfect," she said, turning back in a flourish like a game show model with one hand to invite the students to comment. "Isn't it children?"

"Yeee-eesssSister!"

"Not too warm not too cold," Sister continued. "We are just content, just like Goldilocks. Right children?"

"Yeee-eessSiii ...,"

"Yes-Sister," Dave cut in.

"We just need to talk to Johnny ... just for a minute-would that be okay?"

"What is the matter?" Sister put both hands to her chest like a soap opera actress.

They took their heads out of the door and stood straight in the doorway. Dave held his cap in his hands, and Isom's white palms flashed like striped bass in a fishing filmstrip as he rubbed them this way and that.

"Johnny?" Sister turned to Johnny.

He held up his milk carton to say he wasn't done yet.

"You may bring it with you," Sister nodded.

Johnny pushed and pulled himself out of his giant desk keeping one hand gripped on his chocolate milk carton.

He walked up his row, tipping his milk back to drink and weaving like a drunk over to the door, looking out the side of his eyes to see if Jane Lincoln Frogs saw how funny he was.

Sister moved to her desk, taking the opportunity to rest, tired from the effort of being cheerful for the children on this most horrible Monday.

Johnny paused for a moment to tip up his milk and drink.

He wiped his mouth as he got to the door and looked almost straight up at the men.

"Hi."

"We need you," said Dave.

"Yeah," said Isom.

They backed up and waved him out into the hall. Johnny followed as far as the doorway.

Dave squatted down to talk.

"We need you to forget about what we said."

Johnny twisted his jaw to try to remember.

Isom got down on one knee.

"About the boiler. You know, man, Nemo Fatima ... all that?" he smiled and his teeth sparkled in the dark hall like Dairy Queen sprinkles.

"Remember ... strong boys, make ...," Dave began.

"Strong-men-make-a-strong country," Johnny said. "This isn't music," he said. "You said you'd come during music, that's in the afternoon ... on ... Thursday?" He looked over to Sister.

She nodded yes, it is.

"Right," Isom smiled and pointed at Johnny, his perfect fingernails aglow like beating hearts.

"We need you to be strong and ... forget about the boiler and all that, can you do that?" Dave smiled longingly.

"I've been losing weight over the weekend," Johnny said. "I'll be able to fit in there, maybe I could already."

He looked down at his stomach.

He took another swig of his milk, then another to make sure, then stared into the dark hole with one eye.

"No-no-no, see, that's just the thing," Dave said.

"See, it's not real. We were just saying that."

Johnny tilted his head.

"Why?" he said.

"Huh?" said Dave.

"Why would you do that, just say that, lie," he smiled.

"We weren't lying," Dave scooted up a little closer.

"Just having some fun, seeing what you'd say," said Isom.

"Oh," said Johnny. He looked at Isom and Isom stood. Johnny couldn't hardly even see up that far to his face so he looked over at Dave. He stared at Dave, wondering why these grown men with big jobs and big things would bother to take time to try to fool a kid on the day the President is dead.

"Oh, okay," he said.

"Seeya," he reached out his hand to shake with Dave and felt Isom's big hand on his head.

Dave took the hand and held it.

"See ... we just wish it was, real."

"But it's not," came Isom's big voice from above.

"It's dangerous, Johnny," Dave's voice grew deep and serious.

"Promise us you'll never go down there. You can't. You just can't, okay?"

"Yep," said Johnny.

"Okay, well ... then you best get back to school ... then, Mr. Moon, John Moon," said Isom.

Johnny smiled.

"It's all school."

He held his arms out wide.

"Yeah," said Isom. "All school."

Dave waved to Sister Mary-Michael. She smiled and waved and began to rise from her chair. Isom leaned on one leg, grabbed the door frame and stuck his head inside and waved to Sister then to the children.

"Byyyeee-Cooaaach!" they said.

They left the doorway for an instant then both stuck their hands in again and waved to Sister and the kids and said, thanks, thanks, see-you-now.

Johnny walked in front of Sister's desk to the windows then up the line of rows from behind and turned left to get to his safe harbor. As he walked he watched his feet and scrunched his brow and crunched his nose, thinking what was he going to do now.

He had already told everyone.

He had said on the playground the first thing when he got to school and whispered all during Mass and talked all the way back to school and up the steps and while they were hanging up their clothes.

That they would probably be able to go down to the boiler room where Dave kept all his stuff and get inside and ride back into time to see things.

Johnny told them because he just did.

Even though he knew you couldn't go back in time in the boiler and that you couldn't go in there anyway because it's full of old people bones that they only clean out over the summer. But it could be real, real enough for a game and maybe Dave and Isom would play along and it would be fun for a day.

But not now.

Sister took a deep breath, wiped her eyes and nose with a fresh Kleenex and waltzed to the middle of the room, smiling, twirling, clutching her arithmetic workbook to her chest like her own wedding photo book that she wished to show them all.

"What'd he say ... about the boiler?" said Bobby as Johnny walked past.

Johnny shrugged his shoulders without looking.

He hiked up his leg to climb onto the seat of his desk. With both hands he pushed up his desktop. He turned his head left and right inside his dark cave getaway sanctuary and saw nothing that interested him, not rings or gum or markers or ink pads.

He caught movement out of his side vision and saw Jimmy Purple and Jane and Danny with their desks also raised trying to get his attention.

Johnny knew who it was and what they were trying to say, to ask. They believed him. They believed they could go into the past and see things by going into the boiler and they believed they would be going with Johnny soon.

Johnny breathed deep and closed his eyes and remembered when he had started whispering about what he knew about the boiler in the quiet preparation time before Mass. The girls had turned around and told him to shut up.

Jimmy Purple and the other guys had leaned way over to listen to Johnny whisper about what he had found out last week about the boiler room from Dave and Isom.

"That's how the old people do it," said Jimmy Purple. "That's what this sixth-grader told me. I'll bet we can do the same thing when we're alive if you turn off the boiler and let it cool down for a few minutes."

Jimmy saw the sarcastic hue in Johnny's brown eyes and added further explanation.

"It's an old Indian thing, he said, you go on the journey – that's where the old people go – that's what they meant about going back and forward and up and down in time – means you know stuff. That's what you could probably do in there, too, but you'd be dead. Prob'ly."

"How long?" somebody else said.

And the boys stood there thinking, wondering how long the boiler would need to cool down after burning old people bodies all day for them to climb in and take a trip underground and ride down the past, like an underground spaceship along the ocean floor.

They talked about it more on the way to the room from church and even when Michael Irish said he thought they should be thinking about the President and how Oswald was dead and was killed by someone else already on Sunday —yesterday and not about stupid stuff — even then Johnny felt the warm glow of attention. It made his face flush and did not feel like killing himself like he did a long time ago by eating all the ice cream, but not anymore, not for a long time now.

But some of the girls whispered behind their hands and some of the boys were listening to Michael Irish about how Johnny Moon was crazy. They made circles by their head and it made Johnny wonder and it made him think and made him sad.

Because maybe he was crazy.

But how could you be crazy in the third grade. Only older people were crazy, kids weren't crazy. How could you be in only the third grade.

Johnny eased his desk down then put it back up with one hand and fished out his Big Chief notebook, then let it down a little too hard and it made a slamming noise, drawing everyone's instant attention.

Rather than saying sorry he decided to turn very red and stare at the cover of his unopened notebook and began outlining the Indian's feather, over and over.

Sister quickly opened her book and began the lesson with an introduction then swirling to the blackboard and writing big yellow, flaky numbers on the board in a font and style inspirational and magical.

"Today we are going to write," she said. "I want you all to take out a pencil, a sharpened pencil. If you don't have one you may go up ... one at a time."

As all of the children took long turns going to the sharpener by the door and watching into the hall looking for someone they knew while they ground their pencils, Sister M&Ms explained to the children what a journal was and what she wanted them to do.

She walked back and forth in front of the desks and up and down the rows as she had never done before to explain that they should put their feelings about the death of the President and what they think should be done now and talk about current events and things in their lives.

"Just tell me how you are doing, what you are thinking. I want to know.

"No sports or TV shows," she said.

Movies and books were okay, though.

[CHAPTER FOURTEEN]

We choose to go to the moon. We choose to go to the moon in this decade and do the other things, not because they are easy, but because they are hard, because that goal will serve to organize and measure the best of our energies and skills, because that challenge is one that we are willing to accept, one we are unwilling to postpone, and one which we intend to win, and the others, too.

It is for these reasons that I regard the decision last year to shift our efforts in space from low to high gear as among the most important decisions that will be made during my incumbency in the office of the Presidency.

— John F. Kennedy, Sept. 12, 1962, Rice University

*A*t noon recess Sister Mark and Sister Mary-Michael, rather than organizing kickball and pum-pum-pullaway, had the two classes walk in silent, one-line-hands-folded-no-talking-whatsoever procession over to the church.

They followed the sidewalk winding past the playground, darting glances at where they would have been playing, then around the rectory, the rear of the church, past the cannon in the lawn between the church and the convent, pointing out over the avenue and at the Ford dealership across the street.

The river poured into church, breaking neatly into two streams to take advantage of the two holy water font sponge glasses, then up the stairs through the wooden swinging double doors and straight down the middle aisle, remaining in two rows and resisting the

instigating of the sloped floor to break into a gallop like a herd of
wildebeests.

All the way over children in formation around Johnny whispered
to him.

"There's the boiler room!"

And then motioning with their head slyly toward the battered
silver screen door that led to the steep concrete steps of the maintenance basement area and the mystical magical boiler.

The fourth-grade server from the Mickey Mantle card got out of
line to come walk by Johnny.

"Where's my card-huh? Where is it?"

"I don't have it," Johnny looked right up at him in the eyes.

They kept walking.

"You better get it, kid," the fourth-grader said and then ran ahead
to his own line.

Johnny wondered how he was going to follow through on his idea
that he could get the Mickey Mantle card from the dog. What dog?
He had never seen that dog before or since.

Well, if the world ended, then he wouldn't have to. He let his
mind paw at that thought for a bit like a cat in backyard clover.

Johnny pressed his forehead to his fingertips, closed his eyes and
prayed for Russian nuclear bombs, then listened for them, then told
God "sorry," then kept walking, trying not to step on the heels of
Judy in front of him or get stepped on by Michael behind him.

The third and fourth grade took up both sides of the church from
the front to about a third of the way back.

They took position as Sister Mark and Sister Mary-Michael knelt
on the communion kneelers in front, all facing toward the altar.

They smelled the smoke of a recently extinguished red votive candle in the bank of candles on the St. Joseph side that curled around
up toward the face of the statue like the ghost of a dead person who
the candle was lit for and paid five dollars for, but it had not worked.

Johnny felt the softness of the red kneeler and balanced his
elbows on the round pew. He recited the rote jumbo with the others
and withstood the whispers of the boys around him who wanted to
know more about the boiler voyeauge.

The two sisters traded off dragging the group through the Sorrowful Mysteries.

They heard the sacristy screen door slap and the big door brush over the Linoleum, then whistling and banging of closet doors.

Father strode out onto the altar area draping his special red towel over his shoulders, kissing it like it was his very favorite. He half-genuflected in the exact middle of the altar, then pushed open the swinging gate in the communion rail.

Barely nodding to the two Sisters, he smiled at both sides of children and waved with one hand then the other. He pounded up the steep aisle, hitting hard on the heels of his black shoes while the Sisters kept the rosary humming.

Father opened the middle door of the confessional. They heard the sliding door like gallows being prepared and now they knew why they were there.

They locked eyes or took a deep breath or gulped. Some bowed their heads and repeated the rosary Hail Mary responses a little louder.

They were there to go to confession in case the world ended with a nuclear war because the Russians had killed Kennedy because Oswald was a Russian spy that's what their parents had said or it was on The News.

They might die. Or be captured.

They had already discussed in depth on the playground whether they would rather be captured and lined up in a row or killed right away. The voice vote had gone in favor of capture.

The Sisters applied more throttle to the Hail Mary's because they knew Father was ready and did not want to be kept waiting. He probably had to go to the hospital or prepare his Sunday homily or pray for a long time or get his car worked on, so they had better get a move on.

Besides, that's why they were there. Father had suggested they should take all prudent precautions and one thing they could do was to prepare the children for the end of the world.

The rosary ended with a Glory Be drone.

Sister Mark and Sister M&Ms took their posts standing in the aisle next to the back row in their sections.

They allowed one fourth grader and one third grader to tromp up to occupy the two confessional rooms on either side of Father in his post. That way if the one overheard the sins of the other it might not be such a cause for gossip and disruption in the rooms.

When it came time for Johnny to go it was just he and Jimmy Purple left, so they took both of the spots.

Johnny opened the confessional door, turned to make sure it was closed and reached with his hands for the kneeler in the dark. He put his nose on the screen and smelled Father sweating inside like a pig and the shoosh of the sliding door as Father opened Jimmy's side first.

Johnny tried saying Hail Mary's to himself the way Sister had said in order to not hear what Johnny was saying and he tried to hum silently to himself in his mind, and he tried turning his head to look the other way in the dark, but still he heard Jimmy.

"I took pens from Woolworth's … five times. I took gum from Woolworth's … three times, um, fiiivve times?"

Johnny could hear Jimmy over there trying to decide how much to tell, which ones were venial, how many venials to reveal and still get credit for the ones he really needed in order to get into heaven if he died.

"I swore … ten times."

"Did you use God's name in vain?"

"Yes."

"Oh. Go ahead."

"I missed Mass on Sunday … two times."

Johnny heard Father breathe deep when he heard that. It was a good thing Jimmy said it though, that was a mortal and now he was good.

Jimmy cracked his knuckles. He was thinking.

He couldn't remember everything he had stolen and was wondering if a summary would count.

"I stole …"

"You stole, again?"

"Yeah. Uh, mmm, two Snickers at least, and some SweeTarts and you know, that powdered sugar stuff in a straw."

"Pixie Stix."

"Yeah, that."

Johnny could tell that Jimmy was even telling stuff he didn't do, just to cover himself. Sister really said they might not make it through this afternoon. Johnny nodded to himself at Jimmy's good sense.

Father gave Jimmy his penance prayers to do.

Johnny heard Jimmy's door slide closed and his door open and close and Jimmy's quick feet past his door. If he got back to the pew and said his Our Father's and Hail Mary's before Johnny got there he would be done, otherwise he would have to do them at home and then you never did them then and you could go to hell if you died.

Father slid Johnny's door open.

"I was with him," Johnny said.

"Should we try that again," Father said.

Johnny crossed himself in the dark when he saw the faint light and Father's big shadow and smelled him even worse. There were cigarettes mixed with the sweat now.

"Bless me Father for I have sinned, my last confession was one week ago.

'My sins are I was with him," Johnny said. "Except for Mass and swearing. Mine was not as much and different stuff."

Johnny took a deep breath.

He could see Father get closer to the netting and lean down low. "Yes?"

"And I tol' a lie," Johnny said.

"What kind of a lie?"

"Ohh, nothing, just a lie. I don't think it matters, right, huh?"

"It matters to God, Johnny."

Johnny's heart pounded. Father wasn't supposed to know who you were and if he knew he wasn't supposed to let you know.

But now he had to tell, or that's what it felt like anyway.

"About the boiler room?"

Father didn't say anything, but Johnny could see his silhouette getting all grown-up tilted and inquisitive and so interested.

"Oh, just 'bout how you can take rides in the boiler and go see the past and stuff like that ... with the dead old people."

"Who told you that?" said Father.

"But they already volunteered with the church for that ... and."

Johnny gulped and thought.

"Nobody told me, I just made it up. That's why it's a lie."

Father pulled back from the screen and sat erect, letting out plenty of rope through the screen.

Johnny watched Father then pulled his head back at the abrupt blaze of flame as Father lit a match.

The sulfur smell filled the space like kid hell.

Johnny saw Father's face bright and way up close in the small space in the brief light, like night lightning and for just that instant you can see God in his living room, his grayish hair and black glasses, his collar pulled out like a businessman after five o'clock.

Father puffed hard and blew the smoke out, filling his own small room and drifting into Johnny's like gas in the death chamber.

"Please revolve me from these sins and all the sins of my past life," Johnny quick said.

Father puffed again, blew the smoke out his nose and leaned down to give Johnny his penance.

"You must tell your friends that you told them a lie."

"I can't," Johnny said and shut his mouth to try to stop the words.

He couldn't believe what he had said. You can't not take your penance. You can't talk anymore after you say that last thing, after that you're done.

"You must," said Father, "in order to be forgiven in the eyes of Jesus.

"Strong boys make strong men, makes a strong nation."

He put up his hand like a knife and sliced the dark into halves and then quarters.

The little cupboard door closed. Johnny stood in the dark and pushed open his door. He walked out to find his class lined up in the middle aisle waiting for him in the dark church with all the lights off and the fourth grade already left, staring at him like they had heard the whole thing.

The class line moved off and Johnny found his spot at the tail end with Jimmy.

"What'd you get?" Jimmy turned around as soon as Sister at the front had descended the stairs and was out of sight.

Johnny shook his head.

"Nuthin'."

"No, what was your penance?" Jimmy hissed urgently.

"How many Our Fathers? I got ten, already done 'em, how many'd you get, huh?"

"None.

"Hail Mary's?" Jimmy said as he dipped his fingers in the Holy Water at the front door and crossed himself.

"None."

"Glory Be's?" Jimmy was sounding worried. "Once I got a hundred Glory Be's, a frogging hun'red!"

Johnny shook his head as they headed left around the church and the cannon off on the side in the yard, intricate frost coating its black metal.

Jimmy looked angry now, moving to walk backwards in front of Johnny.

"How come? Oh," he smiled.

"You lied."

Johnny shook his head.

"No. I told the truth, everything."

"You have to get prayers to say, or something."

Johnny nodded.

"I have to talk to Mary Pat."

Jimmy stopped. Johnny kept going, around Jimmy, trying to keep up with the class.

Jimmy hurried to catch up.

"Why?"

"I have to tell someone I lied and that's who I'm going to tell," Johnny said.

"You lied about ... what? ...

"Mary Pat?"

"'Cause I have to tell everyone and if I tell Mary Pat, she'll tell everyone and I won't have to go around telling everyone myself or ask Sister if I can talk to the class if I have to do that I will die."

"You will?" said Jimmy, holding the door for Johnny to go in. "Father said that? Huh? Ma-aan."

Johnny nodded solemnly as he entered the school and headed up the grey marble steps.

They walked together, side by side, step by step. When Johnny took two steps, Jimmy took two with him.

Jimmy grabbed Johnny's arm at their floor.

"About the boiler?"

Johnny nodded and walked off. Jimmy caught up and grabbed him and punched Johnny hard in the shoulder and ran.

Johnny accepted it and moved off across the marble floor to the third grade classroom.

The children collected sack lunches from the cloakroom and shuffled to their desks to eat. Sister put an album on her stereo, closed the door and sat down at her desk to eat her apple and say the rosary.

The children talked quietly at their desks and ate while listening to Sister's record: Peter, Paul and Mary, two apostles and Jesus' mom, who sang around Bethlehem, and Jerusalem sometimes.

Johnny solemnly drew his sandwich and cookies out of their bags and placed them in a row with his barbecued Fritos on his desk in front of him. He stared at the food with his hands folded in front of him on his desk.

He selected one of the Fritos and chewed it, looking over at Jimmy who stared back at him hard like Alcatraz lifers across the dining hall.

Johnny took another Frito, brought it to his mouth then put it back. He put his palms on the edge of his desk and pushed himself into the aisle.

He walked to the front of his row and stood next to the desk of Mary Pat Bomb Gardner.

She ate celery and corrected arithmetic papers for Sister with a red pen.

Johnny stood there. She stopped working and looked at him. She pressed the cap back on the pen so it would not dry out.

Johnny watched her chew. He took a deep breath.

"I lied about the boiler room, and the boiler ... and the trips you can take in the boiler into the past and the future, well not the future, that's from the roof of the convent I think above Sister Julie's room not that I know which is her room or where she stands to get dressed, that's not true either."

Mary Pat asked Johnny to explain again and then clacked the papers together and slid out another stick of celery from her Baggie like she was playing Pick Up Sticks.

Johnny returned to his desk and saw the stares out of the very sides of his eyes from everyone wondering what he was doing out of his desk and why wasn't Sister saying something to him?

"Johnny why are you out of your desk?" Sister asked over the sound of the music.

Everyone turned to look at Johnny as the music ended.

Sister crunched her apple.

"I had to talk to Mary Pat."

"We don't get out of our desks during lunch time ... do we?"

"No-Sister."

"Then what were you doing out of your desk?"

"I just had to talk to Mary Pat ... about my paper. I forgot to put my name on it, I thought. I didn't. So I just had to ask her but I did."

"He's lying.

"He's a liar!"

The shrill voice cracked like a rifle through the dry air. The radiator shuddered and stopped, dead. The second hand on the clock stepped around the clock face like someone wanting to sneak away.

Mary Pat Bomb Gardner got out of her desk and stood in front of the class.

"Mary Pat?" Sister said.

"Johnny Moon was lying about the boiler. He told us all this morning and now he said he's lying."

"Aaahh!" the class gasped as one and looked even more intently at Johnny, like a whole class with noses pressed to the glass at the snake exhibit.

He sat with his head down, turning red, his chubby fingers pressing the Baggies on his desk. His heart raced. He curled his toes inside his shoes.

"He had to tell," Jimmy Purple spoke up. "For penance for confession."

"Jimmy-please," Sister said.

"Well, it's true he did," said Jimmy.

Johnny's lips quivered and he forced a Frito between them and sucked it.

"Please finish eating your lunches, class," said Sister.

[CHAPTER FIFTEEN]

At this writing, Dec 27, 2008, I'm 56 years old and John F. Kennedy was MY president growing up. I remember in grade school doing our physical conditioning tests that came from the President's Council on Physical Fitness. It felt like President Kennedy was paying individual attention to ME! When he was killed, I was more sad then than from any family death I'd experienced at that point. So I've always had a sort of curiosity about the details of the assassination. It was personal to me.

(http://forums.catholic.com/showthread.php?t=412461)

*T*he next morning Johnny climbed out of his dad's new Molar White Rambler at the front curb of the church with his brothers and sisters.

Johnny shoved a Twinkie into his mouth and waved to his dad, then turned to step over the big curb.

"Hey, Johnny," Dave said, pausing from his shoveling.

"You riding to school now? No more long hikes, huh?"

"Yeah, I guess," Johnny said.

Another carload of kids piled out as Johnny stopped by Dave.

The kids in the car yelled at Johnny as they hurried past into church.

"Johnny Moon! That's Johnny Moon! Moon! Moon!"

"Nobody can go to the moon."

"To the moon by noon!"

"The boiler. My dad says the boiler is to heat the schools. You can't fly in them, geez, either!"

"You would have to fly past the Alien Vans Radiator Belts, in Hell, to get way underground past them and you can't do that or you would burn up, geez."

"Yeahgeezdon'tyouknowthat?"

Johnny turned to Dave after they passed.

"Hell is underground. That's *it*," he said to Dave. "Everybody hates me."

He shuffled over to watch Dave shave the light snow from the walk.

"I should have got out here sooner," Dave said, huffing and puffing to get the work done before Mass started, or one of the old people complained to Father or the Sisters.

"Nobody really argued about Ground though," he said. "They said that was right here so that was right. And nobody understood how you could see the future from the Sisters' roof."

"Look at my rings. Hey, all ten-see?"

Dave listened with one frozen ear as he flipped the snow into the street until Johnny continued on inside.

Sister Mary-Michael walked across the hall after supper, chores and night prayers.

She wore jeans and a multi-colored M&Ms T-shirt, no shoes, her toenails painted purple.

She knocked lightly on Mark's door, holding a letter in her other hand.

Sister Mark let her in and together they sat in Sister Mark's room, smoking, and drinking Tang.

Sister Mary-Michael started out reading Sister Mark the letter from her twin sister Margaret, but had to stop, then just handed it to Mark and let her read herself, looking away and taking a long pull on her smoke.

She got up and wandered to the window and stared into the dark, down toward the alley.

Mark read the letter then read it again, in a whisper.

The letter recounted Margaret and Susan's day and what they saw when the President was shot and how they ran over, across the street and had their cameras taken and then been interviewed on television.

"We went home and got a little beer and cigarettes and sat on the front porch, not talking, just watching, watching people wondering what are we gonna do now.

"These people. They did not consider all these people out here, now running around like chickens with their heads cut off.

"Or how your children, your students were going through their normal lives, trying to do the best they can.

"Meanwhile, preparations being made to ruin their lives. We have to say something – I know what I saw and I've been talking to other people, a lot of other people, and so has Susan.

"You should have seen him right there, and he smiled right at us – like he knew who we were all along and he was glad we finally met. You should have been there. Really. I think you could have stopped it.

"It's not what they're saying.

"Not at all. Not even close, no-way-Ray.

"*Fuck!* Sister. I mean Mary, sorry. We either have to move to Mongolia or do something. I'm not living here like this and neither is Susan. She's right downtown right now, passing out flyers we made asking people who saw what we saw to come over to our house. We're having a meeting.

"I know you can't come. I know you're a nun, you're not a priest, but say a prayer, huh?

"Seeya and don't let the bed bugs bite.

"And stay away from that tunnel to the priest's house!

"Toodles.

"Hugs and kisses.

"Miss you. Lots!"

[Chapter sixteen]

For the physical vigor of our citizens is one of America's most precious resources. If we waste and neglect this resource, if we allow it to dwindle and grow soft then we will destroy much of our ability to meet the great and vital challenges which confront our people. We will be unable to realize our full potential as a nation.

Many of the routine physical activities which earlier Americans took for granted are no longer part of our daily life. A single look at the packed parking lot of the average high school will tell us what has happened to the traditional hike to school that helped to build young bodies. The television set, the movies and the myriad conveniences and distractions of modern life all lure our young people away from the strenuous physical activity that is the basis of fitness in youth and in later life.

— The Presidents Council On Physical Fitness Press Release

*T*he very next day Sister Frederick-Ludwig Cecilia, the tiny music teacher with the grey nose tufts, stood in front of the third grade classroom introducing the children to the new music for High Mass.

She perched on her Meadow Gold milk crate podium she lugged from room to room.

Usually, Sister M&Ms stayed in the room at her desk grading papers and to make sure Sister Frederick-Ludwig Cecilia did not have any trouble.

This time she was gone.

"Where's Sister?" asked one of the children.

"Timbuktu, for all I know," said Sister Frederick-Ludwig Cecilia.

The children struggled to meet her demands.

"Tantuu-um ... ergooo ... sacramee-entum," they droned away like death row prisoners watching "Sing Along With Mitch."

Dave and Isom appeared in the doorway. They leaned in.

Sister Frederick-Ludwig Cecilia followed the eyes of the children back to the doorway.

She spun on her box and shot her baton at the doorway like a magic wand six-shooter.

"Get out!" she said to the men.

Then asked the children who are those men?

"Daaavvee and Coooaach IiissomSisssteerrr!"

"What do they want?" she asked the children.

The children turned their eyes to the door to ask what the men wanted.

Sister turned to the doorway and placed her folded hands on her stomach to ask the men what they wanted.

"Is-a Sister Mary-Michael here?" Dave said.

"I am here," said Sister Frederick-Ludwig Cecilia.

"We wuz wantin' to speak with little Johnny, Sister," Isom smiled and twisted his hands together round and round.

Sister shot around and found Johnny in an instant.

"Do you know these men?" she asked.

Johnny nodded.

"Why?" said Sister.

Johnny moved his shoulders up and down.

"One a these days, Johnny," someone whispered somewhere.

"To the moon!" someone else completed the line.

Johnny knew who it was and did not look around.

"Who was that!" Sister said.

Sister's eyes searched the children like a shark smelling blood. Her nostrils flared, sniffing for fear, irregular heartbeat, elevated perspiration.

She flicked her head toward the door to tell Johnny to go see what the men wanted while she continued tracking the source of the whispers.

Johnny made his way out of his desk, up his row, in front of Sister, turning left to walk along the blackboard, running his finger across the board and leaving a finger mark he was unaware of.

He walked up to the men and stood in front of them then waved. They backed into the hallway and Johnny followed, out of sight of Sister and his class.

Dave and Isom each went to one knee to look face to face with Johnny Moon the third grade kid.

"How are you guys?" Johnny asked.

"Fine," said Dave.

"I'm good," said Isom.

Johnny stared at them, then smiled, then waved once more.

Dave looked at Isom and Isom looked at Dave.

"We have had a frightening experience," Isom turned to Johnny.

And Isom and Dave both began to speak at once, telling Johnny that they had been at school very early the day before.

"We had to sweep the halls," Dave said.

He explained that Isom sometimes helps him out so he can get done on time.

"And get the Christmas ornaments out for each room," Dave said.

"And we had to take down all the President's pictures," Isom said.

"Really?" Johnny said.

"Yeah," said Dave. "Sister-Something Principal wanted us to do it before all the kids got here because it might upset them."

"Put up LBJ and take the JFKs down to the basement," said Isom.

"Oh," said Johnny.

That did sound sad.

"So," said Dave. "We had a box, big box, old Clorox box," he looked at Isom.

Isom nodded, yes.

"And we had all the JFKs in the box and we was being real careful, both of us hanging on to it, and we set it down on my bench, see?"

Johnny nodded.

"And we had all the new LBJs, the pictures in the frames and they were already here. I wonder how they got here so fast, you know?" said Dave.

Johnny shrugged his shoulders and put his hands up, palms up.

"Well, guess what happened then?" said Dave.

"The box melted and all the LBJ frames and photos melted and we can't use any of them now," Isom said.

Dave scowled at Isom.

"The box melted," said Johnny.

"Yeah," said Dave.

"We set the JFKs down on the floor 'cause I needed my bench for the light bulbs I have to count to see if I have to order any more — can't run out and can't have too many on hand and waste money she says — and kind of moved the box of new President pictures over and maybe it was close to the boiler.

"We went to coffee and when we came back, the LBJs were ruined. Actually had kind of a little fire to put out once we got back. Wasn't too bad. What do you think of that?"

"You might-of set them too close," said Johnny.

"Yeah-but," Dave said. "It's like someone ... or some thing, didn't like the LBJ pictures, and melted them."

"Then we found an eagle feather by the boiler," Isom said, "and someone ..."

"Or some thing," Johnny held up his hands again.

"Yeah," Dave said, "had written your "strong boy" saying into the boiler and even made the "Fatima Nemo" wider and deeper."

Dave took off his cap and put it on, adjusting the tilt.

"To my people," Dave said, "an eagle feather is a strong sign."

Then Isom and Dave began again and stepped on each other's lines and interrupted each other to tell Johnny that they thought the boiler was asking to speak to Johnny and his friends.

Johnny scrunched his eyes and tilted his head so he could wonder how that could be.

"We lied," said Dave.

"Which time?" said Johnny.

"This time," said Dave. "Actually, Nemo Fatima does work. She, it works very well, in fact. We want to go Underground to the past in the boiler."

"We wanna make it up to you," said Isom, "for lying."

"You don't need to tell me," said Johnny. "You have to tell Father. He knows God. Nothing I can do about it," he put up his hands.

"No," said Dave, switching knees. "We told you that Nemo Fatima would take you to the past and tell you the truth."

"And that we could see the future from the convent roof, remember?" said Johnny, smiling again.

"Yeah," said Dave. "And then we said we were lying."

"And now we say we were lying," said Isom.

"Which time?" said Johnny, tilting his head now the other way and scrunching his nose.

"This last time," said Isom.

"Right now?" said Johnny.

"No, just before that," said Isom.

"We want to show you," said Dave. "And you can invite some of your friends."

"Oh, I don't have any friends," Johnny looked at Isom. "I used to, but that was a long time ago. They think I lied to them."

Johnny stood in silence.

He sighed a deep sigh that displayed his dismay at all that was happening and that he was getting a little hungry for lunch.

He could not tell Dave and Isom that he had been in the boiler room with his Big Chief tablet working on his journal and that he had carved that one saying into the boiler. He wasn't supposed to be down there.

Sister Mary-Michael had given them a writing assignment. She asked the children to write about how they felt about the death of the President.

Johnny tried and started to cry when he thought about that day. He thought about the TV and his family at home and everyone else sad and he really did wish that he could go back, go underground to the past and find out why Lee Haahvey Ozwalt had killed John F. Kennedy and he thought by going down and sitting by the boiler that he could write about the boiler and all that.

He had gone after school, taken his time leaving the room, getting on his coat, saying good night to Sister, dawdling down the marble steps, past the nurse's office, and the audio-visual room that he didn't really know what was in there, and down to the side door. Then he had just hoped nobody was behind him to see and kept going around the next corner down to the gym and the hall that led back to the stage and the boiler room.

He had taken deep breaths and held them in to calm himself like Coach Isom had said, then let the last one blow out and let spit fly, and snot, and then he had reached up to the knob and leaned into the bent metal door and gone inside.

It was dark so he waited. Then he could see the long stairs up to the playground and the five-gallon buckets hanging on the walls and the ladder leaning on the workbench.

He went over and wrote the strong boy line in the dust on the boiler and outlined the NEEMO FADAMA in again.

Then he went and sat Indian-style next to the boiler, facing the boiler, and placed his pad just-so in his lap. He had his pencil and he continued to outline the eagle feather while he thought about what he should write.

Then he closed his eyes and thought hard and then he dreamed.

He dreamed of things he didn't even know he knew. He dreamed and he flew and he sat in the White House in his underwear. He rode along behind the ghost dead president on the horse up the big wide road with people everywhere and him just in his underwear and holding on to a ghost who was smiling and waving to the people and they couldn't even see him. They could only see a little boy in his white underwear riding the horse in the funeral procession and they could only assume what that was supposed to represent.

And he flew above the car between the big buildings with the President and his wife in her pink hat and watching them driving in between all the lines of people and he turned right and then left and even put his arms out straight like Superman and then they were going some more and then boom-boom-boom ... boom-boom ... boom!

Johnny startled, but stayed in his dream and used more of his brain and saw the President's car and followed it and because it was his dream he could go anywhere and he went into the room full of people trying to keep the President from dying and Johnny hovered there, in his underwear, flying, dreaming.

And then John F. Kennedy came out of his body and floated up to the ceiling where Johnny was and smiled at Johnny. He smiled and rubbed Johnny's head and then looked back to his wife and the people down there and then he went up through the ceiling and Johnny woke up.

He was leaning on his tablet and had torn the cover from the rest.

He looked around and wondered how late he was, then got up, tried to dust himself off a little, then using the metal rod railing climbed the steep steps and let himself out.

He walked a ways down the sidewalk alongside the school, headed home, then stopped and turned around to look at the boiler room door.

Sister Mark and Sister Mary-Michael came out the side door of the school and turned toward the boiler room door, headed to the convent.

Johnny watched to see if they would look both ways and then go down to the boiler room.

They passed the boiler room door without seeming to notice it.

As they walked Sister Mary-Michael showed Sister Mark a new dance move she had learned, shaking her arms up and down like she was milking a giant cow and squatting almost way down to the ground like she was picking up a quarter with her butt cheeks.

Johnny turned and headed home, walking with his head down, kicking rocks.

Then he picked up his head and began to sprint.

Johnny stared off into space, thinking about all that.
"Hey!" said Dave.
"Earth to Johnny," said Isom.
"Where's all yer rings?" Dave asked.
Johnny looked at his hands.

Johnny shrugged.

"Well, you can get them back, tell them to come with you to the boiler room.

"When?" Johnny looked at Isom.

Isom thought for a moment.

"After school. Meet us after school at the top of the steps by the door, the playground door."

"No," said Johnny. "They hate me. Nobody would want to. It would take a miracle. I think I'll just go home. We got new ice milk last night at Safeway."

Johnny's eyes caught the shape of something behind Isom and Dave, something big, standing a ways back in the dark hallway.

He looked up. It moved closer, right behind the two kneeling men, like the ghost of Catholic Past.

Johnny looked almost straight up with wide mouth and eyes.

"What?" said Dave.

He and Isom turned their heads and swiveled around on the floor, kneeling in front of the apparition.

Sister Mark stood in silence over the kneeling men and the small boy.

She stared hard at them, her hands folded at her waist stuffed inside her sleeves like Houdini in a Franciscan straight jacket, calmly considering the situation.

She smiled.

The boy smiled. The men dropped their heads to the floor.

"I believe you," she said to the men, looking at them, left and right, each in turn.

The lifted their heads and folded their hands at their chests.

"Don't do that," she said, "please, stand up. Here, let's sit for a moment."

She led them to a small set of steps marking the boundary between the old and new sections of the school. She sat on the bottom step. Dave, Isom and Johnny filled in around her.

"You don't even recall, do you?" she looked at Dave.

"What?" he said.

She sighed and nodded, smiling wanly.

"The time I suggested to you the ... um, fairly unique properties of our boiler."

"Yeah, maybe I do," Dave pointed a finger at Sister.

"No you don't," she said. "All the same."

She looked at her watch. Johnny had never noticed before that any of the Sisters wore a watch.

She looked at the door of the third grade room, anticipating Sister Frederick-Ludwig's Cecilia's impatience.

"Oh, bother," she said.

Johnny saw her chest rise and fall under her brown habit and her rosary.

"It's how we got here," she said, putting up a flat, no-nonsense hand to extinguish any gasping or questions or wide-open mouths and eyes.

"We. The Sisters."

She looked at each of them, smiting them afraid to move or blink.

"We are ... not from around here," she said.

"And certainly not from Milwaukee. What utter hogwash."

She adjusted herself on the hard marble step, her knees together and twisted deftly to the side. She ran both hands down her habit to straighten a ruffle visible only to alien eyes.

"Mom said you took the bus," said Johnny. "One time a new Sister came when one got sick and Mom said she saw a whole station wagon full of Sisters headed toward the bus station that one time."

"Yes, that might have been," said Sister Mark, "but nonetheless ..."

She looked down and picked at something on her sleeve.

The men looked as if they understood. Johnny scratched his chin.

"Moses. Flying saucers. Burning Bush. Nemo Fatima," she said. "St. Francis, Franciscans."

She began to make moves to stand.

"We are here to help, mission work, they call it."

She pushed on her knees to stand, then stood straight and brushed her sleeves with each hand.

"These men will help you to understand, Johnny. Am I right in that assumption, gentlemen?"

"Yes-Sister," they said together

"How did you find out?" she took one step away then turned back to Isom.

Isom shrugged and held up his hands.

"I had to tell someone, Sister," Dave said.

"And I suppose you just had to tell the children," she said.

"No," said Dave. "Just Johnny Moon. Just Johnny Moon."

"Johnny Moon," Sister Mark said.

"Yes-Sister?"

"Give it one more good try, okay? Let your friends know that I suggested they go with you," she spoke louder now, loud enough for everyone up and down the hall and in the open door of the third grade classroom to hear.

"And watch out for the ghost class."

She looked seriously at each of them in turn, then her face lightened and she tapped Dave and then Isom each in the shoulder with tight, white, bony nun fist.

"Just give them a little room and don't get run over."

She smiled wide and turned away, then back.

"We in the fourth grade invited them all to our Thanksgiving dinner. It was really quite … interesting."

Again she turned away, then covered her face with her hand. She glided down the hallway without feet or arms or body or anything, only her face inside her space helmet showing any skin like a human being.

"What was that all about?" Johnny asked Dave and Isom.

"That … was the story of life," said Dave. "That right there was the parting of the seas and Noah's Ark and the star of Bethlehem, what you saw right there.

"Woah!" he shook his head and the floor, looked up and shook Isom's hand hard and long. The two men swung their other arms over each other's back and hugged for an instant.

"I told you!" Dave said to Isom. "I knew it. I *knew* it!

Dave picked up Johnny and held him way up, toward the ceiling.

Johnny looked around nervously, afraid someone might see him.

"Dave, c'mon," he said softly.

"Geez."

[CHAPTER SEVENTEEN]

I'm back in the USSR.
You don't know how lucky you are boy
Back in the USSR.
— The Beatles

"*T*hey're saying Oswald was communist," Tom said.
He sat in his usual chair at the regular table at the Corner Café.

Father hurried in, his head bare, unbuttoning his black winter coat.
He sat down to complete the circle. His coffee appeared over his left
shoulder.

"Ol' LBJ's got a tough row to how, with the Russians, Cuba,
Veet-nam," Jim said, sighing, stretching and looking out at his car
in the lot. He touched the keys in his front pocket and his comb and
wallet in his back pocket. He sipped his coffee just as the waitress
appeared with the pot, quickly set his cup on the table and smiled up
at her.

Father nodded for more.

"Yes, please," said Tim.

John put his hand flat over his cup and shook his head.

"Ruby got him," Dan said.

Two people nodded, fingering their cups. One person put his
glasses up to the light then stuck one of the lenses into his mouth.

"Jew-see Voyage?" said Tom to anyone. "We missed it."

One person shook his head, no.

"Big funeral," Tim said. "Looked cold on TV."

Father nodded.

"Big bucks," Bob smiled and leaned toward Father and rubbed his
fingers together.

Father pursed his lips and shrugged his shoulders, took another
drink, holding the cup with one hand, the other hand flat on the
table.

"Can you imagine the people?" Dan said. "Judas Priest, the
crowd."

"Gunsmoke's on t'night," said Bob.

"Celtics play Sunday," said Jim, "Warriors, I think."

Tim nodded and sipped, spilling on his shirt and reaching for a napkin in the middle of the table while keeping a finger on the spot.

[Chapter eighteen]

Also, in the progress report, President Kennedy acknowledged the thousands of letters he and the Council had received. The letters dealt with a variety of issues. The writers wanted to know what could be considered physical activity. A few of the sports mentioned were swimming, skiing, ice skating, golf, touch football, bowling, badminton, social dancing, ballet, sailing, equitation, archery, trap shooting, fencing, canoeing, table tennis, and croquet along with the traditional sports such as track and field, football, baseball, basketball, tennis, and volleyball. Letters from children described poor school gym facilities and equipment, programs in which physical education teachers only came to the school once a week or once a month, and schools with no physical education teachers at all. Many students complained that they had unfair teachers who punished them by keeping them in the classroom during recess or took away their gym classes as a result of poor grades or poor behavior. Jimmy Cannon, a third-grade student in Bakersfield, California, reported his frustration: "We are not having enough physical education in our room at school. If one person jumps out of line, the whole class does not get P.E. Since this happens almost every day, we do not have P.E." Some students questioned why they had to focus on physical fitness when their teachers were overweight and not fit.

(http://goliath.ecnext.com/coms2/gi_0199-10248387/Child-s-letter-to-President.html)

*J*ohnny tried.

He asked the kids if they heard Sister Mark out in the hall saying they should trust him about the boiler in the school basement being able to take them on adventures they had never even dreamed about yet.

They wouldn't buy it. Not in over a million years.

He told himself, why blame them? They were overwhelmed, actually, from the sadness in their homes and on the television, seeing adults crying so much, and just the general disruption of the everything that they could not understand or talk about, but they could feel it, that things had changed, and the undeniable dark-cloud sense that they would never be the same again, ever.

And to have themselves reminded of what they had just lost only days ago, not even enough time to need a new carton of milk in the 'frig at home, still on the same Cap'n Crunch box, the same stick of Oleo, the same loaf of Wonder Bread — it had not been that long — but still the mood had changed. There was a greenish-yellowish tint to the air, but the storm was not on its way, it had come and refused to leave.

The new Crest tube would not run out until it was time to play baseball in Central Park. The world would end by then. That was forever. It would never come. They would never play baseball again ever. The clothes they wore today were their death robes, these astronaut snowsuits, boot and buckle hats.

The kids instead wished to focus like a laser on arithmetic workbooks and the High Mass music and kickball, though the weather was almost too cold to play.

When Sister Mary-Michael tried out one of the new teaching techniques she had read about, putting them all in a circle on the floor and discussing current events and what they wanted to do with their lives, they inched on their butts as far as they could outside the circle. Many other children began to espouse a desire to lose weight. Some wanted to become bankers. One girl said it was now her life's goal to live in Italy and collect shoes. Many boys wanted to be professional athletes and get their photos on the cover of *Sports Illustrated* and have enough money to buy as much gum as they wanted whenever they wanted. One girl wanted to be an actress and another said she knew she would die in a war.

At noon recess Johnny often lingered near the bent and dented grey metal screen door leading down the steep chipped cement steps to the boiler room, hoping someone would come close enough to discuss the matter of traveling back in time.

No takers.

Not until Michael Irish creamed a Sister Mark screwball and it headed straight for Johnny in a spinning, orbiting arc.

It headed straight at Johnny's head and he reached up with both hands.

Smack.

It stayed in his hands.

They burned beautifully. His whole face grinned.

He wound up and with his snowsuit crackling and rubbing he tossed it back to the center fielder, falling ten yards short.

"Nice catch!"

"Way to go"

"Johnny Moooon!"

Johnny thought they might be planning to carry him off the playground on his shoulders when Sister Mary-Michael stuck her fingers into her mouth and whistled.

Johnny watched her and wondered if her fingers had grown. They seemed longer and thinner. Nobody on earth could whistle like she could.

Johnny looked at her sideways these days, wondering how much there was about her that he did not know.

She tweeted, then turned and smiled directly at Johnny. She walked right up to him, put her arm around his shoulders and pulled his head to her hip.

"Good catch," she said.

Johnny felt her hip against his ear and his face burned red to match his hands.

She released him in an instant and squatted down. Johnny was face to face with the woman he loved. He wished he could kiss her cheek, and look at those young, full red lips and those blue eyes. He could see her ears impressed against the white border of the space wimple.

How does she hear?

He looked for antenna places in her headpiece.

"Do you really think we are aliens?" she looked at him, serious.

Johnny nodded.

"I heard what Sister Mark said," she said. "Hmmm."

She smiled and touched her habit as if just discovering she had it on, the sleeve, the starched brown and white helmet, the white bib-thing that ran around her neck and shoulders like an oxygen tank.

He saw her tongue. It was not forked like on "Twilight Zone." Maybe it was at home. This was her school tongue.

Maybe real aliens have regular tongues.

She stayed past the time when Johnny thought she should have pushed off to leave.

In fact, she got down on one knee, even as the children began to mill around like cows nervous to be told what to do, waiting for Sister Mark to announce to the fourth grade playground-duty boys to open the doors for them to flood up the stairs and try to get far enough ahead of the Sisters to punch each other.

"What about an after-school club?" Sister Mary-Michael looked at Johnny.

Her breath was like strawberry Fruit-Stripe Gum. Just a strand of hair had come down. *Blonde!*

Johnny peed himself a little.

"Do you ever watch Mickey Mouse Club?" she said.

Johnny shrugged. He might have. Maybe his brothers and sisters had. Maybe he had.

He nodded.

Sister then gave in to the looming presence of Sister Mark and the rest of the children wanting to go inside. She pressed on her knee to stand, then leaned her head way down low to where her headpiece came around and fell over her shoulder like hair.

Johnny peed himself some more.

"We could do that," she touched his arm. "Think about it."

Johnny would think about nothing else ever.

"Do what?" he thought as he joined the herd headed inside.

They waited for the door monitors to count everyone, by two's and three's, coming to 279, of course, because they would have to start over and ring the bells cuz somebody escaped.

Father came over, made his way through the crowd like he was still walking laps in the YMCA swimming pool with his arms up around his chest.

Johnny saw him head for Sister M&Ms and thought he would go over and say hi.

He stopped when he heard the tone of their voices.

"You just need to be careful, that's all," Father said.

"About the letter," Sister said. "My personal letter from my own sister."

Her face got red and she put her hands on her hips and looked like she was going to put her knee right through Father's 'nads or something.

"Who are you?" she said and stepped back to take in Father more completely.

"Never you mind who I am," he said.

"Listen, don't you have vows or something to guide you?" he said. "Shouldn't you ask Sister Principal to help you to discern, that's all I'm saying."

"I am perfectly capable," she said, and then she began to move automatically as the group flowed inside, searching, scanning, probing for Sister Mark to stare a hole through her head from her forehead way out the back, a huge hole.

Father stopped her by gripping her elbow.

"You seem to be kind of a loose cannon, Sister Mary-Michael, bouncing all over the deck … capable of destroying everything."

She let him have her elbow for a count of one-thousand-two and stared cold into his eyes, trying to see into his mind.

She then gently pulled away and was the last to go inside, as Father lit a cigarette and walked toward the garage.

He timed his steps to approach a left-behind kickball, pounded it, and sent it soaring, higher than the school, over the wires and the rectory, into the lawn, by the cannon.

[CHAPTER NINETEEN]

I grew up in Chicago (by definition a Democrat), and was raised Catholic, so the election and presidency of JFK was a REALLY BIG THING in our house. I vividly remember sitting in my fourth grade classroom when it was announced over the PA system. I had a lay teacher that year, so I don't remember her name, but I can picture her, too, and that she burst into tears. Not too much else was done that day, and we all went home to watch the events unfold on our black and white televisions.

[http://www.librarything.com/topic/59958]

*T*he next day Johnny headed toward the side door.

He held his arms outstretched, ready to hit the lever full-blast on the run, blow right though and keep running until he got home because there was marble ice cream with his name on it.

There was.

He put "Johnny" all over the package in red and green and yellow and purple Magic Marker.

Johnny plowed into the door and banked sharp right, then came to a violent halt. He looked back in horror, thinking he had ripped his snowsuit on the door.

He tore his arm from Jimmy Purple's grip.

"What're you doing!" Johnny roared.

"C'mon," Jimmy said.

"What!" Johnny said.

"C'mon," Jimmy turned to walk sideways away from Johnny over the playground, waving his hand.

"No!" I got to go home.

"No-you-don't, c'mon."

"Yes-I-do," Johnny said as he shook out his arms and began to follow Jimmy.

"What?" he pleaded as Jimmy turned his back to continue over the blacktop toward the priest garage.

Johnny caught up and found Jimmy standing by the little white side door to the garage, behind some peony bushes and lilacs. He squatted down. Johnny squatted next to him.

He saw there were also rose bushes. He fondled one of the big thorns.

"Don't touch those, they'll give you warts," Jimmy said.

Johnny jerked his hand and rubbed it.

"What are we doing?" Johnny whispered.

"The nuns have their station wagon in there," Jimmy hissed. "It's s'pose to just be the Fathers' cars."

His eyes were wild like a French trapper who had just discovered gold.

"They have to put it somewhere," Johnny said.

"Not there!" said Jimmy like Jimmy Cagney making a point, "that's the priestes garage, don't you understand! See?"

"But the Sisters can still use it," Johnny said.

"We're going in," Jimmy said.

Johnny shook his head and planted a knee in the frosty mud.

"No way."

Jimmy took a step and grabbed the black knob on the little white side door.

He melted inside.

Johnny followed.

"Shut that," Jimmy said.

Johnny pressed the door shut and made the dark.

They stood for a while with the black pressing them against the brick wall. Slowly the forms in the garage became comfortable with the boys and showed themselves, a lawn mower hanging from a wall, and big fish underwater, the two priest automobiles, and then right in front of them the Franciscan white station wagon with the Kennedy-Johnson bumper sticker.

It they reached out they could touch it, easily. A real spaceship.

Just think, Johnny thought.

This is how they get to Timbuktu.

Woooaaaahhh …

It looks like it's older and not as good as the priest cars, but it's way better. It can fly and probably disappear and prob'ly fire guns from the bumpers and stuff, and drop tacks out the back, and pois'nus gas and lasers and invisible microphones.

Woaaaahhh …

Johnny felt his heart pounding his shirt and snowsuit, making a little rubbing sound like leaves sneaking over c'ment.

They heard Dave outside talking to someone. A car crackled by just behind them down the alley. Johnny smelled turpentine, like alien spaceship rocket fuel. Ladders and rakes appeared on the walls like someone had just put them there.

Johnny smelled paint.

Jimmy shoved Johnny and pointed at a giant red hedge trimmers hanging from the wall above the hood of the Franciscan Station Wagon Spaceship.

"They cut off kidses dongers," he said. "The boys."

Johnny shook his head hopefully.

"Yeah-huh," said Jimmy. "What else would you use those for?"

He put up his two fingers in front of Johnny's nose and made snipping motions.

"Then they eat them in their soup."

Johnny scooched away and slammed into the garage side wall.

"Donger Soup," Jimmy said. "It's Chinese. Every Wednesday. Space Nuns love their Ding-Donger Soup," he said as he took a step toward the station wagon and put a hand on the passenger door handle.

"No!" said Johnny.

Light poured into the garage.

Jimmy pulled the door and flew inside. Johnny followed him, clamoring to find room on the seat.

Father whistled as he shoved the garage door up all the way. The boys heard a loud fart and turned to each other with wide eyes. They pinched their noses and puffed their cheeks to make gas masks.

Johnny pulled the door shut.

Father's head appeared above his roof, looking toward the Sisters' car.

The boys ducked down, their feet flat on the floor, their backs on the seats, their arms stretched out flat.

Their chests heaving, their eyes shot toward the window like doll eyes. They watched the driver's window for the face of Father, keeping their heads straight ahead.

"Jimmy," Johnny whispered.

"What?"

"Any of the ghost, kids, here with us?"

"No, why?"

"I just wonder why I don't see 'em."

"Maybe you do," Jimmy said, turning his head to Johnny.

Father honked his nose, loud, still over on the far side of the first car, by the other garage wall.

A door slammed, not tight enough, slammed again. Father's engine turned and started. He backed out. The light remained shining into the garage. Another car door opened. They heard the scuffle of good shoes over gravel. The garage door rumbled down and the light went away.

They lay on their backs looking at the car ceiling in the darkness.

Jimmy's stomach almost touched the big steering wheel, a buzz saw and if he moved one inch wrong there would be blood pretty much everywhere.

Johnny ran his feet over the plastic floor mat, trying to figure the pattern.

"This is how they sit when they go into space," Jimmy said.

"No-they-don't."

"Astronauts do, you should know that. You could go to the moon with the nuns, Johnny Moon. You should just stay here 'til they come out and go with them, hide in the backseat or the way back seat, you could."

Johnny thought about stuff.

He felt some sort of wrapper with his feet and rubbed it together with his toes. He considered going to the moon with Sister M&Ms and living there forever, or just going there and coming back and then going home.

Jimmy and Johnny stared at the ceiling, at the plush rooftop stuff and at the dome light.

"You have to pee?" said Jimmy.

"No. You?"

"Nope. Me-neither."

Johnny smelled the evergreen tree on the rearview mirror and watched the magnetic heart and praying hands attached to the dashboard and the ivory statue of Jesus standing up by the window, looking down at them, but also keeping one eye out for Father.

Johnny messed with the window handle and tried to reach up for the dome light to fool with the switch.

"Don't!" Jimmy batted Johnny's hand away.

The dome light shot on. It shined bright into the boys' eyes. They put their hands to their faces and glared into the open door on Jimmy's driver's side.

"What the hey?" Dave stuck his head inside.

"What you guys doing in here?"

"Umm, nothing," said Johnny.

"Yeah," said Jimmy.

They stared at Dave, squinting against the light.

"Father said he heard something in here," Dave said.

He dug at the cement floor with his boot, forever trying to fix up and tidy up.

"Hey! I know what you two are up to!

"You want to ride along to the moon!"

They continued to look at him, seeing nothing to add.

"Hey, you guys got to get out of here right now.

"C'mon, c'mon."

He held the door open and hurried to the side door to let them out.

"Go on, now, I'll tell Father it was mice he heard shutting the Sisters' car door."

The boys ducked their heads at the intense outside glare. They scuffled into the alley. Jimmy walked across to the bushes up against the junior college building.

He unzipped and began to pee, watering the plants and writing his name on the building.

Johnny followed Jimmy, then seeing what he was up to, halted and looked elsewhere. His eyes found the second floor corner window in the convent.

He probably knew just where he was looking. Some boys had speculated on the playground about which room was Sister Mary-Michael's.

And there she was.

Just barely beyond the white lace curtains, he could tell it was her, doing something, maybe looking in a mirror, or prolly something else.

Her mouth moved.

Talking to Jesus.

Woooaaaahhh …

Johnny stood in the middle of the alley, looking almost straight up, his mouth wide open, hands at his sides, in his blue space suit and his corduroy space helmet that buckled under his chin with the little visor and the button on top. He wore one of his gloves. The other dangled from his fingertips.

Johnny felt Jimmy at his side as he kept his eyes glued to the apparition.

"Carlos from public school stood out here almost one whole night instead of going to CCD," Jimmy said. "If you do it too, you'll go blind."

Johnny turned on Jimmy.

"Carlos' not blind."

"He wears glasses," said Jimmy. "He had to go home when his dad came to pick him up."

"We'll stay 'til we need glasses, too," Johnny offered a plan.

Jimmy moved up in line with Johnny and they both stood looking up almost straight up with mouths wide open.

Anything could happen. They might see Jesus come to the window while he's visiting with Sister M&Ms. They might see her naked. They would die if that happened. But they would have seen Sister Mary-Michael naked. They might see her come out her window and catch a ride on the flying station wagon or a space ship from outer space.

An ambulance blared its warning some blocks away and Johnny thought about turning towards home.

And he saw her again. She threw open the curtains!

Aaaahhh! Aaa-aaa. Wooaaah!

Johnny saw Sister M&Ms in her room with hair. It was short and very blonde. His mouth dropped to his feet and he moved forward two, three steps. She was arguing with someone.

Then Sister-Mark-with-hair, black and curled like she had gone to a beauty saloon, came to the window like she was yelling at the window. She looked down and saw Johnny in the alley looking up at them.

Johnny looked down and then squatted on one knee like he had just found the most interesting oil stain in the world.

Jimmy fired rocks at the junior college building.

Johnny counted one-thousand-one, one-thousand-two as time down-shifted into slow motion. He tried not to breathe and wondered where he would live, what would he eat, could he survive outside in the winter, summers he could sleep in the dugout at the baseball field and eat sunflower seeds that people leave under the seats.

"Hi, boys, isn't it gorgeous tonight?"

Jimmy fired one more rock then looked to see who it was.

"Hiii Siiissstteerrr!" he exclaimed, smiling at Johnny who was longingly gazing skyward.

Sister Mary-Michael, in full habit, walked up to Johnny to see what he was looking at.

"What are you looking at?" she smiled.

"Oh, hi," said Johnny. "Nuthin'."

Sister got right down behind Johnny's shoulder to see his line of sight.

Johnny crunched his hand into fists and squeezed them at his sides.

She stood and faced both boys.

"Not many stars out at this time are there?"

She turned to walk briskly down the alley toward the garage. Other nuns came running, walking, laughing out the back convent door, slowing down and shh-shhing each other when they saw the boys, shielding wide grins behind small hands.

"Shouldn't you be getting home?" Sister called to Johnny.

He turned and saw Jimmy at the other end of the alley, searching for rocks to throw, headed toward his own part of town.

"Yeah," said Johnny. "Where you going?" He'd never taken a ride in a nun car or space ship. If they let him and they went to the moon he would really be able to tell Jimmy something tomorrow, or if they just gave him a ride home he might not get in trouble.

"To the Safeway!" she shouted, almost out of range. She put her hands to her mouth. "You don't think we survive just on Ding Dongs and Twinkies do you?"

Johnny's eyes and mouth popped open wide. He hurried into the bushes beside the priest garage.

He hunched down low in the waning light and watched the nun

white station wagon back out of the garage onto the playground. They pulled right in front of him. He watched the car loaded with laughing nuns.

As the back window passed his spot he saw Sister Mary-Michael seated next to the window. She laughed with someone inside, then turned directly on Johnny and smiled and flapped a flirty wave his way.

He looked down and saw that he had peed.

He looked up and the station wagon was gone.

[CHAPTER TWENTY]

I was six and sitting in a tree next to the crosswalk waiting for my older brother to walk home with me. The crosswalk guard told me and I remember climbing down from the tree and just sitting on the curb, very disturbed. It really was like learning that God or Santa Claus had died. Very shocking and hard to absorb.

(http://www.librarything.com/topic/59958)

*T*he next day at school, Jimmy Purple ran up to Johnny as soon as they hit the playground for noon recess.

"Well, what happened?"

"They went to the store," said Johnny. "That's it."

"That's what ah'm saaaying," Jimmy said. "They don't go to the store when they go to the store."

He made double quote marks in the air on both sides of his smiling face.

"Nobody ever sees them there. Did you see them go to the store. No. Seeee."

Jimmy told the kids gathered 'round how they saw Sister and the others get in the station wagon and how they were in the back and traveled to outer space.

"And they were all buck-naked," Jimmy said and then walked away.

The swarm of kids covered him instantly.

Jimmy put up his arms and waved them to shoo them away.

"They were naked and doing voodoo dances like they were out of their minds, like that one filmstrip we saw?

"Then ol' Johnny talked to ol' M&Ms. She was whispering in his ear and they were lookin' up at the stars together."

Johnny glared at Jimmy with wide eyes.

"Yeah-huh," said Jimmy. "Was-so, uh-huh."

Tommy turned to Johnny.

"You need to ask her again about that Mickey Mouse Club," he said.

"Yeah, yeah," the others chimed in.

"NEEMO FADIMA," somebody said.

"NEEMO FADIMA, Hemanooo the Maaab ... nificent," someone else said.

"Club," someone added.

"You're her boyfriend," Danny said to Johnny.

"Yeah, Johnny, get it going."

"The NEEMO FADAMA Club?" Johnny said. "I don't know, not many people would understand."

"That's why you have a club, numb-butts," Jimmy shot back into the middle of the crowd to push his finger into Johnny's chest.

"It's perfect. Only the ones who know, who are in the stupid club, will know what the stupid name means. It's Hemano perfect, right?"

"Right, right, perfect!" the others cheered.

"Tell her it's Latin," someone said.

"She would know," said Johnny.

"No-huh," said someone. "The nuns don't know Latin, only Father."

"Tell Sister NEEMO FADAMA means Lamb of God, or ... she loves you ... yeah, yeah, yeah."

"Too many words," said Johnny, shooting his fingers out of his closed fists to count the words.

He looked up and around the group.

"I don't think she cares," he said. "It was her idea. I think she'll like it."

"Yeah, Johnny!" they yelled.

Everyone shot off for the kickball area, leaving Johnny standing in the middle of the playground by the teeter-totters.

"Okay," he said.

"I will."

That same day Johnny and Bobby laughed together, out on the playground after arithmetic class, banging the big erasers together for Sister.

She whooshed down right past them and they wondered who was up with the class.

They remembered it was music time and this was Sister Mary-Michael's only free hour of the week. She smiled and said "good work" to them as she hurried past on her way to the convent.

Johnny let her get to almost out-of-distance range until he fired.

"Sister!" he yelled, "Hey. Sister."

She turned just her head, trying to keep her forward momentum.

"Yes?"

"Sister?"

She stopped, turned, smiled and clapped her hands together like you'd call a dog.

"What is it?"

Johnny told Bobby he'd be right back and with a big green eraser in each hand and throwing his arms side to side and watching his feet to see how fast he was going, he ran up to Sister and asked her if they could really do the after school club thing that she said that one day.

She smiled and said "that sounds wonderful."

They talked for a little more, then Johnny turned and sprinted back to Bobby, almost invisible within a cloud of yellow dust.

Johnny smiled wide and began banging his erasers together, pow-pow-pow-pow-pow-pow-pow!

On the playground before church the following morning they all gathered early to talk about the brand-new after-school club.

Like cows in a frozen feedlot, the kids pawed at the playground asphalt. Their breath hung in the air. Frost collected on their hats and coats. They moved around with heads down and hands shoved way down into coat pockets.

One's and two's shuffled off then back to the group as if controlled by an invisible dog.

Johnny arrived after walking from home. He moved through the playground gate into a path that appeared in the huddled bunch and closed behind him.

Like gangsters after a restaurant meeting, knowing they were being watched, they talked and laughed and nodded to each other, then punched each other playfully in the shoulders, even the girls, then walked together as a group, hands in pockets, heads tucked down into shoulders against the cold, past the rectory, jumping over the underground passage, past the cannon and around to the front door.

They bypassed the holy water fonts and marched straight up the steps and in a line down the middle aisle, heads up, eyes straight, breaking off into their rows without genuflecting.

During Mass they flashed the finger sign for NF, NEEMO FADAMA, the first two fingers with the thumb in behind, vertical, then horizontal.

They winked and nodded to each other all through Mass, then stared at the old people in back, nodding, sticking up their chins. On the way to communion they winked and nodded this way and that and flashed signs and stuck up their chins to the fourth-graders with the gold platters.

All day long they winked and nodded and strutted: during milk break, walking in front of the class to go sharpen a pencil, back and forth when they raised their desks to fish out an eraser inside, like undercover secret agents expertly signaling each other during a cocktail party in the church basement.

At noon recess the details got hammered out as the kickball rolled around the playground, moved only by a lonely December breeze, looking for someone to play.

Through arithmetic and spelling the anticipation mounted and the knowing nods became more frequent.

When Sister finished giving the next day spelling study words she also could not help but smile.

She sat at her desk, and with the children stared at the brown box on the wall and listened to the announcements from Sister-Principal-Something. They recited the final prayer of the day together as a school.

They stood next to their desks and by rows went to the cloakroom to gather whatever they needed that wasn't hanging drying on the hooks in the hall, then stood in a line from the door back along the blackboard to wait for the bell.

The bell clanged and those in the NF Club fast-walked-but-tried-not-to-run-or-look-like-they-were-in-a-hurry-or-going-to-the-first-ever-NF Club Meeting.

They tried not to leap the last three steps to each landing, but could not always, and they tried not to race each other to the playground, but by the time they rounded the last turn on the first floor they were all running and leaping and flew at the bottom door handle full blast and exploded onto the playground with a whoosh like coming to the mouth of a water slide.

They all watched Johnny and faced Johnny with eyes that said, how does this work, where's Sister-then, where is Dave and Isom, how does this work now, Johnny.

Johnny!

Huh?

Dave pulled up in his pickup right up next to the boiler room screen door and Isom came moseying up the sidewalk. The children formed a semi-circle around Dave's door and he had to be careful not to hit anyone while getting out.

Isom and Dave mingled with the children as they all formed a single line to go through the screen door and down the steep concrete steps.

At first the children chattered to each other to try to hide their nervousness, but the noise of the boiler extinguished all talk.

The ones still at the top of the steps could not see the ones who had made it to the bottom.

"M-i-c … k-e-y," one of the girls tried a valiant attempt.

"Ssshhhh! Ssh-ssh," came the predictable response.

Once all had reached the floor they milled around, bumping into each other, making hanging rakes clang, kicking unseen buckets and bumping into wheelbarrows.

"Shhh!"

"I didn't do it on *pur*-pose!"

Johnny led a delegation to the boiler to show where he had written the club logo.

"That's not how you spell it!" a girl said.

Johnny looked to someone else for confirmation.

"That's how we spell it in this club," Isom loomed above like a bass-voiced skyscraper.

Johnny smiled, relieved.

A shaft of light, Jacob's Ladder, burst into the room.

The metal door squeaked open and all faces turned to watch Sister Mary-Michael glide into the dark room, followed by another Sister.

"Sister Mark," someone whispered, and so it was.

Some of the children were sure everything would be all right now. Some thought things were never going to be all right ever again now. Some were certain that the Sisters were creatures from outer space in human bodies, and two wanted to go home now or in a few minutes.

The Sisters moved together into their midst. Dave and Isom stayed in the shadows, under a shaky rake and a hoe.

They heard scuffling and pounding up the stairs.

The girl paused to lean toward them and say that her mother didn't want her here anyway.

"She said I can't go inside the boiler in my good clothes. Uh, I'm … going home to change-be-right-back."

They heard the pounding up the rest of the steps and the clanging of the screen door.

"Anyone else?" Sister Mary-Michael took center stage and balanced perfectly on her toes to twirl and look around the group.

Some heads shook no and some just stared, some studied the boiler, and two reminded themselves that their parents had told them not to get into that boiler with a Negro, not with your good shoes you will not.

"Well, thank you for coming," Sister Mary-Michael began.

"To the first, uh, meeting," then she found Johnny and said, "of the NEEMO FADAMA Club."

He smiled and nodded, one hand holding his wrist at his waist, his hat cocked at just the angle as Dave's was at this particular moment.

"Well, uh-then," Sister said and this time turned one-half turn, then back-stepped to be able to address them all.

She put her hand into the air.

"How many think that Sister Mark and I are space aliens?"

A few hands went up, a few heads went down, and two pairs of hands shot up to cover wide mouths. One person spotted Dave's hand in the air and Isom's hands shoved deep into his pockets.

Sister Mark stood silently grinning, her hands in her sleeves.

"Okay," said Sister Mary-Michael. "Let's try that again."

She put up her other hand.

"How many think that if we ..."

She turned to Dave and Isom.

"Shouldn't we turn this off? If we get in there now we will be burned up like the old people, am I correct?"

Two girls turned to each other with hands over their wide mouths, knees bent.

Isom nodded and Dave began to hurry around the boiler, switching here and turning there. Wrenches squeaked and clanked on the cement floor. Dave grunted and Isom moved over to squat next to him.

"Yes," continued Sister Mary-Michael, "there's nobody up in the rooms now. Okay. How many of you believe that if we climb into that boiler that we will be able to ride in that boiler ... underground, down through this cement floor, into the ground, down into the earth, for miles and miles ..."

She pushed her own arm up higher and the door that was open to the gymnasium squeaked and closed, leaving them again in sublime darkness.

"They want to play basketball," Jimmy said.

"Who?" said Sister.

Jimmy shrugged and nodded to say she should just go on.

She raised her hand as high as she could and continued.

"And ... that by doing that ... we will be able to see into the past ... and that we will be able to go back in time ... and space ..."

She glanced at Sister Mark when she said this.

"And find out just what happened in Dallas the day the President was shot. How many believe that. Hands now."

Johnny put up one hand as high as his waist.

Isom, kneeling next to Dave, who was on his back twisting on something, looked up at Sister when she spoke.

Some kids looked at Johnny with his hand almost raised.

He felt their eyes and pushed his hand slowly up to his shoulder. He took a deep breath and raised it as high as he could over his head.

Sister Mary-Michael watched him grimly.

"Oh, you do, do you?" she glared down at him.

Johnny remembered hearing his father talk at home during the past weeks and both his mother and father crying, and he thought he remembered something about how excited and happy they had been when John F. Kennedy had been running for president and after he had been elected.

He had heard nothing around home about anything other than that Lee Haahvey Oswalt had shot the President from up in a window of the school booth, positive, and that Oswalt had been killed after that by a guy because that guy didn't want Mrs. Kennedy to ever come back to Dallas ever again.

Johnny knew because the TV was on all night and all day and he even heard his brothers and sisters reading from the newspaper to each other even though he had never seen them read anything ever.

He kept his hand raised and slowly nodded his head, keeping his eyes straight on with Sister Mary-Michael's eyes.

Johnny remembered the President and he remembered wanting to walk to school for the President and he remembered wanting to lose weight and to be a good American and go to the moon like a good American.

"And that's why we are here this afternoon after school, isn't it?" Sister looked directly at Johnny.

Johnny felt a pain in his stomach and the blood rushing down his arm into his face and he nodded again.

He wanted to pee and run up the stairs and race himself home and eat ice cream and crawl under his bed or lock himself in the bathroom and take a hot bath and never come out until supper was nearly ready.

He stayed there, in the school basement in the dark with his teachers and his friends around him and he felt that he was dreaming.

This was not real.

He had awakened from a dream in his room in the night because
he had to pee and he could not make himself wake up and he was
going to have to just pee into the window because there was no door
to the bathroom anymore and here was his dream still right in front
of his wide white eyes.

"Johnny Moon."

Sister Mark moved from the dark into the only light in the basement, coming through from the playground through a crack in one
of the glass blocks.

Sister Mary-Michael glided to the side a little.

Johnny let his arm come down to his side.

"Johnny Moon ...," Sister Mark continued.

"That's not your real name, is it?"

Johnny shook his head and kept his wide, scared eyes on Mark.

"What makes you think we have something to learn from taking a
ride to the underground past?"

Johnny searched the faces of his friends. They looked away. Jimmy Purple answered his stare with his own and seemed to be telling
Johnny with his eyes that Johnny should ram himself right now into
something hard or sharp.

It was his only chance.

"Where did you get this idea?" Sister Mark continued in her pros-
ecutorial pace and cadence.

Johnny looked at Isom and Dave out of the corner of his eyes.
They were standing now next to the boiler, hissing and sighing and
wheezing, shuddering, buckling, letting off steam, like a racehorse
after the run.

Johnny pushed up his shoulders to his ears and held up his hands
as high as his eyes with the palms up. He scrunched his chin so that
it showed a dimple.

Someone sneezed, from the dust maybe, and somebody coughed.
Someone dropped a pen and somebody else knelt down to tie a
shoe, but kept his head up and eyes wide to not miss anything.

"Well, it came from us, me and Isom," Dave stepped forward.
Isom nodded.

"And we heard it from you yourself, Sister."

He took his cap off and put it back on.

Johnny then adjusted his own cap.

Sister Mark smiled.

She breathed deep. The children saw the material on her habit move up and down, so she must have sighed a big sigh, too.

"How can that possibly be?" she asked, first looking at Dave and Isom and then around to the children.

"The Nemo Fatima ... uh, Fadama ... um, club."

She squatted and was right in front of Johnny.

She smiled lightly. He saw her hint of mustache go up and down.

"Johnny Moon, could you explain to the rest of us where you got the name for this club and what it means ... please?"

Isom grabbed Johnny under the arms and Dave hustled over the tall bar stool. They got Johnny all set up. The Sisters sat on the dusty cement floor and pulled their knees to their chests. The children sat down around them. Dave and Isom tip-toed from opposite ways to stand in the rear of the group.

Everyone looked at Johnny, in the light shaft, on the stool.

"Wee-eelll," he began by placing his hands on his knees and smiling.

And he told them the story of walking home on the day of the President's 'sas-nation and talking to Dave and Isom and coming down to the boiler room, and about how they told him this story, but he did not really believe it, because how could it possibly be true.

And he told them the story about Captain Nemo and "Twenty Million Miles Down To The Ocean" and reminded them about the miracle of the mother of Jesus appearing to the little Mexican kids.

"Sister M&Ms, Mary-Michael taught us," he nodded toward Sister in the shadows.

"We had to," they heard Sister M&Ms mumble.

"Fatima," she said. "It's a requirement."

"Continue," Sister Mark said to Johnny.

"And that's ... how you get NEEMO FADAMA," Johnny held up his upturned hands in front of his face to explain.

"But then Dave said Sister said the boiler came from her old school and it's haunted," Johnny said.

"It's complicated," said Michael Irish.

"It really *is*, isn't it?" Susan and Jane looked at each other and nodded in the pitch dark.

Johnny stopped. He sat there and returned his hands to his knees and smiled around the group.

"Haunted?" a boy in the dark asked.

Sister Mark nodded and stood.

"That's what they say."

She shrugged.

"Well?" she looked at Dave.

"Ready?"

Dave touched the boiler with one fingertip, then placed a hand flat against the steel.

"Yep, nice and cool. Not hot anyway. All we gotta do is get this door open and …"

He and Isom worked together to unscrew the big bolts to get the boiler door free to swing open. They grunted and skidded on the dusty cement and pulled the door wide open.

The children migrated toward the opening, pausing far away and leaning to try to see inside.

"Oh, well, let's do this, then. Let's just do it and get it over with," said Timmy. "Just one time though. This is our first and *only* meeting."

"In my old school we weren't allowed inside the boiler," one of the girls said.

Sister Mary-Michael slid up to the boiler door. She squatted pristinely and put out a hand, young and beautiful, sticking it inside the boiler like one of the martyrs.

The children gasped as one.

Sister retrieved her hand and turned to them with her standard smile.

"It's fine," she said. "We can go inside."

All hearts pounded out "Bonanza" hoof beats. Children tried to ooze to the back of the group without moving their feet.

The Sisters looked around the group, at Dave and Isom and the children.

"I'll do it," Sister Mary-Michael and Sister Mark said together.

And they both made a move to duck their head into the opening.

"No!"

"No-I-should-do-it," came a voice from the dark.

Johnny Moon stepped up.

He put a light hand on Sister Mary-Michael's shoulder and looked inside the dark boiler and looked right into Sister's eyes.

"It was kind of like my idea, I'll go."

Sister scooched back a little.

Johnny stepped forward, waiting for the hands that would hold him back and tell him thanks anyway you don't have to here's some ice cream we'll find you a spoon.

He waited at the opening, touching the boiler metal with his snowsuit, rubbing just a little.

He reached both hands out and touched the insides of the circle and stuck his head inside. He pulled one leg up and inside and then the other leg.

He was inside. It was warm, but not hot. He felt the circleness of the shape of the smooth bricks.

He stuck his head back outside and smiled at Sister, who seemed like she was on the other side of the world, far away, like sticking your head into the living room from inside the TV screen.

"It's okay," he smiled at her and waved, and she smiled back and began helping the other children inside.

Dave shined a flashlight inside and Johnny scrunched down to inch to the back of the boiler as the others rustled inside like immigrants into a boxcar.

They huddled in two rows: Jimmy, Johnny, Bobby, Tommy, Timmy, Danny, Michael, Jane and Susan.

And then Sister put a black shoe through and scooted down the middle of the group to the end, next to Johnny, then came Sister Mark.

"Is there room?" Dave stuck his head inside.

"C'mon in," said Sister Mark, "the water's fine."

Dave got in and then Isom.

He pulled the door almost shut, leaving a space for air to get inside.

"You can close it," Dave said. "I've got this."

He showed the big red pipe wrench in his hand.

"We won't get stuck in here long's I got this."

Isom reached out and pulled the door shut with a thud.

Dave's flashlight shined off his face and he showed his teeth.

Sister Mark nodded at him devoutly and he flicked it off.

Each of them sat on the bricks with their legs folded to their chests. All was dark. As dark as purgatory, and if the boiler fired up, they would be in hell, and then they would rather be watching TV or making a snow fort in the back yard.

They sensed each other nearby, but were each alone, in the basement of the school, inside the boiler.

Inside … the … boiler.

Like on "The Twilight Zone." That one episode.

"Eeew! Eeeewww!" one of the girls screamed and everyone jerked.

The cries rang and bounced like gunshots in the bathroom at just after midnight.

The Sisters reached out in the dark to the voice. Dave shined his flashlights. The girl raised way up, scrambling, scratching, swiping at something under her.

"Eeewww-Eeew-Eeew! Bones! Old people bones! Eeeeeewww-ww!"

The children scrambled to get away from her and all raised on their behinds and felt underneath and swept, swept away at the bricks.

"There's hair on them!" the girl screamed. "Dead old people hair!"

Some of the girls began to cry. Two of the boys bit their tongues and one boy peed a little.

Dave crawled to her and scooped up the little bones.

He poured them into this shirt pocket.

"Mice," he whispered to Sister Mark next to him. "Somehow one must have gotten in here, it happens."

Sister Mark began to explain to the group and Dave shined the light on her face, blinding her. He adjusted the light down. Sister told the children the bones were from a mouse and that the mouse was now in Mouse Heaven. She then led them in an Our Father and Hail Mary for the repose of the soul of the "the tiny mouse."

"Where's Mouse Heaven?" somebody asked.

"Same as real heaven," someone answered.

"Is not."

"Is so right Sister?"

"I suppose," said Sister Mary-Michael."

"It is? How can that be? This one doesn't have its bones. How can that be?"

"It does now!" said Sister Mark. "For God's sake!"

Sister Mark then added that Dave wanted to tell them all that he does not burn up the old people in here to heat the school.

"Not any more," she smiled. "Now we use these bricks. The use of old people to heat the school was outlawed by The Vatican Council."

The children gasped and again began scrambling, reaching, sweeping.

"Please," said Sister Mary-Michael. She reached and punched Sister Mark in the shoulder in the dark. "Let's be very quiet," she said.

The boiler shuddered. It rumbled and steam whooshed out from somewhere.

"We're going to cook and burn," one of the boys said.

"Shhh," counseled Isom.

"Give your life to Jesus and the school," someone said.

"Radiator heat. Like the apostles," someone else whispered.

"That's not like the apostles," someone said.

"Yeah-huh, it is."

"It's just the boiler getting settled," Dave said. "It's all turned off. Really. Believe me. It's true. I wouldn't take any chances with any of you, really."

"Thank you David," said Sister Mary-Michael. "We do believe you and we trust you."

Sister Mark hummed.

She nodded at Dave and he turned off the light. Everyone heard everyone else breathing and scooching. Someone sniffled and two people coughed and one person whispered that they were going to die.

"Well, then," said Sister Mary-Michael.

"We are all in an enormous amount of trouble," she smiled in the dark and tried not to laugh.

"No, no," she quickly added, feeling the eyes of Sister Mark.

"I think we should pray, silently … please bow your heads."

Sister Mary-Michael began with an Our Father, followed with a Hail Mary and a Glory Be, and asked them to place their upturned palms on their legs and take a few deep breaths and let it out.

She asked Isom to crack the opening.

"Get some fresh air in here," she said.

Isom turned the crank. Dave handed him the pipe wrench. The children held their breath. The door opened and they felt a little breeze. They relaxed just a bit.

"There," said Sister Mary-Michael.

"This is just like in "The Birds," one of the girls interrupted. "That one scene ... with hundreds of beaks in the door?"

"Dr. No," said someone else. "D'jew see where he ..."

"Psycho."

"Swiss Family Robinson," said Tommy. "It's more like that, don't you think, Sister? We are going on a journey, into places unknown, and we will probably have to fight natives with sticks that Dave and Isom will carve for us by just using their hands and their teeth if they don't have a knife, or they lost their knife in the ocean on the way there, right Sister?"

Sister Mary-Michael said those were all good examples of people going through difficult, unusual circumstances. She then asked everyone to take a deep breath and close their eyes.

"I can't tell if my eyes are closed or not," said Jimmy Purple.

"Wasn't there that one show where the children and the mom and the dad and the grandma and grandpa in that one house got stuffed inside the furnace," Jimmy Purple ran on, certain he would be soon shushed into silence, "by that one man in the black mask, and then the furnace got turned on, and then you saw the house from the outside and the black smoke coming up from the chimney?

"Remember that one show?"

He was shhshed by two good girls at once.

"And now just close your eyes and think of Jesus," Sister Mary-Michael continued. "Think of why we are here today, this first meeting of the Nemo Fatima Club ... to journey ... beyond ourselves and our surroundings ... that's it ... let yourselves go ... don't hold back ... hum to yourselves if it helps."

"Hmm, hmmm, hmmm."

The children hummed.

"We pray," Sister Mary-Michael continued, "that the ... special properties of this boiler may take us ... and help us to be open ... to whatever is out there … as the brave explorer Captain Nemo and the courageous children of Fatima, so long ago."

She hummed the tune to a folk song some of the children had heard coming from the convent as they walked down the alley on Saturday headed to go swim at the YMCA since Catholics could go now.

"Outrageous times call for outrageous measures," said Sister Mary-Michael.

The children who could see a little in the dark looked at her and then at Sister Mark. Sister Mark sat motionless with her head bowed.

"The outright murder of John F. Kennedy," Sister Mary-Michael continued, "nuclear war, the invasion of Cuba, it could be the end of the world for all we know, and what kind of a chance have you young people had?"

The children sensed distress and moisture in her voice.

"Remember what Father said about the boiler and going into the boiler for answers?"

Two good girls nodded in the dark.

"He was joking," said Sister Mary-Michael, "but perhaps that's exactly what is needed. I just thought … that … Jesus might see how truly desperate we are."

"It's like Jonah inside the whale, Sister," said Sister Mark. "He didn't sound like he was joking to me."

Some of the children hummed. The Sisters fell silent and bowed their heads to their chests.

They felt better with the door a little bit open and special at being in such a unique situation along with the Sisters and Dave and Isom and not so stupid and they had already learned that the school was not heated with old people, so that was nice.

Jimmy Purple pinched Johnny's leg and Johnny tried to ignore him, pushing at Jimmy's foot with his foot to tell him to knock it off.

"Fucker-stop-it," Johnny hissed.

"This is just like Hemo The Magnificent," Jimmy said.

"Shut up," Johnny said. "Yeah, you're right, it is," he smiled at Jimmy.

"Shhhhh!" Bobby and Jane hissed.

They sat in silence for two minutes and then for a little while longer and then they didn't know how long they had been in there, inside the boiler in the basement of the school, after school hours.

Some of them huddled up next to each other.

"We should turn on the heat," someone said.

"No!" two people shouted.

"I don't feel nothing," Susan said. "I thought we were going to go back in time in this thing."

"Yeah," Michael said.

"Yeah," said Timmy.

"Johnny Moooon said ..."

"It's more of a spiritual ... um, journey," Sister Mary-Michael began. "Sometimes it takes time to, uh."

"I have to be home pretty soon," someone said.

"I'm not doing this ever again," said someone else.

"Well, one of the reasons we are in here," said Sister Mark, "is that we want to know what happened to the President. Am I correct, Sister?"

Sister Mary-Michael nodded.

"Sister," said Sister Mark, "you mentioned that your sister lives in Dallas and that she has heard some things?"

"Yes, Sister. My own sister, her name is Margaret, lives in Dallas, and she was there that day, at the parade. She was actually there at the, um, where it happened, I believe she said."

Sister Mary-Michael told the children the story that she had heard from her sister Margaret who worked in an office building in downtown Dallas and had been able to go down to watch the President's parade go by.

Margaret and her friend had been at the end of the parade and they had been right there when the President was shot.

"She's only got one friend?" said Susan.

"Weelll, I don'..." said Sister M&Ms.

"They got his blood on them."

"Eeewwww!" all the girls screamed.

"Shhh-shhh," said Sister Mark, putting a strict pointer finger over her own pursed lips.

Sister Mary-Michael continued on, saying that her sister and her *one and only friend* saw smoke behind them and that they thought the shots had come from somewhere else than the television and newspaper were saying.

"So what?" someone said.

"Well," she said, "that just means ..."

And then she began to speak softly and sadly and slowly.

"And, well ..."

Jimmy Purple said, "Let's go, let's get outa here! Blast off!"

"Shhhhh!" all the others turned on him.

"Let Sister talk!

"Just-shhhhuuushhh. For. Once."

"Well," she began again.

"I just ... think it's so sad and so terrible. And it's so frightening. If it isn't Mr. Oswald who did it. And nobody talks about that."

"He's dead. Good, my dad said."

They heard Sister sniffling.

"And I just thought that if we could try this ... it's so strange, sitting inside the boiler ..."

"Yeah," whispered Jimmy Purple. "We're gonna be in big trouble."

"Shhh."

"But I just thought ... that if it really had ... um, different ... um, capabilities, like in Chicago before it came here, that maybe we really could ... you know ... the truth, the 'Big T' ..."

Their eyes were adjusted now and they saw her put her famous double quote marks in the air and they huddled closer together now, not worrying about whether they were scooting close to a boy or girl.

Johnny heard Sister Mary-Michael's voice. His eyes were closed and he was hmm-hmming to himself with his open palms sitting on his legs.

He had a grin on his face that no one could see, as he was way on the end.

He was taking a trip, Underground, zooming, then up above ground, flying.

Johnny sat in the sky, with his legs folded, talking to the Man in the Moon.

Mr. Moon.

"Hi," said Johnny.

"Hello, Johnny Moon," said the moon.

Johnny explained what he was doing with his class inside the boiler in the basement of the school.

"We need to know what really happened," said Johnny.

"Do you know?" he asked.

The Man In The Moon explained that yes, he knew, he had been there.

"I'm kind of everywhere," he said, "just sometimes you can't see me."

"Mr. Moon, Mr. Moon, you're out too ..." Johnny began to sing.

"Yeah, that," said the moon.

The moon told Johnny that he could tell him about what happened in Dallas, but just not today, maybe tomorrow.

"Okay, seeya," said Johnny.

[CHAPTER TWENTY-ONE]

My parents were glued to the TV. Mama was in the kids' rocker. She was crying. I asked what was wrong, and she told me.

I said, "Why are you crying? I thought you hated him?" And she said, "Just because we don't like someone's politics does not mean we want them dead."

I was five years old. I didn't really understand death at that point, having never known anyone at all who had died.

I think that was the first sobering moment in my childhood. I began to realize that death was a serious thing to adults, and might even happen to me someday.

(http://www.librarything.com/topic/59958)

"*T*hat shithead owes me money."

Verlin told Duke as they looked out the fourth-grade classroom windows at Johnny Moon headed home after school.

Verlin and Duke were cleaning Sister Mark's blackboards, windows and counters after being caught taking gum out of her desk drawer while she was out of the room.

"Oh, yeah, the dog," said Duke.

"Yeah. The dog, fuckin' dog," said Verlin.

"I'll be right back," Sister Mark said as she went out the door. "I expect you to have done something by the time I return."

Verlin sprayed the window with Windex and Verlin rubbed it until they could not hear Sister's hard-sole steps on the tile.

"They're up to something, lookit there, look!" Verlin pointed down at Johnny stopped on the corner talking to members of the Neemo Fadama Club.

"They're always talkin'," Duke said.

"Yeah," said Verlin.

"Wait," said Duke. "There's that nigger talkin' to them. I wonder what they're talkin' 'bout, huh?"

"My dad hates that son-of-a-bitch," Verlin said. "Those apes ought to go swim to Africa."

"We s'posed to feed the fish, too?" Duke said.

"Yeah, fuckin' nun," said Verlin. "They're all the same. My Dad said they were the same when he was here, fuckin' nuns, he says. Where's that fuckin' fish food?"

Duke and Verlin walked over to the fish tank in the corner by the supply closet.

"Here," Duke picked the fish food box from the chalk tray and handed it to Verlin.

"Fuckin' fish," Verlin said, "c'mon an' chew on this then," he said as he held the box over the top of the water. The goldfish, Peter, Luke, Matthew, Mark, Martha, Mary, and Noah headed up to the top to eat.

"Forget it," Verlin smiled at the fish and handed the box back to Duke.

"Here," Verlin said.

"C'mon."

Verlin motioned to Duke to go start working on the blackboard on the far side of the room.

Sister rushed inside just as Verlin and Duke began to wipe the board down with wet rags.

"I have to go to a meeting," she told them.

"Can I trust you in here by yourselves?"

"Yeees-Sister," they sang in two-part harmony.

Sister stood by her desk and stared at them for a moment.

"All right then, I believe I can. You are responsible young men. I know you can be."

She scurried to the closet to get her black shawl.

"And if you could just feed the fish, too, and then close the door when you leave, no, don't bother with that, someone will be coming through to sweep."

She searched her desk drawers and then the chalk tray.

"Yes, there it is," she said, seeing the fish food.

"Goo-ood nii-iight Siiissterrr," they said together as she went out the door.

"I hate that stupid club," Verlin turned to Duke.

"What club?"

Verlin punched Duke in the chest.

"That after school club they're always talkin' about, you know!"

"Yeah."

"And I think Isom's part of that stupid club," said Verlin. "Remember when he wouldn't even let us throw snowballs at the stupid third-graders?"

"Yeah," said Duke. "We woulda slaughtered 'em. We had that perfect fort set up, oh, maa-aan, yeah."

"I was there, I know, stoop."

"He's the stupid floor sweeper. Them niggers are the stupid janitors," said Verlin.

"And Dave," said Duke.

"Yeah," said Verlin. "Here's what we do."

Verlin and Duke wiped the blackboard with wet rags then dried them with dry rags while they talked about Verlin's plan.

Verlin and Duke hurried to finish cleaning the boards then ran to the back of the room to throw the dirty rags in the bucket in the cloakroom.

They poured the entire box of fish food into the fish tank, and set the empty box in the closet where the janitors kept their brooms and dustpans.

Verlin and Duke fast-walked down to the library.

Verlin stuck his head inside and saw all the nuns seated around a large table. He spotted Sister Mark and Sister Principal, and Father at the head of the table.

"We're done, Sister," Verlin waved to catch her eye. "Me and Duke are going home, now, leaving the building, right now, seeya!"

Sister Mark matched his wave and smiled, then returned her attention to her meeting.

"C'mon," Verlin whispered to Duke. They walked away from the library, around a corner, and shot up the steps, using the wooden handrail to vault in threes and fours.

They went to each classroom in the building and poured all the fish food in the room into the tank. Each time they put the empty box in the janitor's little closet in the room.

The next morning Sister-Principal Something called Isom to her office and fired him from his janitor job. She also spoke to Father and Father walked over to the school, down to the basement to visit with Isom. Father told Isom that he would not be allowed to stay in the locker room anymore.

"The Sisters just don't trust you," said Father.

Dave spent the rest of the next week cleaning writing from the walls of the boys and girls restrooms about Isom being a "niger," and "kilt all the kidses fish."

[CHAPTER TWENTY-TWO]

Second-grade, heard nothing at school, found out when I got home and found my dad, who was never home early, in front of the television. I was more than mildly put-out that the Mickey Mouse Club had been pre-empted by the news.

This was the beginning of the end of my childhood innocence. After Oswald, Martin Luther King, and Bobby Kennedy, my world changed, believing that assassination was a part of life. It was not the safe haven I had thought.

A seven-year-old should be able to be idealistic for a few more years.

(http://www.librarything.com/topic/59958)

*E*ach day before Johnny went to bed he took down his chart from the refrigerator door and sat at the kitchen table. He used his own pencil from up in his room and wrote down what he had eaten that day.

On top of the paper it said "A Strong Boy Makes A Strong Man Makes a Strong Country." He had made the chart from the lined paper in his Big Chief pad and written the heading across the top. The words started in the left corner and descended to about the middle of the page on the right side, leaving him with about half the page to write on. In that space he made up and down lines and across lines to make a chart the way he had seen Sister do on the blackboard with the nutrition table in secret science class.

On the sides of the paper his brothers and sisters had written: "two scoops ice cream," "candy is brain food," and "moon ... cheese ... must eat ... moon."

Johnny was pretty sure it was his second older brother who wrote vertically along the left hand column from bottom to top: a fat boy makes a fat man makes a fat fatty.

Johnny had put in the days of the week and for a whole week now he had written in what he had eaten at breakfast, lunch and supper: Cap'n Crunch, peanut butter, crackers, apple, soup, and on and on.

Then Johnny headed into the living room while nobody was around to turn on Jack LaLane.

He sat on the sofa and watched him exercise. Then the man pointed at Johnny and said, "Get up off that couch and exercise."

Johnny moved to the side of the room and sat in a chair by the window to listen from where the man couldn't see him.

He peaked around the side of the television.

The very next day Johnny asked the other kids in the club on the playground when there was going to be the next meeting.

"There's not going to be another meeting," Jane said.

"One was stupid enough."

"That was so stupid. I can't believe we did that."

"No, it wasn't," Johnny said. "It wasn't stupid. It was smart."

"Smart?"

"Why was it smart?"

"You prob'ly like sitting in that boiler. Reminds you of hell, 'cause that's where you're going for crawling on the floor in church that one time."

"That will be enough, girls," Sister Mary-Michael walked over, fingering a whistle on a string around her neck. She would be the new physical fitness instructor now that Isom had been fired and kicked out of his apartment in the basement locker room.

When the girls skipped away singing an original jingle about Johnny Moon and the boiler and going to hell forever and ever, "and Michael rowed the boat ashore," Johnny motioned to her with his finger to squat down.

Sister walked over to the slippery slide and took a seat on the steps and Johnny followed her over.

"We have to have another meeting," Johnny said.

Sister looked at him as if to say, go on, I'm listening.

Johnny took a deep breath and let it out. He closed his eyes and took another, which provoked a smile from Sister.

"Oh, well," he said, looking all around and then at the ground.

"Boy, I was dreaming, you know, in the boiler that one day. You can't believe what I saw.

"Did you see that?"

"No, Johnny, I didn't. You had a vision, like Fatima."

"I did?"

"You might have, I guess. What did it tell you?"

"But you don't believe in Fatima," he looked up at her.

"How do you know?"

"Cuz you don't seem like you do. They had special messages," he said. "So it had to be real."

"They only told us about the first two and they seem so, hokey, planned, rosaries, conversion of Russia, burning in hell. It doesn't sound like Jesus to me, Johnny."

"Well, maybe the third sign is Jesus. Maybe those first two were some other guy up there, Jesus' Dad, and all he talks about is old stuff."

She smiled and said, "you are probably right, young man, now what did *your* dream tell you?"

"It said, uh, I don't know. We have to go back."

"Ask for a sign. People always ask for a sign," she said.

"I talked to the moo-oon."

He took another deep breath.

"It's umm. Well, the moon, looks like, kinda like. I think maybe he's ... oh, nothing."

"And what did the moon have to say?" she said.

He looked up at her, surprised. He searched her face, her long eyelashes, her red cheeks, her thick lips, for signs of a snicker.

"He said to come back and he'll tell what he saw, you know, in that place your sister is. Purgatory."

"Dallas," she said.

Sister looked around the playground. Confident everything was in place, she looked back at Johnny.

"Then we'll have to have another meeting, for sure."

"They won't," Johnny said, motioning with his head toward the other kids.

"Why?"

"I asked 'em. They already said no."

"Well," Sister said, "what if we had snacks? I wonder if that would make a difference?"

"Snacks? Like Ding Dongs?" Johnny said. "I don't know."

"Well, not Ding Dongs exactly. But maybe cookies. I could bake some. What do you think?"

"You can make cookies?"

"Sure, I can," she said.

"Like on Bewitched?" Johnny said, moving his nose with his fingers.

"No. Not like on Bewitched. In an oven. I wasn't always a nun, you know."

Johnny's heart pounded and his mouth dropped open. His eyes went wide and he gulped.

"What?" he squeaked softly.

"You be in charge of getting everyone to the meeting and I'll bring the refreshments, deal?"

She reached out her hand to shake. Johnny took it.

"And then we'll all go find out what Mr. Moon has to tell us," she said.

"Oh, yeah," he said. "Oh, okay."

[CHAPTER TWENTY-THREE]

I was ten. We were sitting in class in Catholic school. One of the
nuns came in and whispered to our nun and they both flew out of the
room. They wheeled in the television, turned it on and we watched.
They sent us home early that day. I cried hard from the first
moment I heard. I had a hard time walking home, and I had a little
sister to take care of. The crossing guard tried to calm me down. She
was very nice, but it was an impossible undertaking for her.
We made it home, called mom and put on the TV.

(http://www.librarything.com/topic/59958)

*J*ohnny chewed on his second raisin oatmeal cookie. The noise
echoed inside his head and he wondered if it was that loud to the
others.

He stopped and heard them chewing, too.

They all sat in two lines inside the boiler of Sacred Fart School
like dairy cows, inside a submarine, waiting to be milked.

"Will Sister Mark be attending?" one of the girls asked Sister
Mary-Michael.

"No, Susan. Sister Mark has bayonet practice on Tuesday afternoon."

"Oh," said Georgette.

"How does this work, Johnny?" Sister said.

"Umm, just do like before, let's try that," he said and then closed
his eyes and began taking deep breaths and opening his palms as
Sister coached the others to relax and ask the spirit to enter into their
midst.

"The Holy Spirit?" one of the girls said.

Sister kept her eyes closed and said, try for any spirit.

"It's cold," someone said.

"My dad says the pipes will freeze if we keep shutting off the
heat," someone else said.

Sister opened her eyes.

"You told your parents?"

Three girls nodded yes.

Sister sighed and let her eyelids drop.

Jimmy Purple looked at Johnny and waved his hand in front of Johnny's face. Johnny's eyes were closed. He wore a faint grin on his face.

"Can I go to the moon, um, to you, to see you?" Johnny asked.

"No, Johnny nobody from where you are can come here. I think Mr. Wizard had something on about that. It's too freaking far, for one thing."

"And the radiator belts?" said Johnny.

"Yes! Very good, that's another thing, Mr. Science. Johnny Science, that'll be your new name."

"Johnny Moon's enough," Johnny said.

With his eyes closed Johnny watched the moon.

"Well?" Johnny said.

"It's complicated," the moon said.

"Everything's complated," Johnny said.

Johnny made direct eye contact with the moon and did not talk, which made the moon a little uncomfortable and so to fill the empty space, the moon talked.

"Okay. Well, Long Ago, when God created dinosaurs and boiler heating systems, he knew that people like Dave would be getting up early, early in the morning to come down to make sure the school was warm for the children."

"Like me?"

"Just like you.

"And, he didn't want those guys to be going out in the dark so he gave them the moon."

"You?"

"Me."

"And Isom?"

"Yes, and Isom, too."

"Where is Isom?"

"He's okay, I'm pretty sure."

"And, sometimes, sometimes when it's cold out, really, really, I can, or let's say I just do. Better to ask for forgiveness than permission, right? I come inside to warm up some.

"Those folks in Chicago, well, they just got a little scared, spooked.

"Dave and Isom and your Sisters, they understood maybe just a little more. It seems that way."

"Jimmy Purple said his dad talks to you in sweat lodge in the summer in the park when they have big Indian festivals sometimes, is that right?"

"Actually, people talk to me all the time. They like my look I guess. They say I'm not hard on the eyes like Mr. Sun.

"Don't you recognize me, Johnny?"

"Yeah, you look just like in the sky."

"Oh, okay."

"I still want to keep losing weight and be a good American, Johnny said.

"The moon smiled and said, you do that, Johnny, you just do that."

"Is there anything you can do about this? The truth. The Big T, I mean," Johnny said and put quote marks in the air, placing his hand aside his mouth and whispering.

"Well, I can just keep shining as bright as I can. Actually, I don't make any light at all, Johnny. It all comes from somewhere else. Whatever I am, I'm just a reflection of other things and people, people like John F. Kennedy, and you, Johnny, and you."

"Is it like *The Daily News* says. Or is it like Sister's sister says. What can you tell us about what really happened? I think Sister really wants to know."

"You'll know," said Mr. Moon. He shrugged.

"That's about really all I can say about that. When you start using more of your brain, you just will know."

Johnny told the moon that the other kids wanted a sign.

"They said that there's usually always a sign."

The moon sighed.

"A sign?" he said. "A sign."

He sighed again.

"Okay," he said.

"Okay?"

"Yeah, you'll get a sign."

"Okay," said Johnny. "Hey. Why me?"

"Huh?"

"Why me why are you talking to me?"

"I'm not talking to you," said the moon. "You are imagining this, dreaming this inside your mind. Using a part of your brain that hasn't been used before."

"Yeah, well, then, why me?" said Johnny.

The moon nodded and tilted its chin.

"Because you asked, because you tried," he said. "Out of all the children in all the schools in all the towns who had their President murdered just after lunch recess on a Friday, you asked what was what.

"You got heart, Johnny Moon. You got a whole lotta heart. I give ya credit for 'dat, kid."

"You sound just like my ..."

Johnny smiled wide and Jimmy Purple nudged him.

"I do?" Jimmy said.

"Yeah, you do," said Johnny, smiling, opening his eyes.

"We gotta go," said Jimmy.

"Everybody's freezing, c'mon, move it, let's go."

[CHAPTER TWENTY-FOUR]

The death of President Kennedy had a huge impact on me.

First, my birthday and his were the same which I thought was really cool. Second, as a Catholic and JFK being the first Catholic President, we heard alot in the 4th grade about how people worried when he was elected that the Pope was going to take over. Friday afternoons were our weekly trip to the school library and I was in the library picking out books that I wanted to read when we were told over the intercom that he had been killed. We were sent home immediately and since I lived only two blocks from school, I got home very quickly. I sat in front of the TV all afternoon.

Last, My father worked at the TV station and he didn't come home for two days because of all the extra work that the coverage caused. It's surprising the little things you remember when you sit down to reminisce.

(http://www.librarything.com/topic/59958)

*O*n Monday Johnny assured the others and Sister that the moon said there would be a sign.

"A stop sign," said Jimmy Purple.

On Tuesday perhaps, or Wednesday, Tommy, who got white milk every day during morning milk break, brought around by the fourth-graders and set along the chalk tray, began opening his milk on the way back to his desk and tripped a little and spilled most of his little carton.

Sister Mary-Michael asked someone seated by the cleaning closet to please bring some Bounty towels.

When Danny got to the milk spill he knelt down and looked at the milk.

"Sister, you should come here," he said.

"What is it?" Sister said as she walked over.

She looked at the milk and then calmly knelt on both knees in front of the milk spill.

Not knowing if they should, but doing it anyway, the children crawled out of their desks and filled in around Sister.

They cracked down on their knees and crossed themselves.

While Sister Mary-Michael and her class knelt on the shiny wood floor in front of the blackboard, the children heard sniffles and strained their eyes to see her pulling Kleenex from her sleeve. She blew her nose and wiped and then made the Kleenex disappear.

Tears ran down her face and her nose was red. Her chin quivered.

One of the good girls began to lead them in the Glorious Mysteries to celebrate the miracle of the spilled milk in the face of John F. Kennedy, the murdered president of the United States.

Johnny returned to Mr. Moon and told him that the children still did not believe Johnny was speaking to the moon.

On Thursday or Friday the class said a rosary on their knees out in the hall after noon recess, all staring at the boot slush formed into the manger scene at Bethlehem.

Johnny went to the members of the NEEMO FADAMA Club and explained that this was the moon giving a sign that he was really real and appearing to Johnny Moon in the boiler in the school basement.

He told Mr. Moon that the children still did not believe.

"They say I'm alloos'nating."

"Ha-lu-ci-na-ting," said the Moon. "Well. You are under stress. Like someone in the desert. They start to see things, imagine things."

"They do?" said Johnny.

"Yes, they do. You might be going through more right now than you really imagine."

"Yeah," said Johnny. "They think I'm 'magining you."

"Who can blame them?" said the moon, "this is all very improbable."

"What's improbable?" asked Johnny.

"Everything," said the moon, "just everything that's going on these days."

On the next Monday morning at 8 a.m. all-school Mass on a December day that marked the beginning of Advent, Father marched out of the sacristy sporting bright red robes and vestments, with Verlin and Duke leading the way.

As they got to where everyone could see them, Duke tripped on his cassock and fell on his face on the marble and blood from his nose spread across the floor. Verlin laughed out loud and tripped on his own cassock and fell on his nose and began to bleed all over the church.

Father continued with the Mass, as it could not be interrupted once begun and the Sisters hurried up to kneel by the boys and say the rosary until the ambulance came and picked up the boys and wiped up the blood while Father droned on, his back turned, facing the altar, and the children sang their new song they had learned while the fourth graders were hauled out on stretchers, up the middle aisle.

Johnny told the moon that they still refused to believe.

"Maybe I could make the sun turn around and around real fast?" Mr. Moon suggested.

"That wouldn't be that big of a deal," Johnny said. "No, something *eeelse*."

On Friday of that week the third-graders sat in class fighting sleep. The radiator banged and some of the boys wiped sweat from their foreheads.

"It's hot!" they complained to Sister.

Sister spoke louder to try to overcome the noise of the radiators. She asked them to concentrate on their long division problems.

"After this we will get to diagram sentences," she smiled, "we still have plenty of time."

She turned her head to read the clock.

Each of the children looked up as well.

It said two-o'clock, on the nose. They would not be free until three-fifteen, forree-ever.

"Well, that's about it for today," Sister smiled. "Have a wonderful weekend. There will be no announcements today, Sister-Princi-pal-Something is attending an administrators meeting, you are free to go. Don't leave any coats or gloves or boots over the weekend!"

She walked to her desk briskly.

The children stared up at the clock.

It said 3:15. Big hand on the twelve. Little hand on the three. 3:15.

In stunned silence the children pushed up their desks and tossed in their workbooks, slid out of their desks and walked to the door, casting looks at the clock and at Sister working in her red grade book.

"G'night," she smiled.

In the hall the members of the Neemo Fadama Club huddled around Johnny.

"We believe."

"We believe."

"We believe," they said.

[CHAPTER TWENTY-FIVE]

I was in sixth grade at a Catholic school in Chicago. Everyone was for Kennedy during the elections, it seemed, except for my parents, who were Republicans. I was so embarrassed.

The principal came on over the PA system to say the President had been shot, and we should all pray for his recovery. Later I found out he was already dead. I think that's when I lost my Catholic faith, thinking about how pointless the prayers had been.

We spent the next four days watching TV. I think it was the first time any of us experienced 24/7 news coverage. I remember seeing the lines of people waiting to pay their respects. What shocked me, was my Republican dad saying, "If we get in the car right now, we'd get there in time to be at the end of the line." We didn't, but it taught me a lesson about adult complexity.

I remember my grandmother saying, "This is what they do in Europe. This doesn't happen here."

Only weeks later, I discovered the Beatles, so the memory of the assassination always felt like the marker at the end of my childhood. Then when John Lennon was shot, it was the other bookend. His murder was the end of my youth.

(http://www.librarything.com/topic/59958)

"*T*hey believed that," Johnny said to the moon.

"Okay. Good. Now what?"

"What about the future, Mr. Moon. Where's Isom and am I gonna find that Mickey Mantle card that dog has, huh?"

"Call me Mickey. Mickey Moon, man that guy can hit, huh? Nah, no, Mister's fine.

"Yeah. You can see it from the convent, I guess. I've heard that.

"Isn't this enough for now? If it was me I wouldn't want to know everything. Some people can't handle it."

"Like dreams," Johnny said.

"Like dreams?"

"Like dreams are the future," said Johnny.

"Oh. I don't know. The future. It's complicated," said Mr. Moon.

"Yeah," said Johnny.

"I think it's kind of the whole trying to use more of your brain sort of concept, thing, see?"

"Yeah, said Johnny. "And Ground."

"Yeah, and Ground. Underground, Sky, Ground. Yep, Ground is the now, what you can see, what it looks like from a flat surface looking out over a flat surface. Can't see much can you?"

"Huh-huh," said Johnny. "I can't."

"Nobody can."

"I think that's why they look up at the moon," said Johnny. "We look up at the moon because we have to look somewhere, and then there you are, and you look nice and you have a face and so we just talk. Like that?"

"One of the reasons, sometimes it's other things prolly," said the moon.

"Yeah."

"Get a different perspective, better angle. Maybe I can see things from here that they can't."

"Yep.

"Everything's different now," said Johnny.

"I suppose you're right, John."

"We're still not back the way it was," said Johnny, rubbing his open palm with the fingers of his other hand, running along the lines, noticing the fold marks and the veins.

[CHAPTER TWENTY-SIX]

I was in Sister Florita's seventh grade class at a Catholic school in a western suburb of Philadelphia. I remember being in the cloakroom at the back of the classroom with Michael Sims. We were in trouble for something, I think for playing catch with an eraser when Sister was out of the room, and I remember we were both scared at what we were going to get. I think the principal or someone else from her office must have come into the room and told everyone what had happened, because Sister Florita came back to the cloakroom and let Steve and me off, just told us to go back to our desks and join everyone else in the rosary.

(http://www.librarything.com/topic/59958)

*T*he members of the NEEMO FADAMA Club huddled close together inside the boiler.

Danny sat next to Timmy next to Johnny next to Sister Mary-Michael next to Susan next to Dave next to Sister Mark next to Jane next to Michael next to Tommy then Jimmy.

They heard cars on the playground up above, maybe Father going to coffee or the hospital or nursing home, maybe parents picking up kids. They heard a bike clatter to the ground as the rider flung it down as he stopped rather than take two seconds to put the kickstand down.

They felt the latent heat from the bricks, good heat, comfortable like all had grandma afghans on their knees. They smelled the iron and steal and the rail yards of Chicago and the foundry and the sweat of the men who built the boiler.

Tommy farted and they smelled that.

"Well-then," said Sister Mary-Michael.

"Oh, Lord, Jesus, um, the moon, Mr. Moon, be with us today, this afternoon. And as we seek to be in your presence and the, uh … um, to … ask that perhaps, that we might, um, understand … uh, that which you seek, would like to … perhaps, uh … convey to …"

"Amen," said a good girl.

"Yes, Amen," said Sister Mary-Michael.

Each closed their eyes and rested their palms on their knees and breathed deep and slowly.

Sister Mark hummed a tune that three of them found helpful.

Johnny saw the moon with his eyes closed. It seemed to hover right in front of him, inside the boiler, in full moon orange splendor, the kind you might imagine in the fall, after dark, with geese passing and in the foreground the lights of a combine and the spray of corn rising and falling into the wagon inching along next to the row.

Johnny smiled and took another deep breath.

"Hi," he said.

"Hello," said the moon.

And Johnny could hear the moon differently today. It was not totally in his own head, but more real, like, um, like the difference between watching a game on TV and being right at the game. Maybe it was like that.

"Hi everybody," said the moon.

"Hi," Johnny said again.

"Hi," said everyone in the boiler.

"Hi, Mr. Moon."

"It's the moo-oon," someone whispered.

Somebody pointed.

Johnny opened his eyes.

There was the moon.

In front of them all.

Floating, shimmering, smiling, looking around. It looked happy, and different than it did inside his head.

"Are we going," Bobby said, "you know ... somewhere?"

"We're going down Underground," said Jane.

"We're diving down into the earth, under the school, and come up under the little store on Ninth Avenue, and then we get to eat all the candy we want because we're explorers and we get whatever we want, or else we'll just take it anyway. That's what I heard," said Susan.

"That's stupid," said Tommy.

"It's not stupid," said Sister Mary-Michael.

And the children cheered because they got to go Underground into the bottom of the earth and come up and get free candy at a neighborhood little store.

"It's also not true," said Sister Mark.

"Is it?" she looked at the moon.

"Yes-Sister," said Mr. Moon. "I mean no-Sister."

Verlin and Duke pushed their hands and noses flat against the glass blocks. They lay on their stomachs in broken glass and bird nest parts and concrete bits on the playground, their bikes strewn behind them.

"I saw 'em goin' in there," said Verlin, "just when we came around the corner."

"Yeah," said Duke. "Can you see?"

"Yeah, a little," Verlin said. "No."

From the inside their faces had pig noses from being scrunched up so far and their hands all flat and puffy.

"I think they're inside the boiler," said Verlin.

"They can't be," said Duke. "They'd be dead."

"No, I saw 'em one other day," said Verlin. "I was kind of hiding from some people and I was down there when they all came in, talking and stuff. Then they disappeared and I know I heard talkin' inside the freaking boiler. I did."

"Why do they go in there?" said Duke.

"They're stupid," said Verlin. "That's why. They're fucking idiots, that's why."

"We should turn on the boiler while they're in there," said Duke. "Not really."

"Yeah-but-how," said Verlin.

"I know," said Duke. "I worked a whole Saturday with Dave and Isom one time. I had to crawl inside there and replace some of the bricks. I watched 'em turn it off and then on. It's easy."

"It is?" said Verlin.

"Yep-I-could-do-it. Easy."

"You could?" said Verlin.

Verlin and Dave sat with their backs against the glass blocks of the school, their legs stretched out, tossing rocks and bits of concrete at the drain in the middle of the playground to see who could get closest.

The screen door to the maintenance room opened with a clatter.

Out came Bobby and Tommy and Timmy and Jane and Susan.

They gibbered and jabbered and laughed and slapped hands.

Sister Mark and Sister Mary-Michael were the last to come out laughing. They waved and called goodbye to the children and turned to walk in front of Verlin and Duke.

"Good afternoon young men," said Sister Mark.

Sister Mary-Michael waved from her hip.

Verlin and Duke sat and stared. This was their time. They didn't need to be nice to the nuns after school was over, their parents said.

Verlin tossed a rock, just missing Sister Mary-Michael's head. The rock rolled right up next to the drain.

Sister Mary-Michael knew the game. She knew that it drove Dave crazy because it meant he had to open the drain and crawl down in there every summer and clean out all the rocks.

"Perfect," she smiled and waved back at the boys one more time as she and Sister Mark glided down the walk.

[CHAPTER TWENTY-SEVEN]

I remember the wooden floors — it was the 1960s — and sleigh-like desks, bolted to long runners on the floor. The seat part off the desk flipped up, and the top of the desk opened to store our books in. No lockers needed. There was a place for pencils in the desk, and a space reserved for an ink well, long unused. The front of the class-room had a big blackboard and two door-openings on either side to the cloakroom. There I'd place my coat on a hook, and my lunch box — the Jetsons! Every Friday — egg salad ... ooooh and it got so runny from sitting in the cloakroom all morning! I recall a picture of the Holy Father and one of George Washington on the walls. And a crucifix of course.

(http://forums.catholic.com/showthread.php?t=412461)

S ister Principal-Something stood in the doorway of Sister Mary-Michael's classroom.

She held in her hands a delinquent bill for a T.A.B. book order for one of Sister M&M's children.

Seeing that nobody had noticed her, Sister Principal-Something scooted almost inside the room, her heels on the doorway imaginary line.

Sister Principal-Something took the opportunity to gaze around Sister Mary-Michael's classroom.

Drawings on construction paper decorated everything: black-boards, windows, desks. Each drawing a depiction of the moon, a full moon, quarter moon, half moon, with geese, during harvest, with a smile, with life-like craters, and aliens. One with Moses and a burning bush.

Some children knelt beside their desks, their heads bowed and their hands folded, eyes closed, their mouths moving. Some stood at the windows looking up, through the windows, at the sky, waving, smiling, pointing.

Sister Mary-Michael hunched over someone's desk helping with an assignment.

"Oh, that's wonderful!" Mary-Michael exclaimed. "May I?" she asked the student.

With both hands way up over her head she held the student's drawing and rotated around so all could see.

Yet another moon drawing.

Sister Mary-Michael turned and saw Sister Principal-Something standing by the door looking neglected.

Sister Mary-Michael returned the drawing to the student and hopped and skipped up the row and across the room and skidded like Colorado skiing to stop in front of her visitor.

Sister Principal-Something handed over the over-due notice.

"It's nearly Christmas, wouldn't you say?" she asked.

"Yes! It is!" said Sister M&Ms.

"Wouldn't something more attuned to the birth of our Savior be more appropriate for your room décor, Sister?"

Sister M&Ms looked all around at the moon drawings.

Johnny Moon chugged up to her and put up in front of his face for her to see his new drawing of himself inside a space ship heading from earth to the moon.

"It's simply marvelous," Sister M&Ms said.

"Isn't it so?" she asked Sister Principal-Something.

"Hmm," hummed Sister Principal-Something.

Johnny returned to his desk.

"I'm certain you are absolutely correct, Sister," said Sister M&Ms. "Right this moment I will encourage the children to add Christmas trees to their moons and … hmm, how about … a manger scene on the moon.

"Children! Please look here!" she turned around to the class.

"Sister!" said Sister Principal-Something.

"That is not what I mean at all!"

Sister Principal-Something lowered her voice and ducked her head to peer at Sister M&Ms over the top of her glasses.

"Science class is not part of the curriculum, are you aware of that, Sister Mary-Michael?"

"Yes."

"Good.

"I am sorry to hear about your sister," she said. "I hope you will take the opportunity now to return to reality. The real world needs you and your gifts, Sister. The world of make-believe is only useful in small portions. Then there comes a time to buckle down to business."

Sister M&Ms listened in silence, rolling the papers in her hand tighter and tighter.

"Please have that taken care of promptly," she pointed at the papers, turned and walked away.

"Come back to earth, Sister," she said with her back turned, walking away.

Sister M&Ms watched her go, the methodical click … click of Sister Principal-Something's black hard-heel shoes on the marble out of rhythm with the pounding of her very own heart.

On the playground at noon recess the members of the NEEMO FADAMA Club walked around handing out holy cards before they broke off and joined the kickball and pum-pum-pole-away.

That afternoon they returned to the boiler and the moon again appeared to them while Verlin and Duke pressed their pig noses against the glass blocks and lay in the snow and ice on their bare stomachs with their shirts pushed way up.

"We need 'The Big T'," one of the girls said to the moon, using air quote marks.

The rest of the children nodded.

Sister M&Ms nodded. On the boiler floor next to her lay Johnny's Big Chief tablet with the cover torn off to take notes for Sister Principal-Something, who had gotten wind and wished to be kept in the loop.

The moon then turned serious and began to talk. He paced, moving back and forth in front of them as he talked.

A tear fell on Sister's shoe.

She pulled a Kleenex from her sleeve and reached up to wipe Mr. Moon's eyes.

"That tickles," he smiled. "Thanks, though."

Sister M&Ms turned red and bowed her head to her tablet by her side.

As Johnny walked home that day he kicked a rock.
And worried.

The moon had told them that they needed to tell people about what he had said.

They needed to proclaim, Johnny thought he had said.

At the crosswalk Johnny took a big swing and kicked his rock way across the street. He chugged after it and continued to nudge it along.

Mr. Moon had suggested they tell their parents and the rest of their families and then the people in their church and around town.

They had a list.

The list that Sister M&Ms had written down on Johnny's Big Chief tablet with the cover torned off.

It was the list of things Mr. Moon had told them about what had happened in Dallas on that Friday that President John F. Kennedy was shot and killed and they had gotten out five minutes early from arithmetic.

Johnny kicked the rock and thought. He kicked it over the tracks without it getting caught. He kicked it over another street and then almost lost it when he kicked it into a parking lot full of rocks.

It was the rock the moon had given each of them as a sign. It was a moon rock, he said, show your parents that you talked to the moon and he gave you this rock as a sign. That should do it, the moon said.

But it was just a rock. It could have come from anywhere.

It's not going to work, all the children had told each other as they divided up to walk home in one's, two's and three's.

They all shook their heads and mumbled. Some stuck the rocks into coat pockets, some tossed them in the air as they walked.

"It's not going to work, I just know that," said one of the good girls.

At school the next day the members of the NEEMO FADAMA Club opened their desks as soon as they could and dropped their rocks inside.

Johnny did not see the others hide their rocks under their desk-tops. He just knew he was the only one who had not talked to his parents about the moon and the moon rock and the President in Dallas on that one day that would not go away.

On the playground the members avoided each other, drifting off to play with other people, jumping rope, flicking marbles with freezing cold fingers, and a snowball war being conducted around the corner in secret when the Sisters weren't looking.

Johnny fired two snowballs, one with his right hand and one with his left. He threw at the other team, the enemy, the invaders, the Rooskies. He threw without looking and then he ducked way down and took the incoming blows off his thick blue-plaid snowsuit. The pummeling stopped and Johnny looked up and yelled at the other team.

"Fuckers!"

The others were not there.

Johnny looked up and saw Sister Mary-Michael standing next to him, her shawl around her shoulders and her black-gloved hands forming an isosceles triangle in front of her chest.

Johnny's face was red from the freezing cold.

He looked up and turned white.

"Hello," said Sister.

"Sorry," said Johnny.

"You musn't tell me. Tell God," she said.

"'kay."

"I take it that nobody showed their rocks at home," Sister said.

Johnny shrugged and squatted to re-fasten a buckle that was already tight.

Sister stepped away to place her back against the brick wall. Johnny joined her, staying far enough away so that maybe it looked like he wasn't talking to her.

Johnny asked Sister if she had shown Sister Principal-Something her rock.

"Nooo," she said. "I didn't."

"It's just a rock," Johnny began.

"A moon rock."

"I dunno," he said.

"But it is," she said. "You were there."

"Yabut."

Johnny blew cold air smoke out to see how much he could make.

"Some of the kids want markers, I think," he said.

"Money? For what?"

"Or gum. To do this, what the moon wants, it's hard."

"It's not about markers or gum, Johnny, I thought you of all people knew this. The moon doesn't have money to give."

"He could get some."

"No. I don't think he could."

Sister squatted down and Johnny looked around to see who was noticing him hanging out with Sister again.

"Johnny. You are going to be a fourth-grader soon. You will be serving Mass. And after that you will almost be in junior high and then you will be on your way."

"I will?"

"Yes. It won't be long.

"You might yet go to the moon."

"And lose weight? And be a Good American?"

"Certainly. And get the president's physical fitness award you wanted."

"I think that's over."

"It is? I'm not sure about that," she said.

"Yeah-huh. It is," said Johnny.

"Johnny," said Sister. "Why won't you show your parents your very own moon rock?"

She slid down the bricks on her back and sat on the cold ground.

Johnny looked all around in a panic, wishing she would get up. Sister did not notice his dilemma, lost in her own reverie.

"You know, with the children at Fatima, they ... well, they pretty much just went with it after they saw the Blessed Mother, you know. They told everyone and they prayed and they, just ... really believed."

"That's God," said Johnny. "God's Mom."

"Yes?"

"This is the moon. Mr. Moon. It's different."

"But a talking Mr. Moon. Inside the boiler. In the school basement."

"Yeaaahh," said Johnny, sitting down. He slid his legs to push his knees up and wrapped his arms around his knees to keep them there.

"Yeaaahhh-I-knoooww-but."

He blew cold air smoke out like a train and rubbed his chin with his thick-gloved hand, then folded his hands together over his knees and turned to Sister.

"Sister. You know. And I know."

He touched his chest with his open glove.

"What, Johnny," she swiveled her knees together toward him and Johnny did pee a little and it was cold out.

"Those kids at Fadama, the things they were talking about, well, the things they were predicting … uh, anybody coulda said that. To predict wars, there's always wars, 'polean, Charlie Main, you know."

Sister looked at him with wide eyes. He plowed right through her stop sign.

"These things the-uh Mr. Moon wants us to say, we'll get in big trouble. Nobody says that. Big trouble. It's different."

Sister began to speak. Johnny put a hand on her arm to put an end to all that.

"Those kids at Fadama, that was somewhere else. And a long, long time ago."

"Yes?"

"Well and somewhere else and way long time ago is easier than here. Those kids only had to talk to people far away. We have to talk to people here, and it's hard."

"Johnny, but those children had to do things in their own town, their own people," said Sister.

"Yeah-but, not here. That was Mexico. Right here is hard."

"Oh."

Sister turned and sat back against the bricks. She let her head go back and rest.

"You mean, if Jesus came down right here, right now in this playground … let's say he was accompanied by, uh, say, John F. Kennedy and, hmmm, Mr. Moon as well, and they asked you to do something, you wouldn't be able to do it?" said Sister.

Johnny scrunched his chin and turned his head and looked up.

He looked over at Sister, this time just part way, far enough to watch her shoes, far enough anyway, she could hear him good.

"If Jesus came and landed here and asked me to take a moon rock home and put it on the kitchen table, that would be simple, 'cause it won't never happen," he explained.

"And it would be easy as pie not to say bad things if the Russians came here and tried to make us. I can do that."

He took a deep breath and tried to broach the decades between them.

"See-ee," he thought of how he could make her understand the world. She was so old.

It was no use.

He turned and rested his head against the bricks and looked up. He stared and his mouth fell open just a bit.

"You see that?" he said.

"See what?" said Sister M&Ms.

"That right there, see? You can't see that?"

"No, I don't."

She moved over toward him to look where he was looking.

"Oh, I guess it's nothing," Johnny said. "I thought I saw something."

She scooted back.

"A burning bush?" she smiled.

"Yeah, maybe."

Johnny rolled over to push up to stand.

He faced Sister.

"I'm gonna do it," he said.

He took a big breath and let it out in a giant breath puff.

"A strong kid makes a strong man makes a strong rest of all of it," he said.

"I'll talk to the other kids, too."

Johnny held out his hand and helped Sister up. Then he walked away to track down the other after-school club members.

[CHAPTER TWENTY-EIGHT]

The nuns still wore habits, but the shorter skirts (Franciscans). I can still see Sr. Jeanette talking to the chalk whenever she felt we weren't paying attention. And Sr. Angelita rolling her eyes and waving her hands whenever she was trying to explain something and words escaped her (she was the English teacher, too!) She was also the queen of imaginative surgery... like removing our tonsils through our ears if we didn't stop talking and start paying attention! She was fun. The school closed down last year and the nuns were gone long before then. Friday Mass every week with confessions every first Friday, the segregated playground (boys on one side of the monkey bars, girls on the other), Monsignor coming around every six weeks to hand out grade reports.

(http://forums.catholic.com/showthread.php?t=412461)

"Mo-oom! ...
"Moo-ooomm!
"Mom!"
Johnny hung over the railing to holler downstairs that there was no toilet paper upstairs.
In front of his face appeared a roll of toilet paper, tossed up by someone somewhere.
Johnny later went back to his room. He stood by the window watching the neighborhood in the waning winter light.
He saw neighborhood kids going full blast, engaged in a game with intricate self-made rules involving chasing each other around the house across the street.
Below on the sidewalk running past his house Johnny saw some kids he knew. He rapped on the window to get their attention. He unlatched the window and tugged on it to pull it up. He wasn't supposed to open the window, ever. The screen had been removed for some reason and birds and bats and bugs and who-knows-what could fly in if you opened it.
"Hey!" Johnny yelled at the kids who had slowly walked out of

hearing distance, like a ball on a lake that does not appear to be moving at all and then it's a hundred yards from shore, or a kickball game that lasts all afternoon and then when it's finally over you haven't seen those kids for forty years.

Johnny stuck his head way out and looked around. He had never done this before.

He kneeled and put his elbows on the ledge.

He looked up at the moon and smiled.

He waved with one hand, then two hands held high up.

Johnny smelled the chilled air and sucked it down in a deep breath like a cherry popsicle.

He thought of how he wanted to lose weight and be a good American and walk everywhere and do what President John F. Kennedy had said he should do.

And he looked up in the sky to see if he could see John F. Kennedy and Mr. Moon and Jesus.

They would be friends. Playing kickball and riding bikes and throwing dirt clods at girls.

It would be a long time until baseball season. Johnny saw leaves in the gutter.

"Hey!"

And his toy soldier!

Right there. It looked like it should slide down but it didn't. He looked all around on the porch roof for his balsam airplane, but it was gone for good or on the other side.

Johnny put the whole weight of his head in his hands and adjusted his knees on the floor and let all his air out.

If he really wanted to do this, they would kill him, too, probably.

He would be riding his bike to get a pop at the gas station on about the first day of spring and some guys with sunglasses and guns would jump up out of the bushes at Mrs. Finicky Butt's house and shoot him, flat dead in the street.

If they went around and showed everyone "The Ten Things Of Mr. Moon" on his Big Chief tablet with the cover torned off, he might not be able to live at home anymore and he would be living with Isom in the school basement except nobody knew where he was.

[CHAPTER TWENTY-NINE]

Beyond that frontier are the uncharted areas of science and space, unsolved problems of peace and war, unconquered pockets of ignorance and prejudice, unanswered questions of poverty and surplus. It would be easier to shrink back from that frontier, to look to the safe mediocrity of the past, to be lulled by good intentions and high rhetoric — and those who prefer that course should not cast their votes for me, regardless of party.
— John F. Kennedy, Sept. 17, 1960

*W*ell, now … Johnny talked to the other kids, about how they should all go take their moon rocks from Mr. Moon home to their moms and dads.

He got three kids to do it, to go along with the whole thing.

Jimmy Purple said yes, and then so did Jane, and then at the end of the day as they were walking out of the room, Danny walked up to Johnny and whispered, "I'll do it."

And so they walked together to the coat rack in the hall silently, slowly, like firemen weary of fire, they put on their coats and hats and boots, and trudged together down the marble steps around and around, and around 'til they came to the bottom.

Johnny let Jimmy go first out the grey double doors 'cause it looked like he wanted to.

They stood outside the door in a clump and had to move because a thousand fourth-graders poured out.

Johnny spotted Verlin and Duke and watched them as they picked their bikes off the playground blacktop and took off.

Verlin saw Johnny watching him and flipped Johnny the bird and kept flipping it until he got to the alley and rounded the corner by the garage. He almost hit the garage, but kept his balance while keeping the one hand and finger in the air and looking back at Johnny and then back to steer.

Johnny and Jimmy and Jane and Danny looked at each other,

and without speaking, their little circle broke up and headed every which-way, like those kaleidoscope things.

Johnny dropped his rock and let it roll, then started kicking at it with his big rubber boot toe. It took some concentration. Tennis shoes would have been better, but it was still winter.

Jimmy tucked his in his pocket and headed toward the alley, the same way that Verlin and Duke had gone, confident that moon rock karma was stronger than bandit danger.

Jane headed north, through the desert downtown area, and Danny went south, over long stretches of rolling, worn-out sidewalk past the Meadow Gold milk plant and the retard workshop and the apartment building with the blue doors.

Johnny picked his rock up in front of his house and turned it over and over. It was scuffed and chipped, from the moon maybe.

It is from the moon, he told himself. Mr. Moon gave it to me himself in the boiler in the basement at school.

He stuck the rock into his pocket and kept going past his house. He walked around the block. Nobody was really out yet playing. They were home eating cookies and watching "Leave It To Beaver."

He came up beside his house again, on the corner. He stopped at the anthill next to the concrete drain next to that one tree. He couldn't see the anthill. It was covered in snow. He stared down to where it was though and then kept going. He didn't cut across the lawn to get to his front steps even though it was really only all snow. He went to the corner like a young man not a Wild Indian and then plopped up the steps one giant boot after the other.

At supper time Johnny took his spot in the comfortable armchair farthest from the TV with his food on his TV tray in front of him.

His twin brothers sat closest to the TV, on both sides of the TV, controlling access. The two girls snuggled on the sofa, TV trays in front of them. Johnny's father and mother sat off to the side, almost in the dining room with their chairs and TV trays.

Johnny hunched under the picture of his dead brother dressed in his homemade astronaut suit made out of Tide boxes, oven mitts and his dad's overshoes.

The shades were pulled because that's the way everyone liked it so they could see the black and white screen. And it was almost dark anyway and they didn't need people walking by on the sidewalk just looking in.

The room smelled like meatloaf and onions and Pledge and Tang.

Johnny's other brother sat on the floor on his stomach with his food on a tray, facing the television.

They watched *Gunsmoke*.

Johnny cut his mashed potatoes in half with his spoon and vowed to himself to just eat the one half. He stared at the halves and then cut a little off the left-hand side and pushed it over to the right.

"What are you doing?" one of the twins said to Johnny.

"He still wants to lose weight to go to the moon," said the other twin. "Dork."

Johnny pursued his eating and watching in silence.

"I've got a moon rock," he said.

Everyone continued watching the television.

"I have a moon rock."

"Shut up!" both twins turned to yell at Johnny. "We're tryin' to hear!"

Johnny leaned over to the right and picked up the rock from the floor. He set it on his TV tray.

The brother from the floor got up and picked up the rock. He turned it over and over.

"This from the moon?" he said to Johnny.

Johnny nodded.

"How'd you get it?"

Johnny stared at his brother and took a deep breath.

"The moon gave it to me. Mr. Moon," he said.

"Seriously?"

Johnny nodded.

The brother from the floor took the rock and walked down the aisle formed by the TV trays and posted himself in front of the television screen.

"Hey!"

"Hey-whatayadoin'!"

"Hey, lookout. Move!"

He held the rock up.

"Johnny has a moon rock. He wants us to know."

"A moon rock?"

"Riiigght."

"Move-it!" one of the twins tried to push the brother from the floor out of the way, but was pushed back into his seat.

The brother from the floor turned and pushed the knob and the TV went off.

"Hey! What's this all about!" said the father.

"Yes, please," said the mother, "we're watching the show."

"John has something to say," said the brother from the floor.

John put his hands on his tray and folded them.

He breathed deep.

"Mr. Moon appeared to some of us inside the boiler in the school basement."

Johnny fought the urge to run. He saw the smirks and heard the giggles and the chewing. One person coughed. Johnny sat up straighter and spoke louder.

"This is really from the moon. He gave us each a rock so you would believe we really talked to him. ... We said it wouldn't work, it's just a rock, but it's really a moon rock, see?"

The brother in front of the TV held up the rock with both hands like a game show model with a diamond tiara. He swiveled right and left to let everyone see.

"You *are* nuts," said one twin.

The other twin made circle motions by his head.

"Stop that!" said the mother.

"And he wants us to also ...," Johnny began.

"That'll be enough," said the father.

Johnny looked at his father. He turned a little in his thick easy chair to face his father.

"Mr. Moon wants us to also go tell people. He gived us ten suggestions.

"Moses," snickered one of the girls to the other. "Johnny Moon Moses."

"Ten suggestions that might help people understand what happened to President Kennedy."

"We know what happened," said the father. "He was killed by a nut, Lee Haahvey Oswalt, from the school book building, everyone knows that. That's what the newspaper says, and the TV and the radio, and that's what everyone says. Everyone knows that. What else is there to know?"

"There's more," said Johnny.

"There's way more."

Johnny looked at his father. His father looked at him. Everyone else watched those two looking at each other. The brother in front of the TV held the rock in both hands down by his waist and used the bottom of one foot to itch the top of his other foot. The girls tried to suck the orange Jello from their bowls without making any noise. One made a slurping sound and they burst out laughing. The twins took turns taking swipes at the rock to get it from the brother in front of the TV, but he kept yanking it out of the way just in time.

"I can't believe this. I really can't. Just imagine, in our own house," said the father to the mother.

He got up and walked into the kitchen, carrying his TV tray and food.

"I wonder if we have enough Miracle Whip for the Jello," said the mother. "I hope nobody has eaten their dessert yet."

She carried her tray to the kitchen after the father. She threw her words in front of her, grappling hooks to pull her faster towards the kitchen. Her heels punctuated the wood floor in the dark dining room with paper-piercing periods.

The brother in front of the TV walked back to Johnny and placed the rock on Johnny's TV tray. He returned to the floor and one of the twins reached up to switch on the TV.

The next day in school Johnny and Jimmy and Jane and Danny sat on the classroom floor, their backs against the wall.

It was the day when Mrs. LaDooooo the doctor's wife from the Catholic Daughters came in to teach them art. They had all the desks moved over to the side and the floor was filled with construction paper and newspapers under that and there were jars of finger paint scattered mostly everywhere.

Johnny's fingertips were red. Jimmy's were purple. Jane's were green and Danny's were blue.

They kept their construction paper close-by and whenever Mrs.

LaDooooo looked their way they looked down seriously and rubbed on their papers.

"I did it," said Jane.

"I can't live at home anymore."

"Me-neither," said Danny. "And I have to grow up and learn a thing or two before I try anything like this again."

"I need to get a job and buy my own house and learn to pay my own bills," said Jimmy.

Mrs. LaDooooo headed their way and they all put their heads down and drew lines across their papers with their colored fingers.

She stood directly above them, checked each of their lines, hummed, nodded, smiled and moved on.

They scooted closer together.

"The kids at Fadama got burned in oil," said Johnny.

"That'll be next," said Jimmy.

"No they didn't," said Danny.

"They almost did," said Jane.

"We need to get the list from Sister," said Johnny.

They all stuck their colored hands up in the air and waved to Sister Mary-Michael seated at her desk correcting papers.

She saw them and came over.

"We need the list," said Johnny. "It's time."

"I can get it for you," she said. "I'd like to go with you, do you know where you are going, what you are going to do with the list?"

"Not you, Sister, just us," said Johnny. "The kids at Fadama didn't bring their moms."

She squatted down and they wished she hadn't done that.

"I'm not your mother," she said.

"You know what I mean," said Johnny.

Sister almost-grinned and nodded. With a stage exhale she pushed off her knees to stand. She went to her top desk drawer and withdrew the Big Chief tablet with the red cover and picture of the chief torned off.

She handed the list to Johnny. He accepted it and held it in front of him with both hands, putting red fingerprints along both sides.

"Uh-oh," he said and hurried to put the list inside his desk, using his elbows to lift up the top.

The very next day at noon recess the four Neemo Fadama club members stood on the front cement porch steps outside the screen door next to the big wooden door at the front of the rectory.

Johnny reached up and pushed the doorbell then stepped back in line with the others. He held the list with the red fingertip prints that were still sticky.

The housekeeper, a Mrs. Hula Witch, answered the door and the kids asked if they could see Father.

She left and they stayed in their line, except for Jimmy who went to the far end of the concrete porch and leaned way over the railing to see if he could see anyone on the playground.

"Hey! Ass-face! Face-ass! Ha-Ha! You!" Jimmy pointed and yelled at the playground just as Father appeared in the doorway.

Jimmy ran back to the line.

Father held the door for them to come inside, firing a stern look at Jimmy bringing up the rear.

They walked with Father through the living room. They looked all around at the curtains and the chairs and the TV and Father's office and the windows and the stairs. It was quiet except for Mrs. Hula Witch upstairs vacuuming.

The house smelled like church, like the back of church, like Vick's and candles and cigarettes and Rolaids and perfumed Kleenex.

Jimmy spotted an opened pack of L&M's on the bookshelf and looked for someone to poke.

Father led them to the kitchen and asked them to sit around the little table. They each took a seat with a red cushion and sat and looked at the plate of cookies on the counter with the Saran Wrap tight over the top, probably too tight to give them any.

Father spotted the cookies, too, and reached and placed it in front of them. He removed the wrapping and sat down.

"No, go, please, dig in," he said.

The children reached one each and all marveled at theirs for a moment before biting.

"What can I do ya for?" said Father.

"How may I help you?"

Johnny reached up and brushed the table free of crumbs right in front of him. He set the list down, careful not to let the finger paint get on the table or on his hands again.

"You have a list of demands?" Father smiled.

Jane nodded softly as if to say, yes, we're afraid so.

"No, not like that," said Danny.

"Yeah-huh," said Jimmy.

Johnny twirled the paper around so that Father could read.

He brought his index finger down the paper. They watched his finger, with a strong, confident nail and hair and tan. They smelled his breath like cigarettes and coffee and a cookie.

"Hmmm," he said and looked up.

He twirled the paper around to Johnny.

"That boiler nonsense again, Mr. Moon?"

"Yes, from Mr. Moon," Johnny smiled and took a crunchy cookie bite.

Father stared at Johnny Moon.

Johnny stared back.

"I believe we are done here," Father said.

He collected the plate of cookies and clanked it back on the counter without replacing the clear wrapping.

He let the back door screen bang, leaving the children in the kitchen. They looked at each other. They listened for the vacuuming. They heard the kitchen clock ticking and the refrigerator began to hum.

They heard the children on the playground.

Someone was choosing teams for a game.

Jane and Danny headed for the door. Jimmy grabbed another cookie. Johnny folded his list in his hand and followed, dragging the wooden door behind him.

[CHAPTER THIRTY]

How difficult it is the escape the dread consequences of a regime's calculated and incessant propaganda ... how useless it was even to try to make contact with a mind which had become warped and for whom the facts of life had become what Hitler and Goebbels, with their cynical disregard for the truth, said they were.
— William Shirer, *The Rise And Fall Of The Third Reich*

*T*he next Monday after school Jimmy and Johnny and Danny and Jane stood in front of the newspaper editor's desk where the one lady had left them.

They tried to see over the top of the empty desk and swayed from leg to leg, looking around for cookies.

They gawked all around and over their shoulders at the different desks and all the people moving around and they heard the clacking of the type-typing like indecisive machine-gun fire.

They smelled ink and looked around for a water fountain.

They saw a man in a glassed office talking to another man.

The other man finally came out of the glassed office and sat down in the empty chair of the empty desk in front of them.

He smiled and placed his folded hands on his desk the way Johnny had done when he had tried to make his family believe in him.

The editor looked over the heads and around as if he was trying to find who was in charge of them.

"So, you're on a field trip?" he said.

Johnny shook his head.

They all shook their heads.

Johnny put the "The Ten Things Of Mr. Moon" suggestions on the big editor's desk with the pointed note things and the ashtray and the typewriter and two phones on it, too.

"You want us to put this in the newspaper? Is that it?" he said, now scowling rather than smiling as before.

Johnny nodded.

They all nodded.

Johnny moved around to the side of the desk in order to be able to explain to the editor a little more about the moon and the boiler and the vision they had been given about the assassination of President John F. Kennedy.

The editor prevented that with a hand stop sign and shooed him back around to stand where he was before.

He reached for the phone and called someone.

The Neemo Fadama Club representatives talked amongst themselves.

"He's calling the pres'dent."

"Everyone will know the truth."

"We did it."

"That wasn't that hard. We should do more other stuff."

One after another, three, then four blue and white police cars with lights flashing pulled up to the curb in front of the newspaper office.

The policemen raced inside with guns up and held in both hands. For a moment they could not get the front doors open as they were holding the guns with both hands and tried to use their elbows, their foreheads and their buttocks to open the doors.

Finally, a sports intern leaped two rows of desks to help the police get inside.

The police officers jumped to the floor onto their stomachs then made their way inch by inch, desk by desk, rolling over, somersaulting, calling for backup.

After half an hour the first officers reached the four members of the Neemo Fadama standing in front of the empty editor's desk.

Johnny and the others saw people on the sidewalk with their faces pressed against the big windows trying to see what was going on.

The now four dozen police officers inside the newspaper offices wrestled the children to the floor. Many officers suffered cuts to the heads and elbows from desk corners and from those sharp needle-like things to stick pieces of paper on.

Jimmy kicked hard to try to free his legs from two officers. He sat on the face of one of them and farted. He apologized, regretted it, and let fly again.

The stench from Jimmy's two farts spread across the newsroom like gas over the Argonne.

News reporters, editors and photographers leaned into their waste-baskets and vomited.

Johnny pinched an officer in the stomach. Jane crushed an officer's ding dongs in her fist and Danny sneezed point-blank in an officer's face as he tried to tie his arms with the phone cord from the agricultural reporter's desk.

An ambulance flashed by.

Unable to find parking anywhere close, the driver jumped the curb and landed in front of the newspaper offices on the sidewalk. Emergency personnel dashed inside with a gurney and defibrillator, opening the doors expertly with their buttocks and elbows and foreheads.

The local television cameras set up on the sidewalk along with the local radio reporters. Inside, the newspaper photographers took hundreds of photos of the injured policemen and the ones still wrestling with the children.

The photos ran on page three that day with the headline: Sacred Heart After-School Club Tours Newspaper Offices.

After the police officers let them up, the children walked outside. They stepped through the broken glass doors onto the sidewalk.

They walked to the corner together.

"Hey," they waved at Dave and Isom sitting in Dave's light blue pickup with the rust in two of the wheel wells.

"You alright?" Dave asked.

"You all need to know I didn't kill no goldfish," Isom said, sticking his head out the passenger window.

"Hey, Isom, where you been?"

"We know. It was Verlin and Duke."

"Where you been, anyway, Isom?"

"We thought the Russians got you or maybe you was 'sass'nated."

"Or something."

"Well, as you know, they kicked me out of the locker room. I been staying at Dave's place. Him and his wife have been very generous. I'm still playing basketball and I might be getting to come back to the school, don't know about that yet.

"You guys want a ride?"

Isom got out and let the kids pile into the front seat.

"How'd you know where we were? We been trying to use more of our brains. You think we saw the moon and it was just a dream? Or what?"

"Yeah, so I see. Everybody knows where you were," said Dave. "And Sister asked us to keep an eye on you."

[Chapter thirty-one]

I wouldn't want to do anything to hurt God. He's got enough trouble with the Russians and all.
— Theodore Beaver Cleaver

*A*t the car dealership over in the downtown area, across Main Street, not the one across the street from Church, but a different one, three of the Neemo Fadama children stood in the showroom surrounded by brand new Ramblers in all the new year's colors, tan, cream, white, pearl and opal.

Jimmy stood outside, holding onto the flag pole with both hands and leaning way back, gaping up at the giant United States flag flapping in the wind.

"A pirate wants a parrot, sir, not a bloody parakeet!" Jimmy yelled up into the flag and the sky and the wind. He kept hold of the pole and let himself fall way back and walked and fell around and around, until he fell down in the gravel and the weeds.

He stood up straight and wiped slobber off his chin as he made his way to join the others.

"We need to talk to smart adults," Johnny acted as spokesperson.

"Who know a lot and they care about people and they are smart, I said that, sorry."

He took a deep breath and let it out and took another and let it out. On the second breath he also wet-farted.

"I've got a little gas," he winced at the car salesman standing over him.

"Well, and adults, you smart adults, will want to know this and ..."

Johnny tried to remember what they had all rehearsed at noon recess that he would say.

"And ... that's why the moon, Mr. Moon told us in a vision.

"And it's important."

"Whatcha got?" the salesman flicked his cigarette onto the floor and stepped on it, then stepped forward and put his hand out. "This piece a paper?"

He read the ten suggestions, slowly, going back to re-read a couple, then back down. He took out another cigarette and lit it while he was reading.

"I'll have to go talk to my sales manager to see what we can do about this," he said. "You don't wan' a car or nuthin'? You here alone?"

Johnny looked over at Jimmy licking the front headlight of a new white Rambler, up and down, up and down.

"Yeah, no," said Johnny, "we're good."

The sales man walked into one of the glassed offices all in a row along the showroom floor, reading the list.

Johnny and Jimmy and Jane and Danny saw him talking to another man the way they had seen the newspaper editor talking to somebody else in that one room not too long before they got wrestled by the police.

The man placed on the other man's desk "The Ten Things Of Mr. Moon" suggestions in Sister Mary-Michael's nearly perfect handwriting that the moon had thought that people might want to consider about the killing of their president in Dallas not too long ago that might tell them more about what kind of country they lived in and about history stuff, too.

The man at the desk took out some black glasses and leaned over the list.

When he had finished he looked up at the salesman.

They both screamed and put both hands into the air.

"Aaaaahhh!" the children could even hear it through the glass.

The two men struggled to open the door with their elbows with their hands up in the air and yelling "Aaaaahh"!

But managed to finally get it open after Johnny went to open it for them.

The men ran across the showroom to where Jimmy was standing holding open the glass door to the outside.

The children watched the men run down the street, following by the dealership mechanics and the two office secretaries.

Just as soon as Johnny and the others stepped outside, the Beatles music that had been playing over the loudspeakers in the lot switched to the National Anthem, full blast.

"Aaaaahhh!"

Then another office secretary, who had been in the restroom, ran out of the building with her hands straight up in the air, headed out of the lot and down the sidewalk.

[CHAPTER THIRTY-TWO]

We are living in the future, I'll tell you how you know, I read it in a paper 50 years ago, we're all driving rocket ships and speaking with our minds ... and wearing turquoise jewelry, we're standing in soup lines.
— John Prine

*J*ohnny went in first. Jimmy caught the glass door and handed it off to the other two.

Johnny stood in the bank lobby with his arms crossed, looking up at the wooden railings and the openings up there like a fort. He saw heads.

He looked behind him to watch Jane sniffing and then Danny was sniffing, too. Johnny sniffed to try to see what they were sniffing.

"What smells?" Jimmy asked.

Johnny shrugged his shoulders and they all turned to stand in a line and look around at the giant bank.

Johnny led the others up to stand under one of the fort openings. He looked way up and shouted, holding the list of the ten suggestions as high as he could so she could see.

The bank teller leaned on her arms and smiled and stuck her head through the fort hole and said, whatcha got?

"We are here because ..." Johnny began.

The girl recognized Johnny from the newspaper, dropped back into her station, screamed and went running.

The children stood in the big marble shiny and wood shiny office watching the big clock hands move and the bank tellers and managers and the customers who had been in talking to the bank managers running with their hands over their heads in the direction of the open vault door.

They each dived headfirst into the vault, landed on their stomachs, held their arms out straight and slid on the marble floor as they had rehearsed since learning about The List.

The bank president grabbed the giant grey steel door, and with all his might he grunted and pulled and pulled and the vault door finally made a thud to shut.

Lights flashed and sirens wailed inside the bank.

The children ran to the windows to watch the fire trucks go past.

They watched three then four police cars screech to a skidding, slamming halt in the front parking lot. The police men crouched and ran toward the bank door with their guns in two hands up around their face.

Johnny hurried to hold the door open.

One officer shoved his gun into his holster and began to wrestle one of the children. Another officer had a commando handkerchief over his face and it slipped up over his eyes and he grabbed the first officer by his hair and pulled until they both screamed.

All the officers gave each other instructions and they all ran back outside and skidded away in their cars.

The children waited at the front window, except that Jimmy walked way back to the vault door and tapped on it with his knuckles and tried to hear inside.

"They're back!" Johnny called and Jimmy came running, Colorado sliding on the cool bank floor on the way.

They watched the officers dive out of their cars onto the ground and crouch down and wait for the one officer who had the big net.

They all formed one line and crouched down, holding their guns in two hands up near their noses.

The officer in back ran up to the front and then the next last officer sprinted up.

When they reached the front door, they all tried to help hold the net and that didn't work. They let the one guy bring the net inside. When they got inside they snuck up behind the children who were facing them.

Two officers spread the net across the room and they tossed it at the children. It fell short. They pulled it back and stepped forward a couple of steps together, then said, one, two-oo … three!

Like apostles fishing, the two officers tossed the net at the children.

The net landed over the children, except just over one of Jane's shoulders. She held the net up and climbed under it so she was caught.

The officers directed the children to come with them. The kids tried to walk with the net around their heads and necks and feet. They tripped and fell and started rolling around.

The officers tried to drag the children out of the bank, but it was difficult because first one side would go and then the other, but never both sides at once.

The officers worked for three hours inside the bank getting the children out of the net. They rolled around on their backs and took off their hats and undid their ties and went to borrow a roller creeper from a friend at a gas station. Then they got a wooden C clamp and some number nine wire and a vice grips and then all the tools were scattered over the slick, shiny marble floor with the big white engraving of some initials in the middle.

The children took the net off and stepped out and began helping the officers pick up the tools and clean them a little if they needed it with a moist towel from the restroom.

Just when they got done they heard faint tapping coming from the bank vault door.

"Well, hmm," said one officer to the children. "You want to go anywhere?"

Johnny said how 'bout the school playground.

The kids waved when the officers pulled away after dropping them off by the slippery slide.

[CHAPTER THIRTY-THREE]

Am I asking the people of America to believe this? I'm doing more than that! I am trying to tell the people of America that the honor of this country is at stake. And if we don't do something about this fraud, we will not survive. And there is no way to survive if we don't bring out the truth about how our President was killed four years ago. And the investigation by the Warren Commission wasn't even close.

— Attorney Jim Garrison speaking to Johnny Carson on *The Tonight Show*

*J*im, Bob, Tim, Dan, Joe and Father sat at their regular table in the front window of The Café.

Dan talked about the children coming to the car dealership. Jim talked about their visit to the newspaper office, and Tim mentioned in passing his new ag loan director and how good it felt to feel the sun on one's face.

"They've got to be stopped," Father spoke while holding his coffee cup by his chin, then took a drink.

Bob nodded and Dan sipped his coffee. Two others adjusted their stares to another part of the café.

"They're kids," said Joe the barber.

"Hooligans," Father muttered.

Bob nodded. Dan touched his cup with both hands to see how hot it was. Tim and Jim looked at each other then out at the icy parking lot.

"Don't you have rulers there anymore?" said Joe. "They did when I was there."

"The thing is," Father took another drink, then had to stare at the table and put his hand on his chest to make the coffee stop burning.

"It was a good thing."

"Good thing?" said Bob.

"The assassination," Father said.

Tim and Jim looked at each other then looked at Father.

"He was one of yours, padre," said Dan.

Father shook his head and looked down at his hands wrapped around his warm white coffee cup.

"It doesn't matter who did it," Father said.

"Oswalt," said two of the men at once. The others nodded and looked around, either at other people inside the café or out at the parking lot.

"He was getting out of Vietnam," Father said. "That's how the Communists win."

"He was?" said Dan.

During quiet-read-anything-you-want-just-don't-bother-Sister time Johnny pushed out of his desk and slugged down the aisle, pausing for a split moment to return somebody's blind kick, then scuffled over in front of the room to Sister's desk.

"I'm not sure they're listening," he said.

She kept her head down working on her papers.

Johnny reached up and touched something lying flat on her desk.

"What's this?" he said while picking it up.

It was an orange construction paper moon. It looked just like Mr. Moon, with the crater face and the kinda smile that Sister Mark called Moona Lisa.

Sister Mary-Michael reached for it, but her desk was too wide.

"You made this?" said Johnny, turning it over and around, touching it.

"It's good. You made this?"

It was the size of a giant chocolate chip cookie from the bakery downtown. He put it in front of his face and then peaked out from one side, grinning.

"Johnny Moon."

"Yes, may I have it, please?" said Sister.

"Thank you," Sister said, returning to her chair after having gotten out to walk around the desk to retrieve the moon from Johnny.

"I don't think they're listening," he said.

"Yes, you said that."

Sister put down her pen, folded her hands in front of her and gave her full attention to Johnny.

"What do you think we should do?" she said in a voice Johnny thought sounded tired mad and tired of people.

"We should keep trying," he said. "That's what Mr. Moon said. We should keep trying for John F. Kennedy. We should walk everywhere and lose weight and go to the moon and be a good American."

Sister watched him and waited for him to keep going.

"Maybe we should ask Mr. Moon again," Johnny said.

He waited for her to say something. He touched the desk with a finger and put all his weight on his right leg and tried to balance that way. He raised his left foot off the floor and balanced on his right foot with one finger on the desk.

"Trapeze?" Sister said and Johnny nodded.

He set his left foot down and looked up at her, into the big eyes and long eyelashes that were patiently smiling and watching him.

"Maybe tonight?" he said.

Verlin and Duke appeared in the doorway, each clutching one side of a metal basket carrying the day's milk break cartons.

Johnny looked at them and back to Sister.

"Hello boys," Sister said to Verlin and Duke. They walked in front of the class and began setting out the chocolate and two white cartons along the chalk tray, taking their time.

"Maybe we should go back to the boiler tonight, after school," Johnny said.

"I think you're right," Sister said with a big heave and sigh. "You'll tell the others?"

"Yep," Johnny nodded and spun around.

He decided to walk past Verlin and Duke on his way back to his desk rather than taking the safer behind the rows passage.

Verlin, on one knee by the basket, methodically pulled the cartons out and put them in a row while Duke stood nearby checking their list on the clipboard.

"Hi," Johnny said.

Verlin looked at him and scowled.

"I can't find that one dog," Johnny said. "I looked."

"You better," Verlin said. "You haven't even looked."

Johnny stared at him wondering how he knew that.

Verlin held out his open hand to Johnny.

"Fifteen cents," Verlin said, "hand it over."

"I don't have it," Johnny said, "fourteen."

"Hand it over," Verlin stuck his hand out closer to Johnny.

Johnny took a deep breath and let it out. He looked at Verlin then turned to walk to his row and his desk.

"Thaa-aank-you-Siisssteerr," Verlin and Duke hummed as they walked through the doorway with their milk basket.

"D'jou hear that?" Verlin hissed as soon as they were three steps down the hall.

"She said, bye," said Duke.

"Nahhh! At first. They're going to the boiler tonight.

"You didn't hear that?

After school Johnny sat inside the boiler with Jimmy, Jane and Danny, and Sister M&Ms and Sister Mark.

"It feels cold," said Jimmy.

"It is ushally," said Danny.

Sister asked them to close their eyes and take deep breaths and let them out and invite Mr. Moon to the boiler to help them in their hour of need.

A light appeared in the pitch-dark boiler and they opened their eyes and saw the moon.

Verlin and Duke lay on their stomachs on the playground ice, embedded with rocks and pop can tabs.

"I can't see shit."

Verlin got up and walked to the screen door.

"C'moo-oon," he waved to Duke.

"Fuckin' little kid won't give me my money," he said when Duke got up there.

"Remember you said that one thing?" said Verlin.

Duke shook his head.

"Yes-you-do, c'mon."

Verlin carefully opened the screen and stepped over the concrete threshold placing one tennis shoe and then the other on the top cement step.

The screen clattered shut.

Verlin looked at Duke with brief homicidal rage. Duke shrugged and pushed himself inside to have room to stand on the first step.

"Hear that?" Johnny said into the dark.

"There was a noise," he said. "You hear that?"

"I heard something.

"Did you hear that?" he asked Mr. Moon.

Sister Mary-Michael shrugged her shoulders.

Verlin and Duke took giant, slow steps into the deep darkness of the school basement maintenance workshop, keeping one hand on the homemade railing made of electrical piping or something.

They shushed each other back and forth at their missteps and bumps into each other.

Verlin took a giant step and hit the floor. He grabbed backwards and got Duke's coat and pulled him around, toward the boiler. They heard whispering and talking.

Verlin pulled Duke close.

"Do it," he whispered in Duke's ear.

"It's too dark," Duke whispered back, "I can't see!"

Verlin stepped up to Duke, placing his nose on Duke's nose. He snagged Duke's testicles, the skin, with his long fingernails, and squeezed with one hand. With the other hand he covered Duke's nose and mouth tight. He squeezed with both hands. He snarled at Duke's wheezing and crying, struggling to move his feet and his head.

Verlin let go and said, "I said, do it. Noo-ow."

By the weak light coming through the glass blocks above from the dying winter day Duke tiptoed around the boiler, trying to remember how Dave and Isom had done it.

He found a switch and flipped it up. He spotted a familiar knob and turned it one way and the other.

He bumped a rake hanging on the wall, quick grabbed it and froze.

"I know you heard that!" Johnny said.

"It's Dave," said Sister Mark. "He knows we're in here."

Inside the boiler the Sisters and the moon and the children continued to discuss the ten suggestions list and what they should do with it.

"How about signs?" the moon suggested.

"Yeah!" said Johnny.

"Frogs! A million frogs, that'd be so neat."

194

"And toads," said Jane. "A million toads."

Jimmy suggested falling pancakes and eggs.

"A million eggs," he said.

"Yeah, do it!" the children said.

"Everyone would start using their brains then!" said Jane.

Duke pulled a lever on the wall that looked like it was attached to something hooked to the boiler.

"Clunk-whooosh."

Steam escaped from somewhere and something in the pipes rattled overhead.

"Just Dave," hummed Sister Mark.

"I kinda meant signs," said Mr. Moon, "like the kind you hold, like protest signs, demonstrations."

"Ohhhh," said the children. "Hmmmm."

Sister Mark adjusted herself on the uneven boiler bottom. The moon disappeared for a moment then came back.

"Sorry," said Sister Mark. "I had a cramp."

"That's okay," said Johnny.

"I think frogs is better," he said. "Hmm. How 'bout a flood or …"

"A burning bush?" said the moon.

"Yeah, how'd you …" said Johnny.

"Let's just do the cardboard signs," said the moon. "Trust me. Okay?"

"Okay," said Johnny, smiling in the dark.

"We will."

Johnny heard a drip-drip on the bricks.

He touched his forehead and found it was coming from him.

"It's hot," he said.

"Yeah," said three others.

"Maybe we should crack the opening," said Jane.

"We might lose Mr. Moon," said Sister M&Ms.

"We're done anyway, aren't we?" said Sister Mark.

Sister M&Ms leaned over and pulled down on the lever.

She moved over closer and tried with both hands.

She switched to the other side of the boiler to give her move leverage.

Jimmy moved over to help her.

"It's stuck," said Jimmy.

"What?" said two of the children.

"We can't get out," Sister M&Ms looked at Sister Mark.

"It's getting hotter," Sister Mark said, trying not to say it loud.

They heard laughter outside the boiler and deep rumbling in the pipes and steam escaping.

"I want my fifteen cents!" Verlin got close to the boiler and yelled.

"That's Verlin!" Johnny whispered to the others.

"Tell him to let us out, the boiler's starting up," said Jimmy.

"It wasn't fifteen!" Johnny yelled. "Fourteen! I counted! You said it was fifteen, it was fourteen!"

"Johnathan!" Sister Mark said. "Tell him to get us out."

"Sister Mark says let us out, Verlin!"

"Verlin-Earl-Runnels, open the door this moment!" Sister Mark shouted.

They heard shuffling on the concrete and someone falling down.

They heard running on the steps coming down and then a collision and voices, Verlin and Duke and a deep man's voice.

They heard the door open.

"The boiler's starting up!" Dave yelled. "There's people in there! Turn off the gov'ner!"

They heard cussing and bumping and turning and pushing and grunting.

A big hiss sounded like steam spilling from somewhere above them.

"We are going to cook to death, like the apostles," said Jane. "I'm ready. More than ready."

She folded her arms at her chest.

Her nose wrinkled to try to catch the tears forming in the corners of her eyes.

"No, we aren't dear, come here," said Sister M&Ms.

"The apostles did not cook! I don't believe. Did they Sister?" said Sister Mark.

Sister M&Ms shrugged her shoulders and hugged Jane to her chest.

"Ask the moon to help!" Jimmy told Johnny.

"Okay," said Johnny. "And I'm gonna ask JFK and Jesus, too."

"Just do it," said Jane with her head pressed to Sister M&Ms chest.

Johnny put his open hands on his knees and breathed deep and let it out.

"Any day now, I'm roasting here," said Danny.

"Mr. Moon," said Johnny. "Please, and John F. Kennedy and Jesus. We are in the boiler, in the basement … the school basement … you can come in … the doors are open Dave's here. And save us. Now and at the hour of our death-amen."

Johnny opened his eyes and looked for Mr. Moon and JFK and Jesus.

He looked behind him and up and down in the pitch dark.

"Well?" said Jimmy.

"It might not work now," said Sister M&Ms.

"Why not?" said Johnny.

"Oh, God!" screamed Jane. "We are going to be baked alive! Like in an oven!"

"We'll be famous," said Jimmy.

"Shouldn't we pray?" said Danny. "We should say a rosary."

"Oh! That won't do any …" said Sister M&Ms.

Sister Mark grabbed her robes and duck-walked over to the front of the group. She lay down flat on her back with her feet near the boiler door. With both feet she kicked and kicked.

The crank on the door squeaked. Sister kicked again with her heels, and again. She flopped onto her side and grunted.

"God-dammit!" she said and kicked again.

The children looked at each other's big eyes and grew even more scared.

"God-dammit!" they all hollered at the door to make it go open.

They heard more shuffling and grunting outside. Their bodies squeaked with sweat.

The door wrenched again and they heard Dave and Isom grunting and swearing and it sounded like they had their feet up against the boiler and were tugging.

Squeeek!

A terrible sound like bats being pulled through keyholes.

Light poured in the crack. The door whined again and they saw Dave and Isom and each other.

"God-dammit, way to go!" Johnny said.

Sister Mark elbowed Johnny and shook her head.

"Hi, guys, thanks!" Johnny smiled.

Dave fidgeted with the door using a pliers and screwdriver.

"I don' know why it was so tough. It needs oil."

"May we come out?" Sister Mark said.

"Oh, yeah, geezuz, yeah," said Dave.

Dave and Isom stuck their heads and hands inside the boiler to help the children and the Sisters climb out without bumping their heads.

"Watchit, watchit," said Dave. "There you go, yeah."

"I think Verlin did it, and Duke," said Johnny to Isom in a whisper.

"Yeah, I saw 'em comin' on the steps. They like to run me over."

Dave explained to the Sisters and the children that he and Isom had been upstairs cleaning the rooms when they heard the radiators shaking and bubbling.

"And we knew they wasn't s'posed to be on, that you folks was in there," said Dave.

"We came-a runnin'," smiled Isom.

"And you saved us," Johnny reached up and grabbed Isom's big black hand.

"Yes, sir, we did that," Isom smiled.

"Thank you," said Johnny.

"You are welcome, Johnny Moon," said Isom.

Dave took Johnny's head in his hand and pressed it against his side.

"Jesus, wouldn't we a been in big trouble, tomorrow?" he looked at Isom. "Father and Sister-Something would have skinned us 'live. Cleaning it up would have taken the whole day. Ohh, ma-aan. Wouldn't we a been in big trouble, Isom?"

"That's for certain we would," said Isom.

[CHAPTER THIRTY-FOUR]

ARGO newspaper: What is the renaissance following this long, hard night, that you also spoke about?

Mort SAHL: We'll start pursuing the American dream again. I don't know if we'll ever realize it, but we're supposed to have the right to pursue it. And that's what this country is. It's an active exercise in man reaching his upper limit, as they used to say in the math department. And the renaissance will be that a ground swell of public opinion will flush out the rascals because the CIA has infiltrated every area of our national life. I'm afraid that the country they subverted best was the United States, be they in the various right-wing churches or be they in the Dallas Police Department.

Sister Principal-Something stood in Sister M&Ms' doorway. She held in her hand the milk order for next week for Sister M&Ms' class.

Sister M&Ms walked over, holding out her hands for whatever Sister Principal-Something had to show her.

"Couldn't you have sent someone?" said Sister M&Ms. "It's a long walk from your … well … it's certainly good to see you. Aren't you cooking tonight? Fish?"

"The walk does me good," said Sister Principal-Something. "And I sort of like stopping by here. You always have something … interesting … um, going on. You know?"

Sister M&Ms smiled and turned and waved her arm like a maitre d' to invite Sister into her room to inspect the current activity.

They walked together slowly toward the children, scattered over the room on the floor, working to make signs on white poster board.

Sister Principal-Something bent down and said hello to a student and felt the board.

"The good stuff," she said to Sister M&Ms.

Sister Mary-Michael blushed and began to make apologies.

"It will be better in the wind," said Sister Principal-Something.

"The wind? I did think maybe we might show a couple in the windows, after Father has gone to the hospital. And then take them down of course."

"No," said Sister Principal-Something.

"Outside, next to the cannon. Outside. Definitely outside."

"Won't Father ..." Sister M&Ms began.

Sister Principal-Something shrugged and stuck out her tongue in the direction of the rectory.

They laughed together, putting their wizard sleeves up to their mouths.

"Too bad about Verlin Runnels," said Sister Principal-Something from behind her sleeve.

"What's the matter?" said Sister M&Ms, keeping her sleeve up by faking a cough.

"Too bad we can't stick him in the boiler and turn it on," said Sister Principal-Something. "But if we said anything about what he did, that would mean we would have to explain your being in the boiler. I wonder what the parish council and *The Daily News* would think about that."

"Do we care?" Sister M&Ms took her hand down. "What they think?"

"Perhaps not, but I think your signs here will get you to the same point, without having to explain sitting in the dark in the basement boiler, with Sister Mark and your students ... and JFK, the moon and Jesus."

[CHAPTER THIRTY-FIVE]

We all live in a yellow submarine,
Yellow submarine, yellow submarine,
We all live in a yellow submarine,
Yellow submarine, yellow submarine,

— The Beatles

*T*he sun elbowed through the January clouds and shined bright at the last moment just as the penultimate church bell warnings called out to those wanting to make it to Mass on time.

The newspaper editor checked all his pockets before locking his car up in the parking lot behind the office.

The car dealer said hello to his secretary and lifted the box on the community counter to see what sort of pastries were available, knowing he could only look.

The waitress at the café wiped down the tables from the first wave of coffee klatches.

Father sat in the rectory kitchen with his cup, using a plate for an ashtray at the same time that the bank manager tiptoed outside in his slippers to get his paper off the front porch, careful not to lock himself outside again.

As the old people helped each other over the bumps and edges in the sidewalks and the ice landmines, they paused grumpily, raising their heads to negotiate around a clump already congregated, blocking the front door.

They followed the commotion to a group of children and two Sisters standing on the half-frozen lawn in heavy coats, hats and mittens, holding white signs all around the cannon that was pointed across the street at the car dealership.

"What?" one old person said to another and it was repeated back through all the old people.

Like geese checking out breadcrumbs tossed onto the lawn they waddled toward the children.

"What?"

"What?"

"What?"

The old people whispered to each other and touched each others arms and shoulders. Some walked a bit farther to see what the signs said, then turned around disgustedly, some waving their hands back at the signs to dismiss them.

Sister M&Ms and Sister Mark and the four children of the Mr. Moon vision stood around the cannon, holding their signs and singing "Michael Row Your Boat Ashore," and "she loves you, yeah, yeah, yeah," sometimes confidently and then sometimes wavering to near nothing, until one of them gathered the gumption to encourage the others to be heard.

Each at the same time, as if characters in a play making their entrance, Sister Principal-Something walked out of the back door of the convent and Father out the rectory front door. They saw each other and looked the other way. The way they looked was away from the chilled westerly breeze and toward the sign-holders on the parish courtyard.

Sister Principal-Something smiled and headed around on the south portion of the sidewalk, toward the church, and on a path that would take her right past the signs.

Father fired a cigarette at the sidewalk and pounded away, toward the sign people on a sideways canter, like a horse being taken out of the paddock and in front of the crowd for the race. His eyes were wild and his nose flared from having been too long in the barn.

Father stood in front of the group, one shoe on the frozen lawn, at a sideways stance, leaning slightly forward, his forehead furrowed for reading.

He stood straight and stepped back onto the walk. He shoved both hands into his pockets and smiled and shook his head like Fr. Bing Crosby discovering an unruly child on the playground after hours at Boys Town.

Father sensed Sister Principal-Something getting nearer and turned to meet her. He walked right up and talked to her with his back to those on the lawn, by the cannon, with the signs, singing the songs, seeing how far they could blow their breath smoke.

Father broke off the meeting and followed Sister Principal-Something's previous route to skirt far around the others and make his way to the sacristy.

Sister Principal-Something sauntered over to the group, pulling her scant shawl around her shoulders. She stopped in front of them all and carefully read the messages.

She took a deep breath and turned to go into church, having to take a wide arc around the old people still gathered at the corner of the church, some daring to edge out far enough to read the signs then hurrying back to tell the newbies.

The chimes sounded a last warning. Sister M&Ms and Sister Mark helped the children store their signs in the church basement in the back room with the giant lawn ornaments of donkeys, cattle, sheep and a life-size ivory statue of baby Jesus.

Johnny walked past to put his sign against the wall, snuck a look around, petted Jesus on his curly white hair, then ran to catch up with Jimmy so he would not have to walk past the mad old people alone.

The next morning they were out there again.

Johnny held his sign with one hand while trying with his other hand to get the right grip on one of the donuts that Sister Mark had brought out to share with the Neemo Fadama sign group.

He took a bite and ducked his head a little to the right to duck a snowball, but the snowball landed on the sidewalk, not even making it onto the Grassy Knoll St. Nick area, as the children were calling their spot around the cannon, on the lawn, with the church, rectory and convent forming a "C" around them.

Two of the children held their signs up in front of their faces to shield against the potential barrage of snowballs.

Jimmy held his white poster board shielding his face with one hand, and put his other hand over his privates.

The old people again congregated in a clump at the corner of the church. They fired snowballs at the children. Some threw underhand softball style.

"Go! Go away! Git!" they hollered.

"You don't believe that malarkey do you? Those are fairy tales, they're made-up."

The snowballs flew through the air a few yards. Some landed on the lawn. One old man with a cane with a rubber end, with a hat similar to Johnny's with earflaps and a piece that came down under his chin for tying, sneaked up close with a big, hard snowball in his bare left hand.

He acted as though he were invisible, Johnny thought, like nobody could see him, but he was way out in front of the old people group, way beyond their snow fort they had packed together to hide behind and store their snowballs. Some of them were able to get to their knees to get behind the fort, but most were forced to try to stay in the huddled group and then occasionally shuffle out to take a crack.

The brave old guy got close to Johnny.

Johnny waved and smiled.

"Hi."

The old man's face filled like a fish trying to make itself look big for protection, with blue veins and giant eyebrows. He needed a handkerchief and he fought to get the words out, he was so angry.

"You are just trying to bring America down!" he shook his finger and then his fist at Johnny.

Sister M&Ms, leaning against the cannon, squatted, keeping an eye on Johnny and the old man.

The old man put one foot on the frozen lawn. Johnny saw his lips were cracked and he had hair coming out around his colored T-shirt top.

"President Johnson is a good man! A good man! One nut killed the president! And that's that! That's it!"

He swept his hands out like an umpire making a safe sign, still keeping the snowball in one hand.

Johnny saw the man in danger of falling over, either from the ice or the breeze or a heart attack. He stepped toward the man.

The old guy's eyes flew wide and startled, like he had just discovered a Japanese soldier hidden in the grass.

His eyes focused on Johnny.

"You! You!" he yelled as loud as he could and took a step back off the grass, perhaps afraid Johnny was a demon getting too near.

The man cocked his hand to fire the big hard snowball from point-blank range.

Johnny opened his mouth and his eyes wide and stopped.

From her knees Sister M&Ms fired her snowball with her left hand and nailed the old man square in the chest, throwing him off balance.

He struggled to keep afloat.

He dropped his snowball to the ground, turned and scurried back to the group, casting frightened glances back toward Johnny to make certain he was not being followed.

"Sister!" hissed Sister Mark.

"Siiisssterrr," said the children, putting one mitten hand over their mouths and letting their signs droop for a moment.

The old man arrived safely back at the church corner. The others welcomed him, as a hero returning from the South Pacific after all these years.

Sister M&Ms used the cannon to pull herself up, all the while staring hard at the old people.

On the third day, the first of the morning's snowballs dotted the sidewalk.

A station wagon pulled up to the curb in front of church.

Everyone recognized *The Daily News* red lettering on the front door.

Two men crawled out, their eyes on the sign group on the lawn, around the cannon.

One held a notebook, the other a camera. The camera man shot pictures of the old people throwing. He took photos from in front and behind. He got on his back on the sidewalk and then on his stomach on the snow and ice.

The reporter talked to the old people, taking notes, with one eye on the sign group on the lawn.

The bells chimed. Sister Mark looked at her wrist.

A screen door chattered and they heard Father's quick, chippy steps down the rectory steps and then another old screen when he entered the sacristy.

Sister Principal-Something walked up behind them on the grass and stood visiting cryptically with Sister M&Ms. They each kept one eye on the reporter and the photographer.

The reporter broke though the Congregated Clump and began making his way over the short bit of sidewalk and onto the grass. He positioned himself in the middle of the group and surveyed them all, reading the signs, taking notes.

Johnny noticed he did not wear a hat or gloves and only a light, unbuttoned coat. He wore buckle overshoes, big buckle overshoes.

Johnny smiled and waved with one hand and then quick grabbed his sign when it fell.

"Hi," he said.

The reporter stepped up to Johnny, the closest of the group.

"So," he began as the photographer moved around the group,

snapping photos, standing on his tiptoes, kneeling on one knee, both knees, flopping to his stomach.

The reporter talked to Johnny, taking notes, then moved around to visit with each of the children, then back to the three Sisters at the cannon.

Sister M&Ms stood with her arms hanging at her sides, an iceball in each bare hand.

The reporter asked the Sisters a few questions then returned to Johnny.

"So," said the reporter. "You're Johnny Moon, huh?"

Johnny smiled and said, yeah.

He told the reporter about how he was walking to school before and he still was and that he was trying to lose weight. And he told him about the chart on the refrigerator and how he needed to still do what he ate from the last three days but he thought he still remembered.

And he told the reporter about a strong boy makes a strong man and stuff.

"And we talked to the moon in the boiler," Johnny said and then wiped his nose with the back of his gloved hand.

The bells chimed loud and the reporter smiled.

"Oh, yeah?" he said.

He got on one knee in front of Johnny and asked Johnny what he meant by that.

The Sisters watched the reporter talking to Johnny.

Sister Mark made a move toward them. Sister M&Ms put a firm hand on Sister Mark's elbow and shook her head, no.

Sister Principal-Something nodded at the hard grass as she walked in front of Sister M&Ms and Sister Mark to move into church for the start of Mass.

Sister M&Ms let her snowballs drop and Sister Mark took her thumb and made the sign of the cross on her own forehead.

"How do you spell that?" the reporter asked Johnny.

"T.H.A.T.," said Johnny.

"You're funny," said the reporter, marking a straight line in his notebook with his pencil.

"N," Johnny began.

"Okay."

JOHNNY MOON

"E."
"Yeah."
"E."
"Uh, okay."
"M."
"Yep."
"O."
"And Fadama, just like it sounds. F-A-D-A-M-A. Fadama."
"Why only inside the boiler," asked the reporter.
"Why not right here, right now?"
"I don't know," said Johnny.
He looked behind him toward the Sisters.
"Maybe that's just the only place we really asked," said Sister M&Ms.
"Asked?" said the reporter.
"Asked?" said Johnny.
"Asked the moon to talk to us. We only asked while we were inside the boiler," said Sister.
"Could you ask now?" said the reporter.
"Yeah, could we?" said Johnny.
Sister M&Ms looked up into the sky.
"I believe it's too soon, too early. The moon just went to bed."
"Mr. Moon, Mr. Moon, yer out ... hmm, hmm," Johnny sang softly.
The bells chimed. Sister Mark hurried with getting everyone and all the signs rounded up and organized to march it all down the short steps to the church basement.
Sister M&Ms, the reporter and Johnny remained in a cluster on the lawn.
The reporter got up from his kneeling position.
"You really nailed one of the old people," he said to Sister.
"It was an errant toss," she said. "I was aiming for a fence post."
The reporter looked around and behind him.
"There's no fence posts that I can see," he said.
"So there aren't," Sister said, putting her hand on Johnny's back and directing him toward the battered metal door leading to the church basement.

On Friday morning, about a quarter of eight, church bells chimed, banged, rang, hollered down the tundra, skipping across the earth like flat, hard rocks over frozen water.

The sound of tires on snow-packed streets, a harmony of squeak, scratch and roll, took its turn whenever the bells took a breath.

The same scene and scenario of the days before repeated itself in the so-called courtyard of the Catholic Church.

The old people clumped on the front sidewalk right at the corner, huddled against the cold, cattle with snowflakes on their coats and hair.

Like Bolsheviks on the barricades they shouted at the cold and the children, and the Sisters and the signs, and the cannon, and the moon and Jesus and JFK.

"They don't' hate Communism!"

"They are eating snow!"

They raised their bony fists and hurled them toward the Neemo Fadama After-School Club.

"They walk into church … like a herd of cows!"

"Communion! … chewing … cuds!"

"Moooo," hummed Sister Mark, making Sister M&Ms and Sister Principal-Something grin with rosy red cheeks.

A woman in grey hair, wearing a purplish, thick coat and holding a paper towel from home on the top of her head stepped to the front of the group and bellowed.

"They *ALL* think they are going to the moo-oon!"

"Moo-oooon!" hummed Sister M&Ms and Sister Principal-Something.

"They should go to *confession*!" shouted a tall, thin old man wearing a red-plaid wool earflap cap and matching gloves.

Dave and Isom appeared in the back of the group, at opposite sides, with their hands in their pockets, watching the cars and the old people.

"You sure you want to do this?" Sister M&Ms turned to Dave.

"You are standing with the Grassy Knoll Saint Nick Moon Nuts, you know, people will talk."

"Let 'em," said Dave.

Johnny heard behind him a deep man's voice, singing a song from Sister M&Ms' record.

Johnny swiveled and smiled and waved, then turned back and picked up his sign, then looked back again and waved.

Isom waved back.

"Hey," said Dave to Sister M&Ms, "the reason I'm here is I can't find my good stapler, you got it?"

"I might," said Sister.

Then they joined Isom in singing one of the songs from Sister M&Ms' record upstairs in her room.

Dave stared at Sister out of the side of one eye while he sang a little.

"I might," Sister looked at Dave while she was singing. "I might, I'll look."

[CHAPTER THIRTY-SIX]

Supercalifragilisticexpialidocious.

— Mary Poppins

*F*ather's hands surrounded his white hot coffee cup.

Around him the other men talked about the group standing each morning outside the church.

"Itn't that right, Father?" Dan said to him.

Father did not look up, but kept staring at his coffee as if he were expecting the creamer dust floating on top to form into the face of Johnny Carson.

"They say the paper came down and talked to your kids and your nuns," said Bill.

Father looked up and stared at Bill, then back down to his coffee creamer, which had disappeared.

He pressed the sides of the cup, feeling the heat, comfortable, then burning, cutting. He pressed it as if he were squeezing the sides of a nun's skull in her white headdress that they wore because they wished to be men. They wished to be priests, actually. They wished to do just what the priests did and get in the way, making the priests step over them to get where they needed to go. Just making life more difficult than it need be.

"Hey, Padre," said Tom. "My mom goes down there and throws snowballs at the kids every morning. She's kind of getting a kick out of it. She says the kids had a vision, like the children at Fatima."

"Fatima?" said Tony.

"It's a Catholic thing," said Tom, "kids in Mexico, Virgin Mary ..."

"Virgin?" said Bob.

"I know some Mary's," said Robert.

"Maybe you ought to kidnap the kids and burn 'em in oil," said Tom, "you know, like the story, to make them admit it's a hoax."

Tom smiled and sipped his coffee as a reward for his good joke.

"What makes you think ...," Father began, then stopped.

"Make 'em go in there and then turn it on," Bob smiled and then looked at Tom. "Not really, you know," Bob said. "Not really."

Father raised his coffee to his face with both hands, planting his elbows on the table, staring out at the frozen parking lot, the traffic light slowly, dutifully switching to red to green to yellow even in the painful cold, and the moon in the faintest outline of white.

"I already ..." said Father, just catching himself.

Tom looked at him.

Bob followed Tom's stare to Father's face.

"Good story, those kids," Father said. "Yeah, Mexico."

"Hey, Father!" said Bob. "Not to change the subject, but, hey, how about the tunnel, the underground nun tunnel, you know."

Father scowled and looked at Bob.

"Tunnel?" Father said.

"From the priest house to the convent," said Tom, "that one."

"Where did you hear that fairy tale?" said Father.

"That's what we always thought," said Tom, "since I was there. No 'fense, ya know."

"Well, there's not," said Father.

He set his cup down, miraculously found the exact change in his pocket, stood and placed it on the table next to his empty cup. He pulled his coat from the back of his chair and as he was putting it over his arms and shoulders looked down directly at Tom.

"We do have a dumbshit detector, though. It sits in the library, next to the front office. Got all the bells and whistles, lights, laser rays. It hums, shakes. I've heard it."

"They do-oo?" said Bob. "We didn't have one at public."

Father finished pulling on his coat and took one step away, then stopped and looked back down at Tom.

"It's how we get rid of all the children who are too dumb to be Catholics."

He walked away toward the door. He pushed on the door and again looked back at Tom.

"I'm sure they didn't have it when you were there."

The door chimes tinkled. The rest of the men listened to Father's hard black shoes on the sidewalk. Father's car door whined against the cold. They heard his key in the ignition and the squeaking of his tires on the snow.

[CHAPTER THIRTY-SEVEN]

Anybody here seen my old friend John?
Can you tell me where he's gone?
He freed a lot of people,
But it seems the good they die young.
I just looked around and he was gone.
— Dion

*T*he next week, on Thursday, Thursday afternoon, about four, it appeared.

The story about the Neemo Fadama Club, in *The Daily News*.

On Friday morning at the church, when the children arrived yawning and rubbing their eyes, they saw police car lights flashing in the street in front of the church. And police cars, and a fire truck, and a truck from the gas company, and one big ladder truck from the power company too.

They took up both sides of Seventh Street in front of the church, facing both ways and sideways all the way 'til Tuesday.

Like workmen on a job they knew too well the children gathered their tools in the church basement in silence, eyes half open, knowing where to go, what to do, where to pee if they had to, where to stomp their feet so not to get too much snow in the church basement and piss-off The Catholic Daughters, as Sister Principal-Something had implied.

The Daily News story talked about the vision the children had, and about the Neemo Fadama Club, and the Sisters, and what happened to Sister's sister in Dallas, and Johnny's quest to lose weight and be a good American.

"I don't eat Pixie Stix no more," he was quoted.

The children walked to their post at the cannon. Sister Mark brought coffee in little Styrofoam cups, and then after all the children and nuns had their coffee she offered a box of donut holes.

"Not the donut, just the hole," she smiled and repeated to each person as she went around the group, bending low so they could see into the box.

"Where's the donut?" said Jimmy

"I don't know, James," said Sister Mark. "*Do … you* want one?"

Jimmy took his one donut hole that he was allowed and struggled to find a way to hold his hot coffee, his donut hole, and his sign. He saw that most of the others were letting their signs stand up on the ground by leaning against their legs.

That's what he did, too.

They enjoyed their breakfast in silence, watching the dozens of red and blue and white and yellow lights flashing and the men standing around their cars and trucks with their hands in the pockets of their big coats and their shoulders hunched forward, fighting January hand-to-hand.

One police officer walked over in the street to get even with the signs. He took awhile to read all the words, sidled a few steps to read the next one and then the next, then stalked over to his car, got inside with one leg sticking out to the street and turned on his siren.

"Weee! Weee! Weee!"

The first church bells trembled and the initial wave of old people

shuffled up, some appearing to have come long distances by sidewalk, others arriving by car and pickup and station wagon.

Then high above it all, over the church chimes and the police car
sirens, the end of the world siren went off all around town.

The closest siren was mounted on a telephone pole in the alley by
the convent garage.

"Rrrrr! Rrrrrr! Rrrrrrrrr!"

On and on it droned, insistent that it was not kidding.

The old people continued to come, this time gathering in front of
the children on the lawn, facing them. Some knelt on the cold, hard
sidewalk, their folded hands to their chest, heads bowed.

The children waved to the old people and two of them smiled,
which caused the old people to react as if they were on the front
rope line when the Beatles arrived in New York City.

One person fainted. One urped up some breakfast onto her coat.
Just a little bit. Not too much.

The newspaper station wagon pulled up again, and not being able
to find a spot to park in the street, rolled around by way of the alley
and drove up toward the group on the sidewalk, just short of the old
people.

The children looked back to try to find Sister Mark and if there
were more donut holes. Some dropped their Styrofoam cups on the
grass and one crumpled it and stuffed it into her coat pocket.

"Rrrrrrrmmm … nnnnnnn …," the air raid alert siren wound
down.

The police man walked over to his vehicle and stuck his whole
body, with his feet in the air, in through the open window to shut off
the siren.

The church bells played something new, something like a Grego-
rian version of that one record Sister M&Ms had up in her room,
in the back closet, under the homemade sticky felt Thanksgiving
decorations.

Johnny saw everyone looking up at the sky and he looked up too
and then he pointed and his mouth went wide open and he pointed
a little more, harder, jabbing his finger at the sky, looking at Jimmy
next to him to see if he could see what Johnny saw.

They both watched the parachutes swinging back and forth, big
and black and coming straight down like each one was a whole car-

nival big top, with the rope things swinging back and forth, gently, in time like a grandfather clock in grandma's front room.

One soldier landed right behind the old people and the parachute covered them all up.

Johnny and Jimmy saw the bulges and folds in the parachute marking where the old people were.

Like a puppet show by a traveling ex-convict troupe on stage in the basement for Christmas and they were going to get out early and have extra chocolate milk, they saw fists and angry faces and tongues sticking out in the parachute fabric.

The soldier worked the big homecoming funeral dress, trying to bring it all to him, grabbing, grabbing, pulling, stretching somebody's nose and someone's ear and two people's arms.

A big green plane loomed directly overhead, with United States flags on the side. It was so big it didn't hardly have to move at all. It probably was going to hit a tree or the church, Jimmy and Johnny surmised as they watched with their noses and tongues sticking straight up.

One side of the plane opened and three ropes dropped out.

Three men climbed down the rope, chanting something together as they hopped down the air, and jumped and crawled down the rope.

The ropes were not long enough to reach the ground.

The three men in green uniforms and helmets dropped the last twenty feet and landed on the church, the rectory and the convent. They rolled when they hit and then tried their best to stop falling off the roofs and stand up. Each of them looked around and seemed surprised at how that had worked out.

One of the men in the long black boots put his hands on his hips and spread his feet wide and stared at the people in the courtyard like Superman who had just stopped a train. The other two saw that this was exactly how it had been planned and took the same stance.

The children saw a long white station wagon go past on the street with the radio station letters in red on the door. The man yelled into an ice cream with his head outside the window, looking with big eyes at the children and the Sisters holding the signs on the church lawn around the cannon with the Superman soldiers on top of the rectory, convent and church and now the black parachute not covering up all the old people.

The second grade Sister came running out of the convent carrying a black phone in its carriage, the cord trailing behind her. She ran as fast as she could. Her headpiece about to come unmoored from the bobby pins. At the front door to the convent two other nuns worked like longshoremen, intensely engaged in making sure the phone line got out the door and that more kept coming.

Second Grade Sister stopped in front of Johnny holding the phone and its carriage in her hands like it was Johnny's newborn son.

She smiled and reached out with both hands to present the phone to Johnny.

"For me?" he said.

She nodded and continued to smile.

Johnny took the receiver and put it to his ear.

"Hel-lo?"

The second grade Sister, holding the carriage with one hand, made gestures to Sister M&Ms and Sister Mark.

She was drawing letters in the air.

"B," said Sister Mark.

"P," said Sister M&Ms. "P."

And the Sister holding the phone smiled wildly and pointed at Sister M&Ms.

"Pres-i-dent!" second grade Sister whispered as loudly as she could. "Theeee Pres'dent!"

The whole front line of old people kneeling on the sidewalk bowed and put their foreheads to the frozen brown grass.

"Theee President?" Sister Mark looked at Sister M&Ms.

Sister M&Ms shrugged her shoulders. She looked around at the men on the roofs and the newspaper reporter and photographer on their stomachs crawling toward Johnny, trying to crawl with their notebook and camera out in front of them, trying not to get them dirty in the grass, all the while rubbing dirt and snow and ice into their white shirts.

Father stood to the side, one hand in his pants pocket, his white collar half sticking out, with no coat. He held a smoking cigarette down at his side. His sleeves were rolled to his elbows showing his Navy tattoo.

Sister M. Principal-Something moved behind the cannon group to go stand by him.

"There's nobody inside anyway," Father said as he puffed.

He offered the cigarette to Sister. She looked all around and then shook her head and waved her hand in front of her waist.

Johnny had the phone by his ear, then away from his ear.

Second Grade Sister could hear yelling and screaming and cursing coming from the phone. Her face turned sour.

While the voice continued, loud and fast over the phone, she reached and gently took it from Johnny and hung it up, then walked with her head down, carrying the phone and dragging the phone line back to the convent, as if the baby had died.

Sister M&Ms moved up, nudging between people sideways to stand beside Johnny.

Sister draped her arm around Johnny's shoulder and pulled his head to her hip. She stared straight ahead. She took deep breaths and her shoulders went up and down.

"It was the President."

Johnny looked up at her.

She nodded and wiped one eye with the back of her hand and then the other eye.

She looked down at Johnny.

"Yes, I know."

Verlin and Duke appeared right in front of them.

"Not now, boys," Sister M&Ms growled.

"No, we just want to talk to ol' Johnny," said Verlin.

"Not … now," she repeated, putting one arm straight out with a pointer finger that meant business.

"We're sorry we tried to kill you," Verlin said.

"Yeah," said Duke.

"That's okay," said Johnny.

"That's not okay," said Sister.

Johnny looked up at her and then to Verlin and Duke.

"Yeah, it is. It is okay."

"You never told on us," said Verlin.

Johnny shook his head no.

A dog barked and they looked towards the convent and saw the brown dog from the street corner racing toward them with something in his mouth.

He stopped between them, wagging his tail and whining excitedly.

"He's got a baseball card," said Duke.

The dog held out the card toward Johnny.

"No, it's theirs," he said.

The dog held out the card in his mouth toward Duke.

"Nah, you should have it," he waved the dog toward Johnny.

"It's your card," said Johnny. "The fifteen cents, remember?"

"Fourteen," said Duke.

The dog placed the card down in the grass at their feet, turned and ran back toward the convent, then around the convent into the alley.

"Go 'head, take it," said Johnny.

Duke picked up the card.

"Stupid holy card."

"Lemme see that," Verlin grabbed it out of Duke's hand.

Sister M&Ms swiped it.

"Fatima," said Duke. "It's those kids from Mexico. FATima. Fat." He nodded subtly at Johnny.

Verlin shoved Duke in the chest with the heel of his hand.

Duke fell over the back of an old person who had sneaked up on her hands and knees to get close through the dense crowd to see what was happening.

"You really see the moon," said Verlin. "I mean, talk to it?"

Johnny nodded.

"And yer getting' in shape, ya know, for the pres'dent?"

"Not *this* president," snapped Sister M&Ms, still studying the holy card of the children at Fatima.

Duke walked up, squeezing between people, dusting snow from his snowsuit.

"I don't think he's lost any weight," he said, nodding at Johnny.

"Shut up!" Verlin said and took both hands and pushed Duke's shoulders, sending him sprawling over the same old person who was still there.

"The moon told you, to lose weight?" Verlin asked Johnny.

"Nah," said Johnny. "That was just me, well and the other president, the first one, John Fitzgerald Kennedy."

"How's it goin'?" Verlin said. "You look skinny to me."

217

"Yeah, I'll show you," said Johnny.

He laid his sign flat on the ground and got on his hands and knees. Then he kicked his legs out like a sprinter does and perched on his hands and toes.

The old lady on the ground got up into pushup position, too, keeping her straining eyes on Johnny, her mouth wide.

All the old people on the sidewalk and spilling onto the terrace climbed down onto their hands and knees and those who could, strained into pushup position, keeping their eyes as best they could on Johnny Moon. Those who could not, posed on their hands and knees. Three bent and tried to touch their toes. One did trunk twisters and one began doing jumping jacks with just her arms.

Some lit candles they had brought from home.

Johnny's face got serious and he blew out his breath and his face got whiter and his lips turned blue.

He let himself down slowly. The old people followed the best they could. Some smashed their faces into the cold, hard earth. Some passed out. Two of them angrily waved away family members who had come to take them home.

Johnny kept going and almost got his nose as far as the top of the grass, then started to push himself up.

He got to the top and then collapsed.

He looked up at Verlin from his back, smiling.

Duke stood next to Verlin.

"His butt was way in the air. That's not a real pushup. That didn't count."

Duke pointed at Johnny.

Verlin looked at Duke and Duke stepped back, falling over the old woman who had finished her pushup and was again on her hands and knees, watching Johnny.

"That was pretty good," Verlin said to Johnny.

"Yeah, I know, thanks," said Johnny, picking up his sign, sweating, breathing hard, pushing off from the ground to stand.

"I heard yer an alien from outer space," Verlin looked up at Sister M&Ms.

"You heard right, Mister," she said.

"No-oo-you're-noo-ot," said Johnny, touching Sister's elbow.

He bent his head down and looked to see if he had peed a little.

"What's he doing?" some old people nudged each other, and they all bowed their heads down as Johnny had done as the reporter took notes and the photographer's camera flashed in the dim winter morning light.

"And just how would you know?" Sister M&Ms said to Johnny.

"Hey – why don't you guys do a vision right now? Verlin said.

"Like them Fatima kids, huh?"

He pointed at the card in Sister's hand.

"Everybody's here," Verlin said, looking around at the old people still getting up, and the firemen and police and Superman Soldiers on the roofs with arms akimbo, and Father and Sister Principal-Something standing on the sidewalk, closely, their noses almost touching, and the newspaper reporter and photographer crawling on the ground between the feet and legs like bankers through tall grass.

"What's goin' on here?" Jimmy walked over with his sign to stand by Johnny. There was not room for him to hold his sign, so he just clutched it in front of him.

Duke came up from the other side, keeping Sister M&Ms between him and Verlin.

"What's yer sign say?" Duke said.

He turned his head sideways to read Jimmy's sign.

"Oh," Duke said. "I knew *that*."

"I can try," said Johnny.

He closed his eyes and clenched into a fist the hand that wasn't holding the sign. He bent his knees a little and scrunched up his face.

"He's pooping," Duke said.

Verlin reached around Sister and tried to punch Duke.

All the old people flexed their knees and scrunched their eyes and made silent grunting faces.

Duke bobbed away, smiling, then took one more half step and fell over another old person on his hands and knees.

Sister M&Ms rested her hand lightly on Johnny's shoulder.

He opened his eyes and looked up to her.

"Not now," she said.

"I can try," Johnny said and regained his vision stance and pose.

"Johnny, I don't think so, not now," said Sister. "How 'bout later, huh?"

There was no room to move with all the people gathered around, trying to hear what the children of the Neemo Fadama After-School Club visions were actually saying, to hear if they were speaking in tongues, if their eyes were fluttering, their bodies floating, if they had said anything about them.

The reporter waited right below Johnny with his pen on his pad to see what Johnny would say next.

Johnny felt behind him and tried to straighten his underpants with gloves and frozen hand through his thick blue-plaid snowsuit.

"He pooped!" Duke said from somewhere.

Sister spoke softly, as if conversing with a saint, or asking to get into the second floor convent bathroom on a Sunday morning.

"We'll have to uh … we would have to … go to the boiler."

Johnny shook his head.

"Just me," he said. "And the kids."

"No. I need to be with you," said Sister. "You need … a … faculty representative."

"Fer a vision?" said Verlin, leaning in.

"That doesn't sound quite right," said Father, now right up close along with Sister Principal-Something, with her arm tucked inside his.

"On second thought," said Johnny, "I don't wanna go. Nah, it's okay."

"Why?" said Sister.

"Well, cuz-a last time."

Sister Mark appeared behind Johnny.

"I'll keep an eye on Mr. Verlin and Mr. Duke," she said.

"You would have to go with us, Sister," said Sister M&Ms, holding her eyes as wide open as she possibly had ever done.

"No, I think you'd better go alone this time, Sister," said Sister Mark.

"No," said Johnny. "On second thought, no."

Sister M&Ms placed herself in front of Johnny, bending down, trying to make the conversation private with hundreds of people right there, leaning in, hands to ears, butt cheeks pursed, heads between legs, hands on hips.

"Johnny. Johnny Moon. Look at me. We do need to go into the boiler one more time, just you and I."

"You and me," said Johnny, "and we're going to die, bof-ovus."

"No, we're not. I just need you to trust me."

She put her hand around his chubby fist inside his glove, hanging at his side.

He peed.

"I always did," he said to her, straight to her, straight into her eyes, and he smiled and took a deep breath and would not ever-ever let it go until she took her hand away from his.

Sister stood, keeping hold of Johnny's hand and smiling down at him like the Blessed Virgin Mary at Fatima telling him he was just big-boned.

Johnny's cheeks bulged and his face turned white and an old person put her hand on his head thinking she could get some grace.

Sister subtly nodded to Johnny toward the school and led him that way, holding his hand.

[CHAPTER THIRTY-EIGHT]

My life was never the same. The country was never the same. Democracy died that day in Dealey Plaza.

— Penn Jones

Sister walked hand-in-hand with Johnny on the sidewalk, slowly, looking into each other's eyes and smiling, speaking the language of the blessed few, lovers, multi-millionaires and candy store workers.

Behind them followed the other after-school visionaries, then Verlin, then Duke a few steps behind Verlin, and Sister Mark behind Duke.

Next came the old people and the policemen and firemen and above them all the National Guardsmen with the short ropes, on the church, rectory and convent roofs, watching, like a Secret Service detachment.

They all stayed on the sidewalk, walking slowly, a procession.

Father grabbed Duke before he got too far and made him run inside the church. Duke came stumbling out with the big, special gold crucifix on the spear and ran ahead to regain his spot in line, in front of Sister Mark and behind Verlin a few steps.

At the very end of the procession Father and Sister Mark strolled along, arm in arm.

"An underground passageway?" Father looked at her as they walked.

Johnny Moon and Sister Mary-Michael arrived at the rackety silver door for the boiler room.

Dave and Isom were already standing there.

The other pilgrims filled in behind them in a semi-circle, covering the playground.

"We need to use the boiler, please," Sister said to Dave.

"I can't," Dave said. "It's running. It's too dangerous."

"It's not running," Sister Mark shoved up to the front. "It hasn't been running for the past three days. You should feel my room."

Isom moved in front of Dave, rubbing his hands together.

"Well, that's true," he said.

He stepped closer to Sister Mark, trying to place his body to shield Sister M&Ms and Johnny from what he had to say.

"It's just that, all these people. All these folks will not fit into the boiler," he said.

He looked down at his hands, watching them scramble around looking for cover, then looked back at Dave, then back at Sister Mark and scooted in closer as she stood her ground calmly.

"And if they do ... if they do-oo-all ... get into the boiler. And see the moon. And talk with the moon and President John F. Kennedy and Jesus."

He looked both ways, up and down and back and forth before his eyes again found Sister Mark's lighthouse gaze.

"And if they find out what Mr. Johnny Moon knows and what Sister M&Ms knows, and what you and these other kids knows, that will be the end of the world, Sister. And we're afraid of that. Very much afraid, Sister."

"Why is that?" Sister Mark took his hands in both of hers to stop him from fumbling. "Why would that be the end of the world, Isom?"

"It just would," he pleaded, not willing anymore to meet her eyes.

"Why does that make you afraid, Isom, why?"

"Because evil don't like it when good gets going," he said. "When it really gets going. And if you people really get going, something would have to come along and stop you."

Dave stepped up and Sister M&Ms and Johnny turned around to form a tight clique.

"And they would stop you," Dave said. "That's how it goes and we are afraid of that."

"It's easier when evil is a little stronger," Isom said. "You see that? Don't you, Sisters? Just a bit, then it's happy."

He looked back and forth at Sister M&Ms and Sister Mark.

"You got to have seen that.

"That's why John F. Kennedy died," Isom bowed his head and took back his hands from Sister Mark. He grabbed one wrist tightly with his other hand.

"If he just kept down a little," Isom said. "And let evil have most-a the say. He'd still be here today. That's the truth."

"So, we can't let you go down to the boiler room," said Dave.

He turned and walked back to the door and faced the crowd.

"You all will just have to go on home. No school today," said Dave.

"Snow day, yoohoo!" Isom shouted and stuck a power fist into the air.

"Just go on home, now git," Dave said haltingly, bravely.

Johnny Moon let Sister's hand go and walked up to Dave.

He stood right under him and looked up at him. He saw a sweat drop on Dave's nose and dodged like a fighter ducking a blow while the drop sailed past him to the sidewalk.

Johnny reached up and took Dave's hand.

Johnny noticed he did not have as far to look up at Dave as he used to.

He had grown.

He smiled at the thought and then shook his head at Dave.

"What?" Dave said.

"Strong boys make strong men makes a strong nation," Johnny said.

Johnny pointed at his own chest and then at Dave, then he turned and pointed at Isom and at Sister Mary-Michael and Sister Mark, then at Verlin and Duke and the other Neemo Fadama After-School Club members.

Then he turned all the way around and held up his hands high, and even though he couldn't see them, to point his fingers at all those people gathered in the parking lot, then over at the three men on the rooftops.

"That's us," said Johnny.

"We do these things, and the others," he said. "Not because they are easy, but because they are hard, you know?"

Dave nodded and took a half step aside.

"'Sides," said Johnny.

"It's just me and Sister Mary-Michael this time," he said.

"We fit."

Johnny took hold of the old rickety door handle and opened it, then stepped aside for Sister Mary-Michael to go down ahead of him.

He closed the door and the mute crowd outside heard their shuffling down the stairs and a few seconds later the squeaking of the boiler door and the clanging when it was closed, and finally the grinding as the lever was pulled to lock the two inside.

Outside on the playground Sister Mark made Duke stand in front of the door facing the crowd, holding the big gold crucifix on a sword in front of him. She instructed Verlin to stand next to him and together they guarded the door and traded off holding the enormous gold cross.

Sister Principal-Something and Father mingled with the crowd and asked them to be seated on the playground, and those who did not ignore them said that it felt strangely warm, as if it were heated and spongy and comfortable and comforting, not like it was hard and frozen and stiff from many months of a tortuous winter.

The Supermen Soldiers-Something on the roofs tossed a nerf football back and forth that Sister Mark had hurled up to them.

The entire membership of the Neemo Fadama Club, along with the rest of the third and fourth grade class, joined with Sister Frederick-Ludwig Cecilia in encouraging the old people to sing Christmas songs.

"That's what they like," Sister Frederick-Ludwig Cecilia whispered to the students. "It will make them happy."

The old people sat on the playground, some sang along with the students, two said it wasn't even close to being Christmas time, some lay flat on their backs looking up at the sky, three did deep-knee bends and two did pushups from a kneeling position. One old woman did what she had been wanting to do for a long while and walked over to this one old guy, grabbed him by the hand and together they snuck over to the school, lay flat on their stomachs and pushed their noses against the glass blocks to try to see what was happening inside.

"It's dark," Johnny said.

"Yes, are you all right?" said Sister.

They nestled in on the bricks and somehow found a comfortable position on the concave boiler floor.

"Yeah," he said. "You?

"Hmm-hmm, listen, Johnny," she said.

"Do you hear him?" he said.

"Uh, no."

"Listen. I think I see him. Close your eyes, Sister," Johnny said.

"Hi," Johnny said as he raised up his hand in the total dark and waved.

He felt a hand on his arm.

"Mr. Moon?" he said.

"No. Me."

"Sister. You?"

"Johnny. I have to talk to you."

"'kay."

She heard the heels of his tennis shoes scratch the bricks as he stretched out.

He put his hands back and rested on the heels of his palms. He could do that for a while.

"Hello, Johnny."

"Mr. Moon!" he said.

"Where are you? How you doing, there's a lot of people outside, see 'em?"

"Johnny, it's me."

Now he heard Sister's voice.

"It's me. I'm Mr. Moon."

She sat in the dead dark silence and looked hard, trying to see his face. He looked straight ahead, not really wondering, more like realizing what he already knew and just taking his time.

"Oh. ... I guess I kinda ..."

"You knew?" she said.

"Ohh, I sorta knew you were a vent-willer-quest, why did you do it?"

Sister explained that she and Sister Mark had gotten the idea of the boiler and visions from Father's sermon way back in the school year about the boiler and stuff and special things happening.

She said they had been inspired by President John Kennedy and Pope John Paul and Vatican II and ... the Beatles.

"And then my sister's letter, well we had to do something.

"And we tried to think of a way to inspire you children as well, I'm sorry.

"It was kind of far out."

He scooched and reached in the dark. He found her knee, her leg and then her hand. He held it. She gripped his hand back.

"Don't be sorry," he whispered. "Far out in a good way."

"I'm 'spired and so are the kids and those other people. They're all 'spired."

He asked her how she got the moon to appear in the boiler, though.

Sister M&Ms explained that it was just colored paper that she held up, and when Sister Mark was with them she shined a tiny key ring pen flashlight from inside one of her sleeves.

"I didn't do it very well," said Sister.

"Yee-es you-do. You do it goo-ood."

Johnny saw her bright white teeth as she smiled in the dark.

"How about when I saw it, the moon, in my head?" he asked.

"Well, maybe you really did," she said.

"Yeah," he said.

"Ya know, I was thinking maybe the moon is my brother."

"That's a nice way to put it, Johnny."

"No, not really. My real brother. Joe was in the ghost class, Sister. He burned and died. I always look for him in the halls, but even Jimmy Purple never sees him.

"But the moon looks like my Joe. I miss him, a lot. He's the nicest brother I ever had."

"Oh, my God, Johnny, I never knew. I'm so sorry. … But isn't it wonderful that you got to talk to him?"

"Yeah-huh. And now I can talk to him anytime. That is far out." She hugged him tight.

"There's way more in our heads than we use," he said. "Maybe I was using it, huh?"

"Yeah, maybe," she said. "Yee-aahh, I'll bet that was it."

"So, you think the Fatima kids really saw something?" he said.

She drew over closer to him and pulled her knees to her chest.

Johnny switched around to sit next to her and grabbed his knees to listen.

"I think they saw something," she said. "But I don't know for sure what."

"I guess that's faith, huh?" Johnny said.

He could hear her humming like she was thinking.

She turned to him in the dark. Johnny could not really see her, but he knew it anyway.

"I wanted to do something, somehow. There is no way I could have except through you and the other children. They wouldn't let me. Forgive me, please. If you can."

"President Kennedy was still a good guy, right?" Johnny chirped.

"Yes. He was."

"And when we did Grassy Knoll St. Nick, that was a good thing, huh?"

She hummed a yes.

"But I still can't get why you did it," he said.

"Me?" she said.

"You're not a boy," he said, drawing it out like saying the words was helping his thought process.

"You can't be a astronaut.

"You don't need to lose weight, and you can't get the physical fitness 'ward.

"So why?"

She grabbed him and propped him up on her lap and he could see her. He could see her fine, her face and her headdress and her nun suit.

"Oh, Johnny, Johnny. Mr. Johnny Moon ... I also want to be a good American, like you, Johnny Moon."

She hugged him tight and he held his breath until she let go.

She released him and he climbed back down to sit next to her.

"Sisters can do that," she pleaded. "Or don't you think so."

The second hand on Sister's new wristwatch ticked, ticked.

"Yeah, prob'ly," he said.

"You whistle the best and Sister Mark can pitch like the majors. They call her Sister Koufax, well some do. I guess me-too. But I like the Yankees."

"She'll love that," said Sister.

"And I didn't know you could throw. You really nailed that old guy."

"Thanks. I rarely get the chance."

She rubbed her shoulder.

"And you know that my own sister died," she added.

"She did??"

"Yes! You remember when I went to Dallas for the funeral and Sister Matthew covered for m ... uh, took charge of the room in my absence. You must remember that."

"Yeah. I guess I do, now."

"Johnny, can I tell you about my sister? She was my twin sister, Johnny. That means we were close."

Johnny nuzzled in closer to say, yeah, go 'head.

"It's not nice," she said.

He nodded his head like a bull-rider in the chute.

"Yeah, I'm ready," he said. "You should hear some of the stuff Jimmy Purple says."

He nuzzled closer, now for safety.

Margaret and Susan, well, they usually worked the same job, usually, not always.

This day they had been in different office buildings downtown. It was a Friday. They had both been at their jobs about a week and felt like celebrating. This is all what I got from Susan's mother. She's been so kind to me, even carrying all her burden.

Margaret was at the bus stop and Susan did not show. Margaret went ahead, thinking that perhaps Susan had gotten off early and was already home waiting for her.

She walked in and found Susan in the living room in a pool of blood and then she killed herself by taking a whole bottle of pills.

They found her on the floor next to Susan the next morning. This is Susan's mother again. She was to pick the girls up and take them out shopping. She had come to town for a long weekend. She said she had been frightened for Susan. She just didn't sound right over the phone.

Well, she doesn't believe the suicides and neither do I.

Of course they didn't have a gun. Or they might have. But it wasn't a terribly bad neighborhood. And to just take a whole bottle of pills without calling the police about finding Susan's body?

It all just seems highly unlikely.

I think it was those cameras, and what they saw, and the interviews they did on TV.

I wonder what they said to the TV. I would like to know that now.

"They killed my sister, Johnny."

"Who?"

"That's what I think, the same ones who killed the President."

"Why?"

"Because she knew things she wasn't supposed to know, thought like they didn't want her to think."

"She was using her brain," Johnny said.

"Yes." Johnny saw the big white glow in the dark again. "She was."

"Will they kill me, too," said Johnny. "I'm using my brain, and the other kids."

"Johnny," she put both hands on his head and was quiet for a second, like she was saying a prayer or something.

"I don't think so. No, I'm here. I'll watch out for you and bofovus."

"Thanks," he said and reached up to pull her hands off his head and shake on it.

"You like ice cream?" she asked.

Johnny nodded.

"Well, good then."

"Oh. We might not have ice cream. You like donuts?"

Johnny nodded.

They crawled out of the boiler like astronauts out of a capsule and trudged up the cement stairs slowly, as if not really wanting to return to earth.

Sister M&Ms and Johnny held hands and walked silently between the others, who parted for them, then closed immediately behind and followed, gospel authors listening close for needed copy to fill many blank pages.

They walked down the sidewalk, in between the rectory and the garage, and turned right down the little walk to the back door of the convent.

"He's joining the convent," some kids whispered behind them and the word spread through the group.

"Just like the kids at Fatima, they all became nuns, too."

"They musta really seen something this time."

Jimmy and Verlin and Duke elbowed and cursed their way through the thick crowd up to where Johnny and Sister M&Ms had stopped on the little concrete porch next to the back door of the convent, like the caboose. They stood next to a black iron railing, as if waiting to address the crowd.

"Don't do it, Johnny!" Jimmy hollered when he got within range.

"Look out! Beat it! Move!" Verlin shoved and slapped his way through the old people and the firemen.

He got up right under Johnny on the porch, looking all holy and creepy and his eyes were big and dilated.

"Hey, Johnny! Hey, over here."

"Hi, Verlin!" Johnny waved.

"Kids can't be nuns," he whispered. "I don't know what she told you, but don't go in there, I'm serious."

"Yeah, don't be stupid," said Duke, standing just a few steps behind Verlin.

Verlin reached and shoved Duke in the chest. Duke flipped over the back of an old woman hiding in the peony bushes, trying to get up close and maybe touch the buckles on Johnny's boots.

"It's a miracle!" the old woman shouted and then fainted into the snowy cold peony bushes.

Some people looked at her. One fireman used his big boot to push her foot off of the sidewalk so he could stand.

"He's joining the convent!" the old people pulled out rosaries from back pockets and billfolds. Some did jumping jacks.

"Excuse me!" Sister Mary-Michael put one hand up high, three fingers. It was the sign for absolute immediate silence, the children knew.

She put her fingers into her mouth and whistled loud.

The waters stilled. All eyes on her.

"Umm, we are going in to have a little bite. It's been a long day already for all of us. You may all go home now. I believe Mass has been postponed until tomorrow morning? *Is that right?* Yes, yes, tomorrow, goodbye, now. That's all for today, thank you for coming, bye."

She waved and Johnny smiled and waved from the back porch like it was an alien space ship nun float in the Fourth of July Parade.

Some firemen held out their yellow helmets for Johnny to sign. Johnny pulled out his colored markers and Sister waited by his side.

She nodded at Father and Sister Principal-Something and Sister Mark and flapped a wave from her waist for them to come on inside.

Johnny asked Verlin and Duke and Jimmy and the other visionaries to come inside for ice cream.

"It's a miracle," Johnny whispered with his hand beside his mouth.

"Well, I'm not sure we've really got …," Sister stammered.

"Okay, bye-bye now!" she waved over her head at the crowd as the invitees formed a line to head inside.

"I'm not joining," Verlin looked up straight into Sister M&Ms eyes as he passed her.

"That's what you think," she said, and stepped in right behind him.

The group huddled in the narrow hallway.

Sister Mark and Sister M&Ms hurried around the red and white kitchen with the red and white table and chairs and curtains, pulling chairs from the dining room, shoving the kitchen table into the center of the kitchen.

Sister M&Ms put one hand into the air to aid her in making a general announcement.

"We do not have ice cream or chocolate milk, I'm sorry!"

"Ohhhh."

They heard M&Ms mumbling with Sister Mark.

"Six? Six!"

"Six. Six."

"But! We do have donuts and ... juice. And ... if Father will give us a blessing ... we will be able to turn these ... six donuts into a hearty breakfast for us all."

"Father?"

"Ohhh," said Father. "What? No. Really?"

Father bowed his head and folded his hands and asked them to pause right where they were, in the kitchen and in the hall and wandering down the hall, peeking into the dining room and the other interesting nun nooks and crannies.

"Oh, heavenly Father ... be with us this day ... morning, as we come together to ... go to the boiler ... as a group ... and, uh, to seek your, uh, Mr. Moon and ..."

Sister Principal-Something whispered something to him and he raised up, relieved.

"Dominus vobiscum," Father said.

"Please," Sister Principal-Something used her hands like a shepherd crook to herd them into the kitchen.

The Sisters got everyone seated and took orders for milk, coffee and donuts.

The screen door slapped and they saw Sister Mark running down the sidewalk, into the alley and around to the garage.

They watched the station wagon skidding around the corner and hurtling down the alley.

"Donut run," Sister M&Ms smiled when everyone leaned and craned their necks to see where Mark had gone.

"Who needs juice?" M&Ms held up a big red plastic pitcher.

"Where's Johnny?" she looked all around.

Someone nodded toward the back door.

She edged that way through the crowd, went outside and saw Johnny giving a donut and a stick of Fruit-Stripe Gum to an old man over the railing.

"All right, come inside," she said.

She walked behind him with her hands on his shoulders and made sure he sat down at the table with the others.

Father stood in the doorway, half in the hall and half in the kitchen, fondling a white cup at his chest.

"Well, Johnny, what did Mr. Moon have to say today?" he asked.

Johnny sat with the other kids, his hands and arms on the table, ripping a donut apart as if it were a science experiment.

"Nuthin," Johnny mumbled.

"Nothing?" said Father. "Really? Nothing?" he looked around for Sister Mary-Michael.

"They're not goin' away."

Jimmy and Verlin and Duke leaned over the sink, looking out the window.

"Who?" somebody said.

"The old people. They're everywhere."

"They got donuts," Duke said, standing on his tiptoes, leaning over the white porcelain sink.

"They got a lot of donuts," Verlin looked out, too.

"They're all chewin' gum and eatin' donuts," said Jimmy.

"And layin' all over the lawn and the sidewalk."

"They're not leavin'," said Verlin as he left the sink to find a place at the table.

"Tell them to go home," Father said to Johnny.

"How can I tell them that, Father? Some have come a long way and they've had nothing to eat."

"They've got gum," said Father.

All the children gathered around the table nodded their heads as they ate.

Sister Mark bustled inside carrying two Safeway sacks in her arms.

"Well, have you all been keeping your journals?" Sister M&Ms asked the children.

Verlin shook his head.

Some children took a drink of juice, some looked toward the hallway where their wandering stares bounced off Father standing in the doorway watching them.

"Yeah, kind of," Johnny said, raising his hand at the same time and also returning a kick to Jimmy under the table.

"You were supposed to write about your feelings," Sister recounted the assignment in case any had forgotten.

"About the killing of the President."

"And then we were going to talk about them, and there are no
wrong answers," Michael repeated the rest of the assignment.

"Yes, I believe that's it, exactly," Sister said, looking over her
shoulder, helping Sister Mark get the goodies going, "thank you,
Michael."

Sister M&Ms passed plates and then donuts around and talked
while she worked, turning the kitchen into her classroom.

Father stood in the hallway, one foot in the kitchen, an unlit cigarette in his hand at his side, looking down the hallway for two bed
sheets to tie together.

"We don't have them with us," said Timmy.

"Yes," said Sister.

"I suppose that's a problem. Does anyone remember what they
wrote?"

"Gentlemen," they heard Father say to someone and they heard
greetings, men's voices, then Isom and Dave appeared in the hallway as Father's head moved down the kitchen sink window along
the walk outside.

"One line," Sister Principal-Something said to Sister Mark.

Sister Mark nodded, knowing that meant the principal and the
priest had come together on a long feud over whether to have one or
two lines at communion.

Sister Mark gave Sister Principal-Something the thumbs up and
Sister Principal-Something smiled and turned to welcome Isom
standing behind her in the doorway.

"Isom! Dave!" the children shouted, scooting their chairs and
demanding that Isom and Dave sit next to each of them.

Sister Principal-Something turned again to Sister Mark and ad-
dressed her as if they were the only ones there.

"He really didn't know there was a tunnel."

She shook her head and looked down.

"Didn't even know."

She looked up and directly into Sister Mark's eyes as Sister Mark
worked with a dishrag at the sink, nodding.

Sister Principal-Something just shook her head and sought to busy herself with something to do with her hands.

Dave moved over to stand next to Sister M&Ms. They leaned with their backs to the kitchen counter, facing the children and all of the activity.

"You scare me," Dave looked at Sister, bending his legs a bit to make it evident he was looking right into her eyes.

"All those people out there."

He shook his head, took off his cap and let his hands play with it for a while to keep them busy.

"Evil ... will hear about this," he said.

"Evil," she said.

"And they will find you."

His hands pushed his cap inside out and folded it and then did it again.

"You have about this much time," he said, putting his index finger and thumb close together in front of her face.

"To celebrate," he said.

Isom moved over to stand with them. He held a plain brown donut in halves in his hands and chewed contemplatively.

He screwed his jaw up, chasing a crumb and watched Dave and listened and nodded.

"Oh, well," said Sister.

"We want to give Johnny something," said Isom.

"What is it?" Sister Mark pushed her way into the group.

Isom quick-tossed the two donut halves into his mouth. They bulged his cheeks. He pulled a worn paper sack from under his arm.

He tried to talk, but couldn't while he pulled from the sack a plaque.

He handed the bag to Dave and held up with both hands a square plaque on a brown board background.

The Sisters nudged in to read it and Isom moved it to see if it might help with the glare.

Sister M&Ms read out loud.

"Johnny Moon."

She could see that Johnny's name had been etched in freehand with some sort of fine tool over "Isom Butler."

"Physical Fitness Award.

"A strong boy, makes a strong man, makes a strong nation!"
She smiled and looked up at Isom.

"I guess he wasn't the first to think that up, huh?"

"I guess not!" Dave smiled.

The dates were also changed as well as possible.

"You think if you don't give this to him, right now, that he might not ever get it, is that what you're saying?" Sister Mary-Michael said.

"Yes'm," said Isom.

"He'll never-ever get it, otherwise," said Dave.

"Hogwash," Sister Mark stuck her head into the circle, then left to go pick up dishes full of donut crumbs.

"He-ll-o-oo!" Sister M&Ms put up a hand.

"Another announcement to make!"

"Do-nuts! Do-nuts! Do-nu ..."

The children pounded their fists on the table and stopped when smacked by death-ray laser-looks from Sister Mark and Sister Principal-Something. Isom stepped into the middle of the kitchen holding the plaque. He motioned with his finger for Johnny to step forward. Johnny pointed to his own chest and pushed his chair back.

He came around the table to stand by Isom in the middle of the crowded, tenuously quiet kitchen.

"For you, Johnny Moon."

Isom presented Johnny the plaque.

"Read the inscription," Sister M&Ms whispered.

Isom took back the plaque and showed it all around the room, then read.

"To Johnny Moon.

"Physical Fitness Award.

"A strong boy makes a strong man, makes a strong nation."

Then he held out the plaque again and showed it, slow enough that they could all see the impressive gold and wood and fast enough to hide the handmade etchings.

He handed it back to Johnny.

Johnny smiled and said thanks.

"Wow! I did it," he looked up at Sister M&Ms.

She squatted next to him.

"You did it, Johnny Moon, you did it."

"There's no such thing," said one of the children at the table.

"Why'd he get it?" said another.

"You didn't even go to the moon, Johnny Moon, that's a made-up name," said someone else.

Johnny kept looking into the glistening eyes of Sister Mary-Michael.

She smiled and her teeth were Rambler White.

"You didn't lose a bunch of weight, Johnny Moon," someone whispered behind him.

"He didn't lose any-probly."

"I'm doing better, prob'ly," he said to Sister.

She smiled and wiped her eyes with the backs of her hands and nodded.

"Yes, you are," she said.

"The moon came to me, huh?" said Johnny.

She laughed a little and her lips quivered.

"Yep, the moon came to you."

Johnny mouthed the secret word and it made Sister take a deep breath and let it out.

"Will it keep evil away, too?"

"Oh, you don't need to listen to those guys," Sister said. "Nothing's going to happen."

"There's still lots of people outside who think I can talk to the moon," Johnny said to her.

"I know."

"And they think I know things about when they killed the President that even none of the old people know or the newspaper or the radio or any of the firemen."

"That's true."

"But it came from you, Sister. You know those things, just by using more of your brain, right?"

"I guess so, Johnny, you might be right."

"What're we gonna do?" Johnny said.

"They might come and do something to us like they did to your sister, do you think?"

She nodded softly.

"And burn us in oil?"

She took his hand in hers and stood.

She excused herself through the crowded kitchen, dragging Johnny along behind by the hand.

They walked to the far end of the hall, away from the crowds outside, to the front door of the convent.

Johnny smelled incense and saw kneelers, a basketball, and a bulletin board with funny cards and notes and handmade drawings.

He followed Sister out the front door, down the cement steps and toward the church.

They walked together ducking their heads into the wind, her hand on his shoulder.

They stomped up the middle of the back steps and through the wooden double swinging doors.

Johnny started to ask what they were doing.

Sister shushed him with a finger to her mouth and guided him to slide into the back pew.

Together they knelt and watched as two people stood by the big red votive candles on the St. Joseph side.

They heard them mumbling and fumbling for change and then the cascade of coins tumble down the pipe into the metal box.

One person lit a match.

They saw in the almost-dark church it was Isom and next to him Dave.

They lit two candles, the five-dollar kind, which meant they had a lot going on.

The silent pair finished with their task, blew out their matches, genuflected one at a time, all the way down, then climbed carefully down from the elevated altar area, the squeaking floor guided them out the side door.

"In the name of the Father, and of the son, and of the Holy Spirit."

Sister began as she pulled out her rosary, kissed the crucifix and etched the sign of the cross into her forehead with her thumbnail.

Johnny sat up straight, pulling his behind off the pew seat, perching on the red kneeler, next to Sister Mary-Michael.

He looked straight ahead in the dark church and began his part.

The wooden double doors behind them thunked and swung.

The church bells chimed loud, boom-boom-boom-boom ... boom-boom.

Like gun shots.

238

CHILD'S LETTER TO PRESIDENT JOHN F. KENNEDY
ABOUT PHYSICAL FITNESS

On March 3, 1963, nine-year-old Jack Chase of Torrance, California, wrote a letter to President John F. Kennedy. In his single-page note, featured in this article, Jack described his plans for staying physically fit. He said he would walk to school, the store, and the library "because I know a strong boy makes a strong man and a strong man makes a strong country." His statements echoed many of the ideas contained in Executive Order 11074, signed two months earlier by President Kennedy.

(http://goliath.ecnext.com/coms2/gi_0199-10248387/Child-s-letter-to-President.html)

About the author:

Mike Palecek has worked on newspapers in Minnesota, Iowa, Nebraska and South Dakota. He also produced Penn Magazine, and was a co-founder of Moon Rock Books, along with Jim Fetzer, as well as co-hosting, along with Chuck Gregory, The New American Dream Radio Show. He has written several novels, information about those available here: https://mikepalecek.newdream.us

Now retired after working for twenty years with the disabled, Palecek also served five terms in jail and prison for protests against U.S. military policy, and was the Iowa Democratic Party 5th District candidate for the U.S. House of Representatives in the 2000 election, receiving 65,500 votes.

(Banned from Canada.)

(Palecek video presentations)
Freedom of the Press False Flags & Conspiracies Conference 2020
https://www.bitchute.com/video/PBDaf07tMm5K/

Freedom of the Press False Flags & Conspiracies Conference 2021
https://153news.net/watch_video.php?v=WGDSDUSWSM78

Archives for The New American Dream Radio Show
https://newdream.us

About the artist:

Anthony LeTourneau

"Can you sit for a minute?"

That's something his three boys heard quite often growing up. Illustrator Anthony LeTourneau always wanted some more time to fi nish his drawings of his boys. Even now he draws or paints every day and spends his free time learning and reading about being creative. Anthony (or as his friends call him, Tony) was raised in the suburbs of St. Paul, Minnesota, and later moved to the Minnesota north woods where he resides today. As a young artist, he studied the works of Norman Rockwell, Howard Pyle, and N.C. Wyeth.

He has an active home studio where you can fi nd laughter from his boys, loud music, good coffee, and great food cooked by his wife, Michelle.

For more information on Anthony LeTourneau and his work visit:

www.anthonyletourneau.com.

www.ingramcontent.com/pod-product-compliance
Lightning Source LLC
Chambersburg PA
CBHW030921120626
46554CB00001B/225